The Only Child

S Englefield

For Hollie and Daniel

Prologue

The car horn cut through the sounds of the rush-hour traffic creeping along Ladbroke Grove. The fast-food delivery drivers weaving in and out on their bikes and scooters, and the hundreds of commuters trying to get home were nearly enough to drown out the sound, but not quite. A few people looked around, and one man even swore in a language Anthony couldn't quite place but thought might be Polish, yet the doorway of their cosy four-bedroom Notting Hill townhouse remained empty.

They were running late for their table. Anthony always hated to be late, thinking it the height of rudeness. When the car horn failed to draw out his wife Joanne, Anthony sighed, turned off the ignition and headed back in to see what was keeping her.

'Come on!' he yelled from the doorway. 'We're going to be late! What's the hold-up?'

Eventually, after what felt like minutes to Anthony but

was in fact only a fraction of that, Joanne appeared at the top of the stairs, brandishing a couple of jackets on their hangers. 'Which one do you think goes better with this dress, the cream or the yellow?' she enquired, thrusting each jacket out in turn.

'What does it matter? You're going to take it off as soon as you get there. It's only dinner with John and his new girlfriend, not the bloody queen!'

'I want to look my best,' Joanne retorted, the pitch of her voice dropping as her brilliant blue eyes narrowed a little, the jackets drawn back like a shield.

'Just hurry up,' Anthony snapped before retreating outside.

Realising that he was fighting a losing battle, Anthony dug out his phone and texted John, explaining that they were caught in traffic and might be a couple of minutes late. He hit Send and looked back at the house, admiring its cast-iron railings and stucco detailing yet again. The commute to Royal London Hospital might be a pain sometimes, but they had never considered moving. They both loved the area too much to ever think about leaving.

Barely a minute went by before his phone vibrated. A reply from John: *She's still not ready then?*

Anthony smiled and took a deep, calming breath. The calm didn't last long, however, as the first drops of a shower started to fall.

'In July? Great,' muttered Anthony under his breath as he hurried to the car.

Eventually, Joanne closed the front door and dashed to the car as fast as her heels would allow, trying to cover her hair with her new Saint Laurent clutch. She climbed into the Range Rover, shut the door and inspected the bag. 'Happy now?' she demanded, wiping the drops of rain from it with the sleeve of her yellow jacket.

'I would have been happy if you'd been ready twenty minutes ago when I told you we needed to leave!' Anthony replied. 'We're going to be late now and this rain won't help.'

'As you said, we're only dining with John and his new girlfriend, not the bloody queen, so what does it matter?'

'You know how much I hate being late.'

An uncomfortable silence descended and Anthony pulled out into the slow-moving traffic. After a while, Joanne asked, 'You're not going to be like this all evening, are you? You've been irritable all day.' Her voice had softened.

Anthony sighed and looked at his wife. Even after twenty-three years of marriage and a child, she was still a knockout. Her naturally blonde hair was streaked with grey and crow's feet were starting to appear at the corners of her eyes, but at fifty-one she could still turn heads. He often wondered how he'd managed to win her heart. He certainly hadn't been the only one vying for it when they'd first met, but somehow he'd triumphed. Middle age had been kinder to her than it had been to him, he reflected. Once he'd been handsome, but now his hair was more grey than brown and had started to recede at the temples, with his waistline a further reminder of his advancing years and that he wasn't running as much these days.

'I'm sorry, sweetheart,' he said, taking her hand and already regretting his earlier outburst. 'I promise I'll be on my best behaviour. It was worth the wait; you look amazing.'

Joanne blushed and smiled the smile that had won his heart nearly thirty years ago. She squeezed her husband's hand.

Returning the smile, Anthony pulled out onto the A40.

According to the witnesses, it all happened in the blink of an eye. Anthony pulled into a gap in the traffic just as the driver of a lorry coming up on the inside dropped his travel mug of coffee into the footwell and stooped for it, taking his eyes off the road. When he looked up and saw the Range Rover he slammed on the brakes, but it barely had an effect. The fully loaded truck slammed the Range Rover into the metal railings that bisected the two carriageways. The ambulance reached the scene in less than three minutes, but by then it was too late. Dr Anthony Simpson and his wife Joanne were pronounced dead at the scene.

* * *

The music, a combination of hip-hop and alt-rock, blared out of the three-bedroom terraced house that Amelia Simpson shared with her university friends. The exams that marked the end of their second year at Brighton University were over and everyone was in the mood to party.

'Come on Amelia, try it. You'll love it!' Jodie told her, trying to put the joint in her hand.

'I'll stick to this,' Amelia replied, waving her bottle of Corona in the air. The lime wedge in the neck of the bottle kept the beer in, though a few drops splashed onto her clothes.

She stumbled out of the living room and into the kitchen where Paul, her other flatmate, was raiding the fridge. He reappeared holding three more bottles of beer and immediately handed one to Amelia. Then he closed the fridge door and half-leant, half-fell against it, knocking fridge magnets and postcards all over the laminate floor.

'You heading home tomorrow, then?' Paul enquired, slurring slightly as the combination of weed and beer took its toll.

'Yeah,' Amelia replied. 'If my hangover allows, that is.'

Banging came from the wall behind them.

'Piss off, you miserable old cow!' Jodie shouted from the

living room. Paul and Amelia rolled their eyes, then started to laugh.

'Next year, shall we shall we find a house away from Jodie?' Paul asked with a wink.

'Don't!' Amelia said, punching Paul lightly on the arm. 'She'll get upset if she hears you; she won't realise you're joking. Then I'll have to spend my evening comforting her instead of packing.'

'I can't wait to be rid of that old bag!' Jodie shouted in the direction of the banging as Paul and Amelia re-entered the living room.

'You know we won't get any of the deposit back thanks to the smell of your weed, right?' Paul told Jodie.

'That'll be the deposit we lost when you put your heel through the plasterboard last month, trying to walk the length of the room on your hands,' Amelia replied, smirking.

'Hey, whose side are you on?' Paul replied, feigning hurt.

Before Amelia or Jodie could reply, there was a knock at the front door. Paul peered through the threadbare grey curtains half-closed over the bay window. 'Shit, she's called the cops!' he cried, and shut off the stereo.

'Who?' Jodie stubbed out her joint in a nearby beer can and waved her hands to clear the smoke.

'Who do you think?' Amelia cried. 'It has to be that moany old bat from next door!'

A second knock, this one more urgent than the first. Eventually, Paul opened the door to find two uniformed officers standing there. Sergeant's stripes were clearly visible on the lead officer. The curtain of the house next door twitched and he caught a fleeting glimpse of an eighty-something woman smiling in triumph.

'I'm sorry, officers,' said Paul. 'I promise we'll keep it down from now on. We're just celebrating the end of our exams.'

'Does Amelia Simpson live here?' the sergeant asked.

'Um … yes?' Paul, mystified, led them down the hall and into the living room.

'Amelia Simpson?' the sergeant asked the two women. His colleague stifled a cough as he inhaled the sickly sweet smoke.

'Ye-yes,' Amelia offered. Her dark-brown hair and eyes were a stark contrast to the paleness of her face.

'I'm Sergeant Wilde and this is PC Collins. Can we go somewhere private, please?' His tone was a suggestion rather than a command.

Amelia, trembling and a little unsteady on her feet, led them to her bedroom and closed the door.

'Please take a seat, Ms Simpson,' said Sergeant Wilde.

Amelia pushed back a half-packed suitcase and a small bundle of clothes and sat down on the double bed. Her hands twisted together. 'I'm heading home to London tomorrow for the summer,' she offered in way of an explanation.

'Are your parents Dr Anthony Simpson and Mrs Joanne Simpson?' he asked. His voice was soft now, his grey eyes sad.

'Yes. What about them?'

'I'm sorry to have to tell you this, but they were both involved in a traffic accident at 17:19 this evening, at the intersection of Ladbroke Grove and the A40.'

'Are they OK?' Amelia asked, her voice wobbling. The blood drained from her face.

'I'm so very sorry to tell you this, but they were both declared dead at the scene.'

'No, you're wrong.' Amelia's eyes filled with tears and she grabbed her phone. 'I spoke with Mummy earlier. They were going out to dinner with John tonight, and we're all going to watch a show tomorrow evening. To – to celebrate the end of my exams.' Tears ran down her face and her voice cracked.

She scrolled to her mother's number and hit Call. After ringing six times, the call went through to voicemail. Amelia's phone clattered onto the floor.

* * *

Hundreds of mourners filed out of the gothic South Chapel at the City of London Cemetery, following the twin cherrywood caskets carried by friends and colleagues of the late Dr Anthony Simpson and his beloved wife Joanne. At their head was Amelia, tears streaming down her cheeks. She clutched at her maternal grandmother, her last remaining family, as she slowly completed the last journey she would ever take with them. Though the midday July sun was beating down, the majority of the black-clad mourners showed no sign of the heat.

The cemetery was quiet, the noise of the city far off, as if the place, respectful of the occasion, muted the signs of everyday life carrying on oblivious outside the cemetery walls.

The grieving mourners were granted a moment's reprieve from the summer heat by the ash trees that lined the avenue leading to the graves. A faint breeze caused the leaves to sway, their rustling joining the birdsong.

The priest delivered the final prayer and blessing and the caskets were gently lowered into the ground. Amelia stared, unable or unwilling to look away.

Near the back of the mourners stood a woman all in black, her long brown hair in a simple ponytail. She was crying silently, her tears running free, mascara carving lines down her cheeks. Her face, which normally would have been pretty, was a mask of pain and grief. Beside her stood a girl in her mid-teens, her arms wrapped around her mother as if she were the only thing keeping her from falling. Her eyes, though, were not focused on the lowering caskets but boring into Amelia's. Her face was not racked with grief, but with something else entirely: something not found amongst the rest of the mourners.

Something blacker.

Hatred.

Chapter 1

Detective Inspector Jennifer Stone wandered out of the small kitchenette that made up part of Ryde police station on the Isle of Wight. The building itself, a brick and cladding cube straight out of the 1970s, was all function – no thought had been given to its design. She was dressed in a grey suit with a fitted blue shirt, her shoulder-length blonde hair tied back in a ponytail. At thirty-nine years old, she was attractive, although the bags under her eyes suggested that sleep had been difficult to come by of late.

She stifled a yawn, her second coffee of the day clutched in her hand as she made her way through the crowded control room. She offered a small wave to a couple of her colleagues before entering the team briefing room. The room was rectangular, with grey carpet tiles and ageing green paint on the walls that Jenny thought was overdue a freshen-up even before she joined the force, let alone now. It had a floating ceiling, a TV on a stand, a couple of whiteboards at one end with the rest of the team sat in a cluster of chairs spread out in loose rows facing them. At the front of the room, Detective Sergeant Emma Marie glanced at Jenny and absentmindedly tucked a lock of her long red hair behind one of her ears before she continued.

'As I was saying, we had a couple of burglaries and the usual drunk and disorderlies. All in all, a fairly standard weekend,' Emma told the assembled team.

'What do we know about the burglaries?' Jenny asked from the doorway, and took another sip of her coffee.

'The first took place in Arundel Close between 3am and 6am on Saturday morning,' Emma replied. The strip lighting made her look even paler than usual, the freckles that dotted her cheeks standing out starkly.

'What was taken?' asked one of the team, a uniformed officer by the name of Steve Mann.

'An Apple MacBook laptop and an iPad Pro,' she told him.

'How can we be sure of the time?' Jenny asked.

'The daughter remembers seeing both when she arrived home that night at 3am,' Emma replied.

'Where had she been?'

'Out drinking in Ryde.'

'So she's hardly a reliable witness,' said Jenny, which drew a few nods of approval.

'She got a taxi home. We've spoken to the firm and confirmed the drop-off time,' Emma replied. 'The theft was reported by her mother when she arrived home from work that morning at six. She works as a nurse at St Mary's hospital and was on the night shift.'

'Do we know how they got in?' This came from another member of the team, a young detective called Simon Michaels.

'The front door was open,' said Emma. 'We think the daughter didn't close it properly when she got home. It was like that when her mother came back.' This brought collective groans from the assembled room. 'Probably opportunistic – somebody coming home after a night out spots the open door, sees the laptop and tablet, and thinks it's their lucky day.'

'Any cameras in that area?' Detective Constable George Bancroft asked.

'Unfortunately not,' Emma told the group. 'However, given that the theft took place in a close, our working hypothesis is that the thief is someone who was either returning to or leaving the close. We've started door-to-doors and we've had no luck tracing the devices either. They've both been switched off since they were taken.'

'Where was the second burglary?' asked Jenny.

'A house on Salter's Road in Haylands was broken into last night, with cash and a games console taken.'

'Does anything suggest that these are connected?' Jenny leaned forward, her coffee momentarily forgotten.

'I don't believe so: they look like isolated incidents.'

'A couple of burglaries and some drunk and disorderlies. Is that it?' Jenny asked Emma, as the team departed.

'You're not in the Met any more boss,' Emma laughed. 'You should be used to the slower pace by now; it's been a couple of years since you transferred here.'

'I don't know how you stand it! Don't you ever get bored?' Jenny asked.

'At first, maybe, but I've come to realise that there's a challenge to policing an island like this.'

'I'm still not convinced,' Jenny muttered as she pulled up her seat, straightened her shirt and sat down.

'Be careful what you wish for!' Emma told her with a smile as she took the seat next to her and logged into her computer.

* * *

By early afternoon Jenny was still sitting at her computer, but her eyes were starting to glaze over. She looked around at her colleagues, all focused on their screens.

Why did I take this transfer again? she thought. *Seriously, I gave up the Metropolitan Police for this?* She glanced at the framed photo beside her computer screen to divert her thoughts from the dark place they were heading for. The photo showed a younger Jenny in full-dress uniform, her arm around a beaming girl of five or six: her daughter Sophie, long blonde hair falling to her waist. Behind her stood her husband, Greg, one arm round Jenny's waist, his other hand on his daughter's shoulder.

I came here for Sophie; I came here for us. London is no place to raise a small child. She needs parks, sand and sea air, not pollution, teenage gangs and crime. Besides, there are still plenty of opportunities for progression here. Jenny stared at the picture for nearly a minute before she put it down.

Sergeant Fischer came in, his gaze darting from one area of the room to the next. 'Are you OK, Sergeant?' Jenny asked.

'Sorry, ma'am, but have you seen Inspector Evans about?' His demeanour radiated a nervous energy uncharacteristic of his portly form.

'I haven't, I'm afraid.'

'I think he had to pop out,' said Emma. 'I saw him heading to his car about an hour ago and he hasn't returned.'

'Shit.'

'What's the matter, Tony?' Emma asked him, both detectives now fully focused on him.

'We've just had a call through. A car has rolled and collided with a tree down Beaper's Shute.'

'Emma,' Jenny called as she reached for her jacket, grateful for an excuse to leave her computer.

'Right behind you,' said Emma, her jacket already on.

* * *

Trees lined the road, casting long shadows in the mid-afternoon sun and giving the impression that it was much later than it was. Jenny pulled in behind one of the parked patrol cars and got out of her Vauxhall Astra. Even from this far back, she could tell that the crash was serious. The car, a blue hatchback, was on its side with the front pointing towards the road, its crumpled roof having come to a sudden and violent halt against a tree trunk. It was clear from the detritus strewn all over the road – broken glass here, a shattered mobile phone there – that the car had rolled a couple of times before coming to its final resting place, and the damage to the car confirmed it. The treacherous stretch of road had claimed many lives over the years.

Jenny and Emma flashed their warrant cards at the young PC manning the edge of the cordon as they ducked under the blue and white crime scene tape and approached the stricken car. Detective Constable George Bancroft spotted them and hurried over, his expression grim.

'What's the situation?' Jenny asked the young DC as Emma took in the scene.

'Two fatalities, a man and a woman, approximately eighteen or nineteen years of age.'

'RPU officers called?'

'Road police unit is on its way, forensic collision are already here. I've closed the road,' he added.

'Good work,' Jenny told him.

'Who phoned in the crash? Do we have any witnesses?' Emma asked.

'No witnesses have come forward. The initial call came from a Mrs Melanie Woodgrove, who was heading in from Brading and came across the car. She stopped and checked on the occupants but she says that it was obvious they were dead.'

'Where is she now?' Jenny asked. She looked around, but could only see police officers and the forensic team.

'She's been taken to hospital to be treated for shock,' George informed her.

'We'll need to speak to her.'

'I've got her address and phone number.'

Jenny and Emma took a slow walk around the scene of the crash, both pulling on latex gloves and overshoes as they did.

'We've got dark tyre marks starting here,' Jenny said, pointing, 'and ending here, just before this sharp left.'

'No sign of heavy braking on the other side, though,' Emma replied.

'No.' Jenny stepped back. 'It looks as if the driver misjudged the road, either because they didn't know it, or through inexperience. Tried to brake, but when it became obvious that they wouldn't stop in time, they wrenched the wheel round, which made the car roll.'

'They must have been going at some speed to do that much damage,' Emma said, gesturing at the car.

They walked towards the vehicle and Jenny stopped next to the battered mobile phone. She touched the fractured screen, which lit up with a shattered image of two people, presumably the driver and passenger of the vehicle. They were smiling, cheek to cheek, oblivious of the fate soon to befall them, and no doubt believing that they had their whole lives ahead of them. Not realising that they would be cut so tragically short.

At the car, the forensic team had already retrieved a handbag from the floor by the broken windscreen.

'We've got a student ID card,' the forensic officer told Jenny as she approached. 'Our female victim appears to be

Kelly Wilson, seventeen years old and a student at the Isle of Wight College.'

'The registered owner was one Stephen Blackmoor,' George told the detectives as he came over to join them.

'That matches with the driving license we found in the footwell of the car,' the forensic officer confirmed.

* * *

When Jenny and Emma returned to the station, the afternoon shadows had lengthened even further, and their mood was considerably more subdued than it had been when they left. No matter how many fatal accidents they attended, it never got easier to see the senseless waste of two young lives so full of promise.

Back in the office, Jenny took off her jacket, draped it over the back of her chair, and sat down with a sigh. Next to her, Emma did the same. Jenny picked up the photo next to her screen and stared at it, her fingers caressing Sophie.

'Jennifer, do you have a moment?'

Jenny looked up. DCI Thomas Edwards was standing in the doorway of the office in the far corner, surveying the team. Jenny put down the picture and got up.

When Jenny walked into the office, DCI Edwards was already seated behind his desk. The office was modest, functional. His desk occupied the nearside wall, holding a computer and a couple of framed photos. The far side of the room was taken up with a chesterfield sofa and chair and a small coffee table. On the wall behind the desk were a number of framed awards and diplomas. In his mid-forties, with cropped salt-and-pepper hair, DCI Edwards gave off an air of confidence. Once fit and trim, middle age and life behind a desk had begun to take its toll: the beginnings of a paunch strained the buttons on the expensive black shirt that complemented his grey, tailored suit.

He gestured towards the chair opposite him and Jenny sat down.

'How are you doing?' he asked her. His fingers were steepled, his steel-grey eyes boring into hers.

'OK, thanks, sir,' she said, after a moment.

'Sergeant Fischer filled me in. It's never easy when they're young, is it?'

'No, sir, it isn't.'

'Have you been able to identify either of the victims?'

'Yes. The car was registered in the name of Stephen Blackmoor. The driving licence confirmed that he was in the car but I need to check with the paramedics on exactly who was driving at the time of the crash. There was also a student card in the purse of the female occupant identifying her as Kelly Wilson. Both were from Ryde.'

'Have either of the families been informed yet?'

'Not yet. I was just about to ask DC Bancroft and DS Marie if they could do it.'

'I would prefer it if you informed the families, please, Jennifer.'

'Sir?' she replied, and groaned inwardly.

'I think it would look better if an inspector were to do it.'

'Yes, sir.'

Jenny strode to her desk, grabbed her jacket and snatched up her keys.

'You going somewhere?' Emma asked, looking up from her report.

'Yeah, Edwards has asked me to inform the families. George, grab your coat, you're with me.' George, sitting two rows away, groaned, and Jenny couldn't bring herself to admonish him. No one wanted to tell families and loved ones that their beloved son, daughter or partner would never come home again. The look on their face as their whole world collapsed was not one a detective could easily forget.

'Don't you have Sophie's music club performance this evening at half past six?' Emma asked.

'Yeah.' Jenny sighed in resignation.

'It's nearly five already; you'll never get back in time.'

'I'll have to try.'

'I don't mind going,' said Emma. 'All I've got on this evening is a date with a microwavable cottage pie and half a bottle of Pinot Grigio. Edwards will never know.'

'Thanks, Emma. I do appreciate the offer, but the DCI asked me to do it, so I will. I'll just have to try my best to get out on time.' Jenny walked out of the office, George following in her wake.

* * *

Jenny screeched into the car park of Town Park Primary School, frantically looking for a space. 'Come on come on come on!' she cried, and whacked the steering wheel with the palm of her hand. The dashboard clock said 19:15.

The visits had been as unpleasant as she feared. Both families refused to believe that their child was gone, sure that there must have been a mistake. She had felt time ticking away, but what could she do? She could hardly tell them that she couldn't stay because her own daughter had a school event she couldn't miss. The least she owed them was her full attention for as long as they had questions that they needed answering.

Jenny pulled up outside the main doors into the school, killed the engine and abandoned the car, relying on her warrant card to get her out of any awkward questions regarding her parking. She bounded up the steps.

'You're too late. It's just finished,' said a voice behind her.

17

Greg walked over; his face showed tiredness rather than anger, and this worried Jenny all the more. She preferred it when he was angry. Anger fades fast: tired resignation is far more insidious.

'I'm so sorry I'm late. You wouldn't believe the afternoon I've had—'

'I don't want to hear it. You promised Sophie that you wouldn't miss her performance only this morning.' His voice was still quiet.

'I couldn't get away! There was a big crash on the outskirts of Ryde. I had to attend—'

'I get it, your job is important. I can handle taking second place, but Sophie is too young to understand, and she deserves better.'

'Where is she now?' Jenny asked, glancing around her.

'She's having dinner at Kerri's. I'll see you at home.' Greg headed for his own car, leaving Jenny standing in the school car park, feeling wretched.

Chapter 2

Amelia, wearing a pale-yellow summer dress, arrived at her boutique flower shop and rummaged in her bag for her keys. Despite it only being late April, the early-morning sun warmed her shoulders. She caught sight of herself in the glass of the door and ran her fingers through her dark brown hair. She used to wear it down but had recently had it cut into an angled bob and was still trying to decide whether she liked it or not. She produced her keys with a little cry of triumph and let herself into the shop.

She had been the owner and manager of Flowers by the Beach for ten years now, and she still loved the smell of the shop every morning as she opened the front door and stepped in. The shop was all reclaimed wood and pale pastels, highlighting the splashes of colour from the flowers that filled every available surface.

Amelia put down her bag and made for the back room. As she switched the kettle on, she heard the jangle of the little bell by the front door.

'Morning,' called her assistant Maria as she entered. In her early sixties, with short grey hair and an easy smile,

Maria was a permanently cheerful woman who had refused to let the death of her beloved husband four years earlier dampen her youthful spirit. In her own words, 'Me and Mark had forty wonderful years together. He wouldn't want me to waste the rest of my life moping around and feeling sorry for myself.'

'Kettle's on,' Amelia called.

'No thank you, had one before I left,' came Maria's reply, her coat already off and a broom in her hand as she prepared to open the shop for another day.

The swish of the broom on the tiled floor and the rising pitch of the kettle was drowned by a crash, followed immediately by the tinkling of broken glass.

Amelia rushed out. 'What was that?' She looked in the direction of the noise. One of the shop windows, the one that bore its name in lovely quirky letters that Amelia herself had designed, had been smashed. The pane had spider-webbed into a thousand small fractures, stretching out from the centre like ripples on a pond whose calm surface had been broken by a careless pebble.

'Are you OK?' Amelia asked Maria. Her shop assistant was white, her hands clutching the broom handle, the sweeping forgotten.

'I'm fine,' she told Amelia, swallowing.

Outside, Amelia stared at the mess that was her front window. The sticker bearing the name of the shop had thankfully held most of the pane intact. On the pavement, in the midst of the broken glass, lay the cause of the damage: a fist-sized stone. Amelia glanced up and down the road. At this early hour Cross Street in Ryde was deserted and the only traffic was the delivery vans coming and going from the other businesses that lined the street. There was no sign of the assailant, although Amelia already had a pretty good idea of who was to blame.

'I bet it was that bitch down the road,' Maria said as she emerged from the shop, seemingly having read Amelia's mind.

They looked in the same direction. Flowers by Kirstie was shut, the blinds closed, and the lights off. To the casual observer there were no signs of life, but Amelia knew better. She couldn't prove it, but she was sure that Kirstie was behind this attack, and all the previous ones as well.

* * *

'What happened?' said a voice behind her.

It was mid-afternoon. Amelia was standing outside her shop while Dan, Maria's sixty-year-old neighbour and the latest in a long line of people trying to catch Maria's eye, screwed a large sheet of chipboard over the damaged glass. She turned to see Megan, her best friend of the last eight years, clutching two takeaway coffees from Ellie's. In her early thirties, with long, mousy-blonde hair, Megan was a PA for the finance director of an engineering firm on the other side of town.

'Why aren't you at work?' Amelia asked, smiling as she gratefully accepted the hot drink. The sight of her best friend lifted her spirits.

'I told you I had today off,' Megan replied, rolling her eyes. 'I've been on the seafront painting the castle.'

Megan was an aspiring artist; she claimed she was only working as a PA until her inevitable career as an artist kicked off. They had met eight years ago, when Amelia had attended an exhibition of local artists. She had just said how much she liked a watercolour of The Needles when Megan introduced herself as the artist and they hit it off. They left the exhibition early to go for a drink and had been best friends ever since.

Amelia brought her up to speed with the morning's events.

'It was her again, wasn't it?' Megan seethed.

'Yes, it was,' said Maria, having appeared from the shop with a cup of tea for the grateful Dan.

'We don't know that,' said Amelia. 'There was no sign of anyone by the time we made it outside.'

'I agree with Maria. Who else could it have been? What did the police say?'

Amelia said nothing.

'She didn't call them,' Maria replied, standing a little closer to Dan than was strictly necessary.

'Don't you have any work to do?' Amelia asked her. A look of faux hurt crossed Maria's face.

'Why didn't you call them?' Megan demanded.

'Don't you start,' said Amelia. 'I've had this all morning from Maria too.'

'Well, she's right,' Megan replied, and Maria smiled at her.

Amelia sighed. 'There's no point. They didn't do anything when paint was thrown over the front of the shop, or when my delivery van had its tyres slashed.'

'You can't let her get away with this: it's harassment. Maybe she'll back off when I've had a word.' Megan took a step towards the second flower shop, its blinds now up and its front door open.

'No, don't! Please!' Amelia cried out, grabbing her arm. 'You'll only make things worse. I'm sure she'll get bored eventually.'

Megan turned back to Amelia. 'I won't if you promise to come out for a drink with me later?'

'I'd love to, but I can't,' said Amelia. 'I promised I'd spend the evening with my gran.'

* * *

Amelia climbed the steps to her second-floor flat and opened the front door which creaked. Within seconds James was there, winding himself around Amelia's legs and purring contentedly. She'd bought the flat outright when she moved down, having been sold straight away on the views of the Solent from the living-room balcony, Portsmouth's Spinnaker Tower visible in the distance. In the early days of their relationship, she and Sam had happily spent summer evenings out there, a bottle of red wine open, enjoying each other's company and the view, the sea air the perfect complement to the wine.

'Hello,' Amelia called as she reached down to scratch the tabby-and-white cat behind his ears, which were slightly too big for his head. She'd found him at a rescue centre shortly after moving to the island. While completely devoted to Amelia, James and Sam had spent the last five years adopting a 'you stay away from me, I'll stay away from you' kind of relationship. Since Amelia would never part with her beloved cat, Sam tolerated him as best he could.

'Hey, in here,' came the answering shout.

Amelia made her way to the rear of the flat, trying not to trip over James, who was still winding around her legs. Sam came out of the living room wearing an old t-shirt, shorts and flip-flops, and holding a PlayStation control pad in one hand. He leaned in and gave her a quick kiss.

'How was your day?' he asked. At just over six foot and thirty-five years of age, Sam was still in pretty good shape, which he attributed to playing football twice a week.

'I've had better days,' admitted Amelia. 'Someone threw a rock through the shop window this morning.'

'What?' Sam said, his brow wrinkling in confusion. 'Was it *her* again?'

'Maria and Megan think so although I have no proof.'

'It sounds like you need cheering up,' Sam told her as he took her jacket and draped it over the arm of the brown leather sofa.

'I do,' admitted Amelia.

'Why don't we go into town for a drink, maybe get something to eat? You could text Maria and ask her to open up tomorrow. I'll ring in sick and we can have a lie-in together,' he told her, wrapping his arms around her waist and nuzzling his face into her neck.

'That does sound nice,' Amelia said, wrapping her arms round him.

'Great, where do you want to go? I kinda fancy trying the new Indian at the top of the high street.'

'As much as I'd love to, I can't,' she told him with a sigh. 'I've already promised Gran I'd go round tonight.'

'For God's sake.' Sam let go of her and stalked towards the living room.

'What's the matter?' Amelia asked, following him into the room.

'I fancied a night out.'

'I've already promised. Why don't you come too? She would love to see you.'

'She doesn't like me.'

'Yes she does,' Amelia protested feebly.

'I've been working all day. The last thing I want to do with my evening is spend it with a boring old woman!'

'Well, I'm going, even if you won't,' Amelia snapped, her cheeks flushed. She grabbed her jacket, walked out of the flat, and slammed the door behind her, leaving James gazing at his empty food bowl mournfully.

* * *

'Hi Gran, only me,' Amelia called as she let herself into the two-bed detached house.

'In the kitchen, love,' came the answer.

Amelia headed in and found Frances drying up. Though Amelia had protested numerous times, Frances still refused to take it easy. At seventy-eight she was still very independent, refusing to let anyone do anything for her. A member of several social and charitable groups, she said that keeping busy helped to keep her young and that she wasn't ready to lay down and die just yet, which suited Amelia fine. As her only living relative and link to her beloved parents, Amelia doted on Frances. Indeed, she had moved down to the island after university to be closer to her.

'Just you?' Frances asked as Amelia walked into the kitchen.

'Yes, Sam wanted to come, but something came up. He sends his best, though!' said Amelia, missing Frances's eye-roll.

'What happened? Was there a beer and computer game emergency?' Frances asked.

'Gran!' Amelia slapped her lightly on the arm. 'He really wanted to come!'

'If you say so my dear, but I do wonder why you put up with that idiot. You could do so much better, you know.'

Amelia felt her eyes prickle with tears and turned away. Frances put down the plate she was drying and went to her granddaughter. 'I'm sorry, OK? You shouldn't take any notice of a stupid old woman like me. If you're happy, then I'm happy,' Frances told her gently.

Chapter 3

'Here you go, hun. You want anything else with that?' the waitress asked Megan as she put her coffee on the table.

'No, that's all for now, thanks,' Megan replied with a smile. The server smiled back and moved on to the next table.

Megan sipped her black coffee and returned to staring out of the window. Ellie's was a small local business in Ryde, not one of the big chains, and Amelia and Megan liked it all the more for that. The shop front was one large window, with dark grey boarders and the name of the shop painted above in white. The dark window frame highlighted its warm-looking interior; a combination of wooden tables, stainless-steel chairs, leather sofas and cosy little corners, where you were encouraged to while away a lazy afternoon with coffee or tea and a book. As it was just down the road from Amelia's shop, Amelia and Megan spent many an afternoon there, putting the world to rights, but that wasn't why she was here now. No, this afternoon she was waiting for someone other than Amelia, but she was a little early.

Megan pulled out her phone and idly scrolled through

Facebook, but soon put it down again, bored. She glanced at the time – five thirty. According to the website, Flowers by Kirstie closed at a quarter to six. She had fifteen minutes to wait.

She glanced out of the window again. From her vantage point she could see the purple front of the little flower shop and the owner, in the process of closing up. She continued to drink her coffee, but her thoughts were interrupted by a rattle from the table: her mobile phone. Taking a quick look across the road to make sure that Kirstie wasn't about to leave, Megan looked at the message:

Do you fancy meeting up tonight? Yours or mine?

Megan pondered for a minute or two before hitting Reply:

OK, come to mine. I'm out at the moment so better make it 7

She hit Send, put her phone down, and took another sip of her coffee, resuming her surveillance.

About ten minutes later, Kirstie and another young woman left the shop and Kirstie paused to lock the door. Kirstie was a couple of inches taller than Megan, perhaps five feet eight, with shoulder-length dark-brown hair. She deposited the keys in her grey canvas messenger bag and slung the strap over her shoulder before moving off.

Megan gave them a thirty-second head start, drained her coffee, and headed after them.

Hands in her pockets and walking as if she hadn't a care in the world, Megan followed them down Cross Street. Kirstie stopped, pointed to the wooden board covering half of Amelia's shop front, and said something to her companion. They burst out laughing and carried on. They walked away from the high street, chatting, unaware that they were being followed. When they hit the corner of Melville Street and Nelson Street, they stopped for a moment before going their separate ways. Kirstie continued down Melville street past the rows of houses with their low brick walls and overhanging trees, now talking on the phone, Megan maintained the distance between them, Kirstie's friend all but forgotten.

At the bottom of the road, now finished on the phone, Kirstie turned right and continued down Monkton Street. About twenty metres on she stopped outside a dated-looking terraced house – black paint on its railings peeling, front garden on the verge of being overrun with weeds – and started to rummage in her bag. Spotting her chance and making sure that no one was watching, Megan lengthened her stride.

Kirstie walked up to her front door and inserted her key in the lock. Megan reached her just as she opened the door. She pushed Kirstie inside and followed her, slamming the door shut.

Kirstie staggered and crashed against a sideboard, knocking over a vase, but managed to stay on her feet. She turned and saw Megan. 'W-who are you?' she stammered.

Instead of answering, Megan advanced on Kirstie, grabbed her shirt and slammed her into the wall. The antique mirror above the sideboard shook, but didn't fall.

'I'm a friend of Amelia's-'

'What? She can't fight her own battles?' sneered Kirstie. 'She sent round her goon to-'

Megan let go of Kirstie's shirt and slapped her hard across the face. Kirstie's brown eyes widened with fear and shock and her hand moved to her cheek, where an angry red welt was starting to appear. Megan grabbed her again and slammed her into the wall. The mirror gave up and fell onto the sideboard before it tipped forward and hit the floor with a crash, shattering into dozens of pieces.

'Got anything else to say?' Megan asked, her lip curling.

Kirstie shook her head, eyes still wide.

'Good.' Megan let go of her shirt and Kirstie slumped to

the floor. She stepped over the broken mirror to the front door, opened it, and turned to face Kirstie.

'I know where you live now. I'd better not hear of any more accidents happening to Amelia, or anything belonging to her. If I do, I'll be back round to see you.'

With a final look at the stricken Kirstie, Megan left, closing the front door behind her.

[1]

London, May 2012

Ashley and her friends walked along the towpath that ran alongside the Hertford Union canal. The late-afternoon sun warmed their shoulders, a faint breeze making the branches of the trees sway lazily. It was a slightly more convoluted route home, but the girls enjoyed taking the canal path to their homes in Bow. They liked to look at the graffiti that lined the wall: some minor works of art, some nothing more than a collection of lines and letters drawn in haste, with no thought other than anarchy. What all the paintings had in common, however, was that they added an explosion of colour to the surface they adorned. Ashley liked them for that reason alone: their juxtaposition to the greens of the trees and the blue-green water of the canal itself.

A canal boat drifted lazily down the waterway as they walked, piloted by an elderly couple. On a normal day they might have elicited a wave from the girls, but not today.

Today the small group of friends had something much more important on their minds: the upcoming high-school prom.

'So have you asked him yet?' a raven-haired girl by the name of Katie asked.

'No, I'm waiting to see if he asks me first!' replied the girl beside her, a strawberry blonde haired girl called Erica.

'What about you, Ashley?' Samantha asked.

'I might ask Tom. Then again, I might not,' Ashley said casually. She tucked a strand of dark-brown hair behind her ear and continued along the path.

The girls giggled and exchanged a couple of knowing glances. 'Yeah, yeah.' Katie laughed. 'I've seen the way you look at him.'

Ashley gave her a little shove and the girls laughed harder.

* * *

The girls, with Ashley at their head, walked past the little corner shop and turned right onto Hewlett Road. They went past the estate agents and the fried-chicken shop until they reached the small terraced house that Ashley shared with her mother. The front of the house had once been pretty, with its cast-iron railings and large sash windows, but now it had seen better days. It needed a little work, a little love. The paint was peeling from the railings and the white wooden window frame looked tired.

Ashley unlocked the black front door and in traipsed the girls.

'Hi, Mum!' Ashley called out as they dumped their school bags in the hall and went into the living room.

'What're you going to wear?' Samantha asked Erica as they all found seats in the small but cosy room.

'Me and Mum went out last weekend, and I saw this

lovely pale-blue dress in Topshop. She says if I'm good all week and help out around the house then we can go and buy it this Saturday!'

'What about you, Ash?' Samantha asked, and the girls turned to look at her.

'Well, there's a dress I've seen in New Look, but you've forgotten the most important part: how we're getting there. We've got to arrive in style. I've looked online, and you can hire a limo for £350!'

'That would be so cool!' cried Katie, and all the others nodded enthusiastically.

Ashley's mum, in her mid-forties with short dark-brown hair and pale blue eyes, came into the room. 'You OK, girls?' she asked the group, with a small smile that didn't quite make it to her eyes.

'Yes thank you, Mrs Johnson,' they replied in unison.

'What're you all talking about?' she asked.

'We're just discussing the school prom. It's in just under two weeks, Mrs Johnson,' said Katie.

'We're looking at limo rentals!' Ashley cried, beaming.

'Oh, Ashley,' her mother replied, her words tinged with sadness. 'I've told you we can't afford anything like that any more, not since—' Her gaze dropped to the floor. 'I don't mind you going, but you'll have to wear something you've already got.' She looked up but refused to meet her daughter's gaze.

'You can't expect me to go to my own summer prom in any old random dress!' Ashley shouted. 'I'll be so humiliated! Why do you hate me?'

She stormed out of the room, stomped upstairs and flung herself into her bedroom. The door crashed into the wall with a bang that echoed around the house.

'Stupid Mum, I hate her!' she muttered and swiped

angrily at the tears in her eyes. She sat down heavily on her bed, which groaned in protest.

It wasn't always like this, she thought to herself. *Back when Dad was here, when we were a normal family, we could afford things. He'd have bought me a new dress and paid for the limo!*

Ashley picked up a framed photo from the cabinet by her bed and stared at it. It showed a younger Ashley at a football game with her dad. He was smiling for the camera and Ashley was beaming next to him, her head on his shoulder. She had a hotdog in one hand, and her other arm around his waist.

That was a good day. Dad turned up with no warning and told me and Mum that he had managed to get away for the day and had got us all tickets to a game. Standing there, eating hotdogs with him and Mum, then on to the fair – a whole day together! For the first time in ages, it felt like we were a proper family.

Her eyes glazed over and her expression hardened. *But that was a lie, wasn't it? We were never a normal family; I was just too young and too stupid to know any better. In a normal family, the dad doesn't only see his daughter when he can get away. No, Dad had a dirty little secret, and it was me.*

There was a knock on her bedroom door and her mother walked in. Ashley's posture stiffened and she looked away, partly because she didn't want to see her, and partly because she didn't want her mother to see that she was nearly crying.

'Your friends have gone.'

Ashley still refused to look round.

'I'm sorry about the dance, I really am.' Her mother sat down on the bed next to her. 'I'll see if I can get a couple of extra shifts at work. If I can, we might be able to buy you a new dress.'

Ashley stayed silent, but her shoulders softened slightly.

Her mother gave her knee a little squeeze and left, closing the bedroom door behind her.

Ashley got up and paced around her room. She never brought her friends up to her bedroom if she could help it; she was too embarrassed. Her TV was an old-style bulky model when they all had the new slim ones, her computer barely even turned on, and her phone was practically an antique. When her friends were proudly showing off their latest upgrade, she told them that she liked her old phone and didn't want to get rid of it, when the truth was that they couldn't afford a new one.

Maybe if she did extra shifts more often, I wouldn't be stuck with all this outdated crap! she thought bitterly, then reconsidered. *No, Mum isn't to blame: she's always working. And her stuff is even older than mine; she's doing her best. When Dad was alive, we might not have been a typical family but we could afford things and we were happy. We always did something together when he was here and Mum was happy, I can't even remember when I last saw her smile, not properly.*

Her eyes narrowed, and her hands clutched her phone so tightly that her knuckles were white. *Mum isn't to blame and neither is Dad. It's her fault. If it wasn't for her, Dad would still be alive and we'd still be happy. I'll make her pay for what she did to my family.*

Chapter 4

Amelia closed her front door and hung her jacket and bag on the hook next to it. She scooped James up and cuddled him as he purred contentedly, nuzzling her face with his.

With the cat in her arms she walked to the living room. The noise from the TV was already deafening: machine-gun fire interspersed with explosions and the death cries of virtual terrorists.

As Amelia entered the room, Sam spotted her and paused the video game, making it unnaturally quiet. The only illumination came from the TV; all the other lights were off. 'Oh hi, I didn't hear you come in.' He put the PlayStation controller on the coffee table, stood up, and moved towards Amelia, but faltered as James hissed at him. Sam retreated out of range of the razor-sharp claws and James resumed his nuzzling.

'How was work?' he asked, eyeing the cat warily. 'Any further incidents with Kirstie?'

'No, thankfully, nothing. Hopefully she's finally got bored.'

'I'm sure she has,' Sam soothed. 'So what shall we do

tonight? There's that new police drama on Netflix – we could get a takeaway and watch that?' His voice was light, his tone hopeful.

'You know I always go round to Gran's on a Thursday,' Amelia reminded him as she put the cat down. James gave her a reproachful look then trotted out of the room, no doubt heading for his food bowl.

'Can't you give it a miss for once? She wouldn't mind. Just tell her you're not feeling too well.'

'I'm not lying to my gran! Look, why don't you come with me? She was disappointed you weren't there last time.'

'Yeah, I bet she was,' Sam muttered.

'I tell you what,' Amelia wheedled, 'if you come with me tonight, then tomorrow we'll get a takeaway and do whatever you like.'

* * *

'Hi, Gran,' Amelia shouted as she pushed open the door.

'Hello, dear,' came the reply from the living room.

Amelia and Sam took off their jackets and headed in the direction of the voice. Frances switched off the TV and turned as Amelia came in, a smile spreading across her face at the sight of her granddaughter.

'Hi, Frances,' Sam said as he entered the room behind Amelia.

The smile on Frances's face faltered, then faded. 'Oh, hi Sam,' she replied, her tone noticeably cooler.

After Amelia had made them all a cup of tea, she and Frances started to chat about the latest meeting of the over sixty-fives' Scrabble club that Frances had been to that afternoon. Before long, Sam's eyes started to glaze over. Bored and restless, he dug his phone out of his jeans pocket and started to play with it.

'So how are you then, Sam? How is work?' Frances asked, her tone polite but uninterested.

'Yeah, all right,' he replied, his gaze never leaving the phone in his hand.

'Amelia was telling me that your five-a-side team are doing well?' said Frances, her patience already wearing thin.

'Yeah, not too bad,' he replied, not looking up.

Frances shot Amelia a look.

'You might win your league, you said so the other day,' Amelia offered, her face flushing.

'Maybe,' said Sam, still engrossed in his screen as his fingers flew across it.

'It's rude to play on your phone while people are trying to talk to you,' Frances snapped, her normally abundant patience having run out.

With a theatrical sigh, Sam put the phone on the coffee table and looked at the women. 'There you go. Are you happy now?' he asked, and Amelia's face turned a deeper shade of red.

'What are you doing with this loser, Amelia?' Frances asked her granddaughter.

'What the fuck's your problem?' Sam replied, his face now as red as Amelia's.

'Don't swear at my gran!' Amelia gasped.

'What? She started it,' he countered, raising his hands with a shrug.

'Gran, you apologise too,' Amelia demanded.

'Come on, Amelia, he's been messing about on that phone since he got here,' she said. 'He clearly doesn't want to be here.'

'Yes he does,' said Amelia. 'You do, don't you, Sam?'

'I only came because you made me,' he replied. 'What would I talk to an old woman about, bloody Scrabble club? Give me a break.'

'If you've got somewhere better to be, you can get out of my house right now. I'd hate you to waste any more of your precious time talking to an *old woman*.' Frances's eyes blazed and she pointed at the door.

'Fine.' Sam snatched his phone up off the table and stormed out. The front door banged and the sound echoed through the tense, thick atmosphere.

'That was a little harsh, wouldn't you say? At least he made the effort to come round,' Amelia said eventually, trying to keep her tone level but not entirely succeeding.

Frances got up, went through to the kitchen, and eventually returned with a glass of water. She sat down and took a small sip, then set the glass on the table, her hand trembling slightly.

'Amelia,' she said, finally. 'Seriously, why are you with that idiot? You could do so much better than him. You're a lovely girl, and so pretty. I hate to see you wasting your life on someone like him.'

'I love him,' Amelia replied frowning, her hands on her hips.

'The old Amelia would never have put up with someone like that,' Frances said, her voice soft. 'The old Amelia would have kicked him out years ago. Hell, the old Amelia wouldn't have given him a chance in the first place.'

'The old me?'

'I know your parents' death hurt you, a lot, but that doesn't mean you should always take the safe option in life.' Frances took Amelia's hands in hers.

'What do you mean, the safe option?' Amelia withdrew her hands, her eyes narrowing.

'Don't get me wrong, I love having you here, but did you really study so hard at university to open a little flower shop on a little island? Is that really what you want to do with the rest of your life? You are so talented; I hate to see you wasting your time.'

'And that's what you think I'm doing, is it? Wasting my time?' Anger started to creep into Amelia's voice.

'I just think you could be doing so much more; I don't want you to get to my age and then wish you had. You should be running your own graphic design agency and married to a doctor or a lawyer, not going home to someone whose definition of romance is a takeaway and a fondle – that's if you can pry him away from his video games.'

'I happen to love Sam and my little flower shop, and unlike you, I don't think I'm wasting my life!' Amelia shouted, the pitch of her voice rising as tears threatened to overwhelm her.

'Amelia!' Frances cried, but she had already gone.

Chapter 5

Amelia glanced up from her phone as Megan pushed through the Saturday-afternoon crowd, placed two large glasses of white wine on their table – the second pair of the day – and sat down opposite her. Their local was busy: it was nearing the end of the football season and half the occupants were focused on the projector at the far end of the room. Sound blared from the large speakers on either side of the screen. People were drinking and cheering, enjoying their time away from the worries and stresses of the working week.

The bar had originally been a typical run-of-the-mill pub. Amelia and Megan had chosen it as a meeting place years ago, because it was roughly halfway between their houses, but after a while they actually began to like the place, appreciating its character and its characters. Recently, though, it had been bought out and modernised. Gone were the sticky carpets, fruit machines and dartboard, replaced by a stainless-steel bar, polished hardwood flooring, an expanded wine selection and imported bottled beers. There was even a tapas menu and a pie of the week. They were still adjusting to the change, unsure yet whether they liked it or not.

'Thanks,' Amelia said as she sipped her overpriced Sauvignon Blanc. Unfortunately, with the updated layout came updated prices: another point against it. 'I need this after the week I've had.' They'd been in the bar a while and were starting to relax into what threatened to become a big night out. For the moment it was just the two of them; Sam was playing football and had promised to meet them later.

'Have you had any more trouble from that cow down the road?' Megan asked, her tone light.

'No, thankfully.'

They continued to chat and drink, putting their week and the world to rights. The second drink gave way to a third, their spirits rising in line with their blood-alcohol level.

Amelia glanced at her phone and Megan raised her eyebrows. 'What's going on? That's the sixth or seventh time you've looked at your phone in the last hour. Are you expecting a call?'

Amelia put her phone on the table, her face pink. 'Sorry.'

'What's going on?' Megan pressed.

'I had a stupid argument with Gran on Thursday and stormed out. I haven't heard from her since.'

'What did you argue about?' Megan asked, curiosity getting the better of her.

Amelia shrugged. 'It was stupid. She said she thought I was wasting my life. I told her that I like my life the way it is and she should stop meddling.' She cringed at the memory.

'Whoa, that doesn't sound like the Frances I know and love,' said Megan, leaning back.

'She had a go at Sam as well.'

'Sam was there? OK, that makes more sense. Why did you take him? You know they don't get along,' Megan sighed and took another sip of her wine.

'I'm sure that if they just spent more time together they'd grow to like each other,' Amelia replied. 'There's nothing wrong with expecting the two most important people in my life to get along, is there?'

'Hey!' Megan replied in mock indignation.

'Sorry. You know what I mean, though.'

'Why don't you ring her?' Megan asked.

'That's the weird thing. I've tried several times, but she hasn't answered, or responded to my messages.'

'Maybe she's still mad?' Megan suggested. 'She might need a bit longer to cool off. I'm sure if you go round tomorrow she'll be over it.'

'I'm sure you're right, but it isn't like her to let something drag on this long. To be honest, I was surprised not to see her the next day. I looked up every time the shop bell rang, expecting to see her standing there looking sheepish.'

Despite her reassurances, Megan could tell her best friend was still worried. She took her hand and squeezed it. 'Come on, let's have another drink. I'll get them in.'

Amelia nodded, still staring at her phone and willing it to ring or buzz, but like the proverbial watched pot, it remained silent. Megan grabbed their glasses and pushed through the throng.

A cheer went up from the bar and Amelia looked over, forgetting her phone for a moment. The majority of the crowd were jumping around, cheering and hugging, while a small handful sat looking crestfallen at their drinks. She guessed someone had scored a goal, and their celebration managed to elicit a smile in spite of her worries.

Amelia's phone started to buzz. She snatched it off the table, certain it would be Gran ringing to apologise, but stopped short as she saw the number. It was a landline number she didn't recognise, with an Isle of Wight dialling code. After a moment's hesitation, she swiped across the screen to accept the call and raised the phone to her ear. 'Hello?'

'Hello?' said a quavering, high voice. 'Is this Amelia? Amelia Simpson?'

'Yes, it is,' Amelia replied. 'Who is this?'

'My name is Heather. I'm sorry to bother you; I found your number on your website.'

'How can I help you, Heather?' Amelia asked.

'I'm a friend of Frances's; we met at the church committee. We were meant to meet this morning for coffee, but she didn't turn up. I tried her mobile phone, but she didn't answer. I was a little concerned so I went round to her house. She didn't answer the door, and the curtains were still closed.'

'Have you rung the police?' Amelia asked, clutching the phone even tighter.

'No, I didn't want to trouble them. I'm sure it's nothing,' she added hastily.

'I'm sure it's nothing too, but thanks for letting me know.' Amelia ended the call and stared at the phone as a horrible feeling snaked through her veins.

Megan arrived back at the table. 'They didn't have any more Sauvignon, so I got the Pinot.' Then she saw Amelia's face. 'You OK?'

'I've just had a phone call—'

'See, I told you she'd ring. I bet the old bird's sorry for making you worry,' Megan said, smiling.

'It wasn't Gran: it was a friend of hers called Heather. Apparently she and Gran were meant to meet up this morning, but Gran didn't show. She went round to her house but there was no answer, and the curtains were still closed.' Amelia's voice wobbled.

'I'm sure it's nothing,' Megan replied, but without conviction.

'I need to go and check; I won't be long. Can you look after my drink?'

'Don't be silly, I'll come with you. I could do with some fresh air anyway; this wine is going straight to my head.'

Megan and Amelia grabbed their bags and headed out, the wine forgotten, the sounds of the bar fading into the distance.

* * *

'Amelia, wait up!' Megan cried as they turned onto Argyll Street.

Amelia was walking like a woman possessed; Megan had tried to get her to slow down but she had barely seemed to hear. Megan jogged to catch up, the combination of white wine and mid-afternoon sun making her feel queasy.

'I can't!' Amelia replied. 'What if she's fallen and hurt herself?'

'Look, I'm sure she's fine,' Megan said, trying to reassure her.

They hurried down the street in silence. Amelia rang her grandmother's number again, without success.

They arrived at Frances's house and pushed the gate open. Sure enough, the curtains were still closed. Through the frosted glass of the front door, Amelia could see that the stair light was on. She banged on the door with the palm of her hand.

No response. Amelia stooped and lifted the flap on the letterbox. 'Gran, are you there? It's me, Amelia!'

Still no answer. Amelia frantically searched through her handbag until she found the spare set of house keys. She fumbled the key into the lock, twisted, and pushed the door open. It swung inwards and bounced off the far wall with a thud.

Amelia dashed into the house and headed upstairs. 'Gran, where are you?'

Megan entered the house and wrinkled her nose at the slight coppery smell in the air, a metallic tang that you could taste at the back of the throat. She tried to place it, but couldn't. She moved towards the living room. 'Frances, are you in here?'

Amelia ran into her grandmother's bedroom. It was empty, the flowery duvet pulled back, and the bedside lamp switched on. She moved towards the bathroom but froze as she heard a soul-shattering scream.

Amelia ran down the stairs, nearly tripping and falling in her haste. At the bottom was Megan, her hand over her mouth, her face ashen.

Amelia pushed past her into the living room and stopped short. On the floor lay the body of Frances Lowes. Her eyes were closed and her blood had pooled into a macabre halo around her, the source of the coppery smell that pervaded the house.

Amelia stood there in stunned silence for a couple of heartbeats before she started to scream.

Chapter 6

Jenny drove down Argyll Street, parked in a space near the crime scene, and climbed out of her car. She groaned when she saw the crowd, knowing that this would be all over the local news and social media before the end of the day. People were already pointing their phones at the house.

It would be a Saturday she thought, with a trace of annoyance. She had been walking along Sandown Pier with Sophie and Greg, trying to enjoy some proper family time and make amends for missing Sophie's performance, when her phone had rung. After the call had ended, she hadn't needed to say anything. 'Just go,' said Greg. Sophie looked disappointed, but gave Jenny a hug before she said goodbye.

No rest for the wicked, she thought as she pushed through the crowd and took in the scene. A blue and white forensic tent obscured the entrance to the house. From what she could see, the property was in good condition. The front garden was well maintained, its small patch of grass recently cut, with pretty window boxes lining the window ledge.

At the front gate stood a young PCSO not much older than nineteen or twenty. Jenny vaguely recognised her: *Jill*

Bennett? She was holding a clipboard and looked mildly harassed. 'No one is allowed in-'

Jenny flashed her warrant card. 'Senior investigating officer.'

'Sorry, ma'am,' she replied curtly and wrote Jenny's name down on her list.

Jenny approached a couple of uniformed officers. 'Close the road, and I want these people gone now,' she said, gesturing towards the growing crowd of onlookers, some pointing their phones at her.

She ducked under the crime-scene tape, entered the tent, and donned a white forensic suit, white booties, a pair of latex gloves and a mask. She pulled the hood up, making sure her hair was tucked inside, and went through the open front door. A number of people were in the hall, all dressed in forensic suits.

As soon as she walked through the doorway, George and Emma came hurrying over. 'So much for our Saturday off,' Emma remarked.

'What's the situation?' she asked George, choosing to ignore Emma's comment; she understood how she felt.

'Our deceased is Frances Lowes, IC1 female, seventy-eight years of age, found dead in the living room,' George informed her.

'Found by her granddaughter Amelia Simpson and her friend, Megan Parkinson. Apparently they hadn't heard from Mrs Lowes for several days, which they say is out of character, and became worried,' Emma stated, looking at her notebook.

'Anyone else live here? Any other family?'

'No,' said Emma. 'Her husband died thirty years ago and her only daughter died in 2011. Her only listed family is the granddaughter.'

'Where are the granddaughter and her friend now?' Jenny

asked.

'Ms Simpson has been taken to St Mary's: apparently she was in quite a state when the first responder arrived. Her friend went with her.'

'We'll need to talk to them ASAP,' Jenny told the two detectives, and headed for the living room.

From the doorway, Jenny watched the CSIs at work. Several numbered place cards identified key aspects of the scene, each being photographed and logged. The body was still in situ, lying prone, head to one side and eyes closed. There was a significant pool of dried blood around the body and Jenny winced at the smell. It didn't matter how many crime scenes you attended, you never got used to it. Next to the body crouched another person dressed in a forensic suit who Jenny immediately recognized as the forensic pathologist, Dr Rahman.

'What do we know so far?' she asked Emma, who had come to stand beside her.

'There is no sign of forced entry. The windows were all locked, same as the back door, and Ms Parkinson said that Ms Simpson had to unlock the front door before they could enter. They found that knife,' - she gestured towards the knife still lying near the body - 'which we expect to be the murder weapon, but so far they haven't been able to recover any prints from it. They have recovered prints from a number of surfaces throughout the house, and we will need to check these against the deceased, the granddaughter and her friend to see if there are any unknowns.'

'Who's our lead CSI on this one?' Jenny asked.

'That would be me, ma'am. Sunil Kapoor.' A tall figure dressed in a forensic suit walked towards the detectives.

'What have you found?' The man was nearly a foot taller than Jenny, broad-shouldered, and appeared muscular underneath the white suit. A rugby player in his free time, Jenny guessed.

'The deceased was definitely killed here: the body hasn't been moved. We have plenty of blood on the carpet around the body and we're going to send a sample and the knife to the lab for analysis. Not sure on the time of death, but the body has definitely been here a couple of days at least. Hopefully we should know more soon,' he said, nodding in the direction of the pathologist.

'Consistent with what the granddaughter has said,' Emma muttered.

'Doesn't appear to have been much of a struggle, nothing was overturned or damaged, and judging by the attire of the deceased I would guess that she was killed either late at night or early in the morning. I would say that she was surprised by her killer.' George nodded at Sunil's assessment. 'Also, there's a knife missing from the block in the kitchen. The make and style of the remaining knives match the one in the living room, which suggests-'

'Which suggests the knife was not brought here by the killer but was grabbed at a moment's notice,' Jenny finished.

'It has all the hallmarks of a robbery gone wrong,' George observed. 'The suspect targets an old woman living by herself, breaks in late at night looking for money or jewelry to steal, gets spooked when they hear someone wake up and come downstairs. They grab the knife, stab the victim in a moment of panic, drop the knife and run.'

'It's plausible,' Jenny conceded, 'but let's not jump to any conclusions just yet.'

She thanked Sunil and walked through the hallway into the kitchen, switching on a light as the room was still shrouded in darkness, Emma fell into step with her.

'I don't like that there are no obvious signs of entry,' Jenny said, looking around the kitchen.

'Ma'am?'

'George's theory… If this was just a break-in gone wrong, where's the break-in aspect? How did the suspect get in?'

The kitchen was immaculate; clearly Frances had been a house-proud woman. No dishes had been left in the sink and the counter was spotless. Jenny went over to the knife block. Sure enough, there was a gap where a carving knife should have been.

They continued upstairs, looking around them. The bathroom was as spotless and tidy as the kitchen. They stepped into what appeared to be the master bedroom, which was the first room that showed some signs of being lived in. Like every room so far, the curtains were closed, but the duvet was thrown back, the pillows on one side were crumpled, and there was a glass of water on the bedside table, a few specks of dust on its surface.

On the cabinet, besides the lamp and digital alarm clock, were a Kindle and a mobile phone, charging. Jenny pressed a button on the side and the screen lit up. Twelve missed calls, most of them from *Amelia Mobile*, two from *Heather Mobile*, and seven text messages, the contents hidden until the phone was unlocked. 'We need access to this,' she told Emma.

'Perhaps the granddaughter knows the code,' Emma suggested.

'We need to speak to her.' Jenny put the phone down. 'We'll know more when we get an estimated time of death, but I reckon the killer disturbed our victim during the night, not first thing in the morning. She strikes me as the kind of woman who would make the bed as soon as she got up, and the curtains would be open.'

They headed downstairs to find George still in discussion with Sunil. He came over to them. 'Sunil and his team are pretty much done for now, and the undertakers are on their way. Dr Rahman has also finished his initial assessment.'

'OK, good,' Jenny replied. 'Let's see what he's got to say.'

Jenny and Emma made their way into the living room and approached Dr Rahman, who was packing up his black medical bag. 'What can you tell us, doc?'

'This appears to be the death scene. Until I can perform a more thorough examination and post mortem, I would say that the cause of death appears to be the single stab wound to the abdomen - most likely carried out using the knife found at the scene - and bled out. The amount of blood and its spread suggests that the victim's heart was still beating when she hit the floor and I haven't found any signs of a struggle. Due to the temperature of the body and the absence of rigor mortis, I would say the deceased has been dead around forty hours. I would put the time of death anywhere between eleven pm on the fifth and two am on the sixth. I should be able to narrow the time of death down further once I've been able to examine the body properly.'

Jenny and Emma thanked the doctor and went into the hallway. 'George, I want you and a couple of uniforms to start door-to-door. Focus on whether they've seen anyone suspicious over the last couple of days or whether they recall anything out of the ordinary, no matter how small. Find out if there's any CCTV along this street: home or business. If there is, I want it.'

'Yes, ma'am.'

'In the meantime, Emma and I will go and speak to Amelia Simpson.'

* * *

Jenny and Emma pulled into the car park of St Mary's Hospital and abandoned the car in the first space they found near the front entrance. A brief conversation at reception confirmed that Ms Amelia Simpson was in an observation room just off A&E.

In A&E, they were pointed towards a small room tucked away on one side. Jenny knocked once and they headed in.

The majority of the room was taken up by a bed, its curtain not drawn. Three people were looking at her: two women and a man. 'I'm Detective Inspector Stone, and this is Detective Sergeant Marie,' Jenny said. The man was sitting on the side of the bed, his arm around a brown-haired woman in her early thirties, her eyes red and puffy. She was sat on the bed with her legs tucked up under her, clutching a cup of tea. Her hands shook, spilling tea onto the bed and fresh tears ran down her cheeks. The second woman, her blonde hair tied back in a loose ponytail, was standing to the right of the bed, her arms wrapped around her stomach. She looked as if she had been crying too but her gaze was direct and she appeared to be holding it together a lot better than the first woman was. *This must be the friend, Megan Parkinson, which means the woman on the bed is Amelia Simpson.*

'I'm the senior investigating officer in the murder of Mrs Frances Lowes.' This brought a groan and crying from the bed. 'Are you Megan Parkinson and Amelia Simpson?'

'You got ID?' the lone male asked, frowning.

'Of course,' Jenny replied, not missing a beat, and with Emma, produced her warrant card. 'And you are?'

'My name's Sam. I'm Amelia's boyfriend.'

'Do you have a surname, Sam, or are you like Beyoncé or Rihanna?' Emma snapped. Jenny shot her a warning look.

'Sam Jones,' he said, scowling.

'We really need to speak to both Megan and Amelia, Sam,' said Jenny.

'Can't it wait? Amelia's in no condition to answer any of your questions. Her gran has just died, for God's sake.'

'I appreciate that this is a difficult time,' Jenny replied, ignoring Sam's snort, 'but the first twenty-four hours are crucial in an investigation like this. I promise we'll keep it brief.'

Sam opened his mouth to protest further but Amelia placed a hand on his arm. 'It's OK,' she told him.

'Thank you,' Jenny said, with a small smile. 'Can you tell me what time you last saw the deceased?'

'Ummm, I think it was around nine pm last Thursday. I always go round to see Gran on Thursdays.'

'And how did she seem?' Emma asked.

'What do you mean?' Amelia asked warily.

'Did she seem worried? Distracted, out of sorts?'

'N-no, she seemed fine. Just normal.'

'Did she have any enemies that you're aware of? Had she fallen out with anyone lately?' asked Jenny.

'Enemies?' said Megan, a look of incredulity on her face. 'She was an old woman in her seventies, not a gangster. What kind of enemies does someone like that have?'

'Was she active in the community? Had she upset someone lately? Argued with anyone?' Jenny kept her tone level. It was always difficult interviewing family this soon after a death, especially in these sorts of circumstances. It required sensitivity, but also persistence.

'No, everyone loved Gran,' Amelia told the detectives. 'No one had a bad word to say about her, but-' She looked down at her hands, clenched in her lap.

'But what, Amelia?' Emma asked gently.

'No, it was nothing.'

'Amelia, any information, no matter how trivial it may seem, could be the key to catching whoever did this,' said Jenny.

'Well, you and Gran argued last Thursday,' Amelia said, looking at Sam. Jenny and Emma exchanged glances.

'Amelia!' Sam protested, his eyes wide. 'That wasn't an argument, it was barely anything!'

'I don't think you had anything to do with it,' Amelia added quickly. 'They just asked if anyone had recently argued with Gran.'

'Would anyone have wanted to hurt her?' Emma asked.

Amelia stared at her then started to cry, burying her face in Sam's side.

'Right, this has gone on long enough,' said Sam, glaring at Jenny and Emma in turn. 'You're upsetting her!'

Jenny sighed, admitting defeat. 'OK, we'll stop there, but we do need to take full statements from both you, Amelia, and you, Megan, as soon as possible.' She reached into the inside pocket of her jacket and handed a couple of business cards to Megan. 'If you recall anything in the meantime call one of these numbers, even if you think it's nothing. Let us be the judge of that.'

The detectives left the room, closing the door behind them. Amelia's crying was still audible.

'He's an aggressive one, isn't he?' Jenny said to Emma as they made their way back to the car.

'He was. Interesting that he and the deceased argued on the probable night of her death.'

'Definitely something we need to follow up on,' Jenny replied. She unlocked the car and they climbed in.

Chapter 7

Jenny strode into the team briefing room with a spring in her step as she did, coffee clutched in her hand. Even at the start of a new case some things never changed, especially to a detective. She looked around the sea of faces. Most seemed tired, rubbing the stubble on their cheeks or the sleep out of their eyes, most cradling coffees of their own. Jenny, however, was full of energy. She always was at the start of a case like this: eager to get involved, to catch the people responsible. It was what she loved most about being a copper. The only other person who appeared raring to go was DS Marie. She was chatting to Claire Watson, a junior DC not long moved up from uniform and eager to prove herself.

'Good morning, everyone,' Jenny said as she made her way to the front of the room. The general murmur died down and all heads turned to face her. She noticed DCI Edwards lingering at the back and momentarily faltered, surprised to see her boss in work on a Sunday. Jenny self-consciously straightened her plain white work shirt and picked at a tiny piece of fluff before she continued.

'As you may or may not know by now, at 15:20 yesterday

afternoon we received a call from a Ms Megan Parkinson. She and her friend, a Ms Amelia Simpson, hadn't heard from Amelia's grandmother for a couple of days and went round to check on her. Amelia's grandmother was a Mrs Frances Lowes, seventy-eight years old. When they gained entry into the house they found Mrs Lowes dead on the living-room floor.'

'What do we know so far?' DCI Edwards asked, his hands clasped behind his back.

Jenny gave DCI Edwards a quick rundown of everything they knew, then continued. 'She was last seen by Amelia Simpson and her boyfriend Sam Jones at around nine pm on Thursday evening. Judging from her attire and the fact that all the curtains were closed, we are currently working to the assumption that she was murdered later that evening. We should be able to confirm this once we get an estimated time of death.'

'What has been recovered from the scene?' This came from another member of CID, DC Simon Michaels.

'The main item recovered so far was the knife. There was a significant amount of blood at the scene, which given the wound, I think it's reasonable to assume that it came from the victim but we're still waiting on sample analysis to confirm this.' Jenny turned to the CSI lead, Sunil Kapoor, who was leaning against the side wall, dressed in jeans and a polo shirt. 'Where are we up to with this?'

'I'll chase up the lab this morning, but I don't expect to get anything back till tomorrow at the earliest.'

Jenny frowned. 'See what you can do,' she told him, and he nodded. 'George, how did you get on with yesterday's door-to-door enquiries?'

'Unfortunately, not well. The woman on the left is in her eighties and nearly deaf. She said she went to bed at nine pm and didn't hear a thing after that. She does remember seeing

Amelia arrive earlier that evening, and did confirm that she comes round a couple of times a week and always on a Thursday. She said that she was going to say hello to Amelia until she spotted her boyfriend. She isn't a fan: apparently he's a nasty piece of work.'

'Interesting,' noted Jenny. 'Anything else?'

'The young couple on the other side said they were awake till gone eleven but didn't hear anything either. There was no sign of any CCTV along the road, and no businesses either.'

'I didn't think we would get that lucky,' Jenny conceded.

'What's our initial hypothesis?' DCI Edwards asked from the back of the room.

'To all intents and purposes, it looks like a burglary gone wrong. The victim woke up in the middle of the night, went downstairs, and found someone in the house who shouldn't have been there. In their panic the suspect grabbed a knife and used it before fleeing the scene. However, there are some problems with this theory.'

'What's that?' asked someone near the back.

'For a start, there were no obvious signs of entry into the house: the doors and windows were all locked and secure. In addition, nothing has been reported missing, although we need someone who knew the deceased well to confirm this.'

'There was that burglary in Pear Tree Close last weekend,' Claire pointed out. 'That's only a mile away from Argyll Street. Maybe they're related.'

'It's worth looking into,' admitted Jenny.

'Have we had a statement from the people who found the body?' asked a uniformed officer.

'Not an official one, no. The granddaughter, Amelia, was in shock, and was taken to St Mary's as a precaution. DS Marie and I went up there to speak to her and Ms Parkinson yesterday afternoon, but didn't get far. Amelia told us that she and Sam had popped round to see Frances as usual on

Thursday but hadn't heard from her since. We did find out something interesting, however.' The corner of Jenny's mouth crept up a fraction. 'Mrs Lowes and Amelia's boyfriend Sam had argued on Thursday evening. I agree with the assessment given by the neighbour; he does seem like a nasty piece of work. Very hostile from the moment we appeared.' Emma nodded in confirmation.

'Do we know what they argued about, or how serious it was?' asked someone Jenny didn't recognise.

'No, but we're looking to get that answered ASAP,' Jenny replied. 'Right, assignments. DC Michaels, I want you and a couple of uniforms to continue with the door-to-door enquiries and expand them to the whole street. Focus on the Thursday night and whether they can remember any historic disturbances. DC Watson, I want you to pull phone and financial records for the deceased and check for any social media presence-'

'For a seventy-eight year old?' Claire raised an eyebrow.

'Don't discount it: more and more of the senior community have some form of social media presence,' Jenny replied.

'Yes, ma'am,' said DC Watson, her expression still sceptical.

'Emma, I want you to look into any CCTV and ANPR for Thursday evening.' Another nod from Emma. 'We also need to know the victim's movements and who she interacted with in the days before the attack. I'm sure I don't need to remind any of you that there's a killer on the loose, and I want whoever did this in a cell by the end of the day!'

'What are you going to do, ma'am?' asked a uniformed officer at the back of the room.

'DC Bancroft and I will speak to Ms Simpson and Ms Parkinson, then get an update from the pathologist.' Jenny clapped her hands. 'OK, people, let's get to it.'

People began to disperse, talking amongst themselves. Jenny noted with a smile that they seemed a lot more energised than when she had entered the room. She was about to leave when she saw DCI Edwards still standing at the back.

'Jennifer, do you have a moment?'

'Of course, sir.'

Jenny followed DCI Edwards down to his office. On the way she saw Emma raise an eyebrow at her, to which she mouthed 'No idea.'

'Please, take a seat.' The DCI closed the door, moved round to the other side of his desk and sat down. 'I'm sure I don't need to tell you that we must get this case wrapped up as quickly as possible.' His tone was sharp.

'No, sir. I want this person off the streets as much as you do,' Jenny replied, working hard to keep the annoyance out of her voice. *What does he think I've been doing?* She took a deep, calming breath.

'We can't let this investigation drag on any longer than necessary. There is already a story on the County Press website about an incident in Ryde yesterday that required a sizeable police presence. It's only a matter of time before it becomes common knowledge that there's a killer on the loose, and then pointed questions about how we've handled this and our response will start to be asked.'

'We're on it sir,' Jenny said.

Chapter 8

Jenny and George walked up the drive to the red front door. Jenny paused and surveyed the house. The front, painted white, could do with refreshing, and weeds had started to push through the cracks in the concrete driveway, but all in all, she thought, not a bad-looking house. She turned around and looked towards the Solent, then turned back to the balconies extending from the first and second floors. 'I bet the view is great up there when the sun's out,' she remarked to George.

George made to press the buzzer for the top-floor flat, but Jenny held up a hand. She gave the front door a little push and it swung open. 'Always worth checking first,' she said, with a smile.

They stepped over a small pile of unclaimed post and went upstairs. 'Must be a pain in the arse with your shopping,' George commented.

On the top floor, Jenny took a deep breath and knocked on the door.

Footsteps clumped to the door and Sam appeared. He didn't say anything, staring at Jenny and George, and Jenny matched his gaze.

'What?' he said, eventually.

'Hello again, Mr Jones. Can we speak to Ms Simpson, please?'

He opened the door fully and stood back. Jenny strode past him into the flat, George following in her wake. She carried on down the hallway until she spotted the living room and went in. Amelia was sitting on a corner sofa, dressed in pale-yellow pyjamas and a pink dressing gown, with a tabby cat curled asleep on her lap. Her eyes were red, and the bags underneath them suggested that she hadn't slept much since Jenny had last seen her.

'The police are here to speak to you,' Sam told Amelia as he entered the room.

Amelia merely nodded.

'How are you doing? Do you want me to make you another cup of tea?' he asked gently, and Amelia shook her head. He moved aside and leaned against the door frame.

'I'm sorry to disturb you again, Ms Simpson-'

'Amelia, please.'

'Amelia,' Jenny amended. 'This is my colleague, Detective Constable George Bancroft. Is now a good time?'

Amelia shrugged, which they took to mean yes.

'Do you mind?' Jenny asked, gesturing towards a couple of chairs.

Another shrug.

'Thank you,' Jenny said as she pulled up a chair and sat down. 'Amelia, I know this won't be easy but I need to ask you about your gran: her movements and activities on the run-up to her death, who she saw, who she interacted with, any clubs she is part of. I also need to know what happened the last time you saw her. I need to know everything you can tell me. Anything, no matter how small, may be pivotal in helping us to catch the person who did this. Can you do this for me?'

A nod.

Jenny pulled a digital recorder from her pocket and put it on the coffee table. 'Is this all right?'

Another nod, which Jenny took as assent.

Jenny switched on the recorder. 'This is Detective Inspector Jennifer Stone, it is ten-oh-six am on the eighth of May and I am here with Detective Constable George Bancroft to take a statement from Amelia Simpson in connection with the murder of Mrs Frances Lowes. Also present is Mr Sam Jones.' She turned to Amelia. 'Can you confirm you're happy for this conversation to be recorded?'

'Yeah, I don't mind.'

'Thank you. Amelia, please can you tell me about your grandmother, Frances Lowes.'

'What do you want to know?'

'Was there anyone who wished to harm her, that you can think of?'

'No, everybody loved Gran. I still can't believe that this has happened.'

'Tell me about the week just gone. What did Frances do? Where did she go?'

'She has the church committee on a Monday-'

'Which church is it?'

'All Saint's, a couple of roads down. She has that every Monday until around three. After that, she normally goes for a coffee with some of the other women.'

'Can you give me any names?' Jenny asked her.

'No. Wait, I do know one: Heather something. I don't know her surname but she rang me yesterday because Gran hadn't turned up for a meeting they'd arranged.'

'Do you have that number?'

Amelia picked up her phone, scrolled to her call log and showed the detectives the number; George scribbled it down in his notebook. 'What else can you tell us?' asked Jenny.

'We normally meet up on Tuesdays. Either she comes to the shop and we go out for lunch, or I go round to hers in the evening. Last week, I went to hers.'

'What did you discuss?'

'I'm not sure: nothing special. We talked about our days, she asked about the shop.'

'And how did she seem?'

'She was absolutely fine; she always was. Nothing fazed her, and if something was going on she wouldn't have kept it a secret. She would have told me!' Her voice rose slightly, and the cat raised his head with an inquisitive look. Amelia absentmindedly scratched him behind one of his ears and he settled down again.

'What about last Thursday?'

'On Thursdays she goes to the seniors' Scrabble club. She says – she used to say that keeping your mind active keeps you young and sharp. That's the thing, Detective: my gran wasn't stupid or gullible. There's no way she would have let someone she didn't know into her house. If someone had turned up claiming to be from somewhere or other, like a utility company, she would leave them outside until she had spoken to someone to verify it.'

'She sounds like a smart woman,' George commented.

'She was. I still can't believe the last conversation I ever had with her was an argument,' she said, her voice cracking. She wiped her eyes with her dressing-gown sleeve.

Jenny and George exchanged glances. 'You mentioned something about this yesterday,' said Jenny. 'Can you tell me what happened?'

'It was stupid, really. I dragged Sam round with me when I went to see her although I know they don't get along. I guess I thought – hoped, really – that if they spent time together they'd grow to like each other. Stupid, I know. Anyway, it wasn't long before they started sniping at each other, then Gran asked why I was with such a loser.'

I really like the sound of this woman, Jenny thought, suppressing a smile.

'So Sam swore at her and she kicked him out. And then she accused me of wasting my life.'

'In what way?'

'She said I should be doing more with my life than running a small flower shop on a small island, and that I'd been playing it safe since my parents died. I took offence and stormed out.' She swallowed. 'I didn't mean any of what I said. I felt guilty and tried to ring her first thing on Friday but I got no answer. I just assumed she was still angry; I had no idea that she was...' She started to cry again.

'There's nothing you could have done,' Jenny told her.

'I tried ringing a few times, and I even sent a couple of messages apologising.'

'Tell me about Saturday, Amelia.'

'I met up with Megan around two at the Horse and Crown. We were planning a lazy afternoon in the sun, drinking wine. You know how it is,' she said, with a small smile.

'Where was Sam?'

'He was playing five-a-side at Smallbrook; he was going to meet us when he'd finished. Megan went to the bar to get more drinks. My phone rang and I answered it, thinking it would be Gran, but it wasn't. It was Heather, saying that Gran hadn't shown up for coffee that morning and she was worried. After that I was too worried to stay, so me and Megan went round there and that was when we...'

'How did you get into the house? Was the door open?'

'No. It was locked but I have a key, so I let myself in.'

'Can we go back to last Thursday, for a minute. You said that after Sam left you argued with Frances before leaving as well. What did you do for the rest of the evening?'

'I went straight home.'

'And then what?' Jenny prompted.

'I had a go at Sam, told him off for swearing at Gran.' Amelia was quiet for a moment before she continued. 'I then got into bed, watched TV for a little while before going to sleep.'

'What did Sam say when you spoke to him?'

'He said that it wasn't his fault, that Gran started it and that he didn't even want to go round in the first place.'

Jenny turned to face Sam who was still leaning against the doorframe. 'What about you Sam? What did you do for the rest of the evening?'

'Nothing much, just played on the computer for a while.'

'What time did you go to bed?'

'I dunno, around eleven I think.'

'OK. I think that's everything I need. Interview ended at ten twenty-four am.' She switched off the recorder and returned it to her pocket.

'Thank you, Amelia, I know that wasn't easy,' Jenny told her.

'You will catch the person that did this, won't you?' Amelia asked, sniffing.

'I promise we will do everything in our power,' Jenny replied. Amelia nodded, apparently satisfied.

Jenny and George got up to leave. Sam went to open the front door, but Jenny stopped and turned back to Amelia. 'That reminds me: we have recovered a phone and tablet from your gran's house. Whilst we can apply to the service provider for the call and text history, that takes time. It would help us greatly if you know the codes to unlock them?'

'0290: the month and year of my birth,' said Amelia. 'I helped set it up for her.'

'Thank you,' said Jenny. 'Would you be able to do one more thing for me, please?'

'Sure, what is it?'

'We need you to go through Frances's house, check to see if anything has been taken. Any valuables she might have, or any cash she's hidden away that's now gone.'

Amelia nodded and Jenny thanked her for her time before she departed, Sam closing the flat door firmly behind them.

'Quite a nice flat: good location, great view. Being a florist must pay well,' Jenny commented wryly as they left the building.

'Where to next?' George asked as they walked to the car.

'Next we visit Megan Parkinson.'

Jenny and George arrived at the two bedroom mid-terrace that Megan had rented for the last five years. The road was busy, and it took a few circuits before they found somewhere to park. 'Not as well off as her best friend,' George noted as they made their way down the short path.

Megan must have seen them coming, because she answered the door before Jenny had a chance to knock. Megan stood in the doorway and stared at them. She appeared more collected than Amelia, but still bore the marks of someone who hadn't slept well the night before. There were dark bags under her eyes and she stifled a yawn.

'I'm sorry to trouble you, Ms Parkinson,' said Jenny. 'May we have a few moments of your time?' Megan nodded and gestured for them to come in.

Jenny's eyes widened at all the paintings hanging in the hallway. Her surprise must have been apparent.

'They're all mine,' said Megan with a small smile, 'by which I mean I painted them all. I'm an artist. An aspiring one, anyway.'

'These are actually pretty good,' George commented, then

blushed as he realised how condescending he sounded.

'I've seen this one before,' Jenny said, frowning at a watercolour of Ryde beach.

'My first-ever sale,' Megan replied sadly. 'That one is a copy. The original is hanging in Frances's living room.'

'I'm afraid that's why we're here, Ms Parkinson. I need you to tell me in your own words what happened yesterday.'

Megan led them to a living room that was also covered in paintings and gestured towards two chairs, taking a seat on the sofa by the window. Jenny pulled out the digital recorder, placed it on the coffee table, hit Record, and completed the formalities and introductions.

'Thank you for agreeing to talk to us, Ms Parkinson. How are you doing today?' Jenny asked.

'I've been better,' she replied, with a feeble smile.

'Did you know the deceased well?'

Megan paused, considering her answer. 'Not really. I mean, I saw her whenever I went round with Amelia, but it was only chit-chat.'

'Do you know why anyone would want to hurt her?'

'No. She was a good woman: she always made time to talk and actually listened when you spoke. When I told her that I was an artist, she made me bring my portfolio on the very next visit. That was when she saw my watercolour of Ryde beach. She said she loved that area and that my painting was really good. She offered to buy it from me there and then and wouldn't take no for an answer. That's the only painting I've ever sold. She cared about people and what they had to say. That's why people were drawn to her.'

'What can you tell me about Amelia's relationship with her grandmother?'

'Amelia adored her gran, and has done for as long as I've known her. It's all to do with losing her mum and dad: her gran is the only part of them she has left.' Megan paused.

'Had left.'

'Amelia said that she and Frances argued on the night when we think Frances died,' said Jenny. 'Did they argue often?'

'No, never – well, very rarely. Everybody has arguments, don't they? It doesn't mean that they didn't love each other.'

'When they argued, what did they tend to argue about?' Jenny asked.

'More often than not, Sam. Frances never liked him; she thought Amelia could do better.'

'Do you think she was right? That Amelia could do better?' Jenny leant forward slightly.

Megan looked out of the living-room window towards the street a few feet away. 'Sam is a nice guy...'

Jenny watched her. 'But?'

'He's a little self-centred and he only really thinks of himself. He does love Amelia, but I also think he loves the easy life he has with her.' George raised his eyebrows and scribbled in his notebook.

'In what way?' asked Jenny.

Megan grimaced and looked away, she thought for a minute before continuing. 'I don't think he pays anything towards the house or the bills and he only works part-time. In his words - *I don't earn much but I don't need much.*'

'Who pays for everything?' asked Jenny, frowning.

'Amelia does.'

'Can you tell us in your own words what happened on Saturday?' George asked.

Megan told them about drinking with Amelia at the Horse and Crown, and how Amelia had received a phone call about her grandmother.

'How did Amelia seem to you after the phone call?' Jenny asked.

'Worried. She left almost immediately and I nearly had to

run just to keep up with her. She was worried Frances might have fallen and hurt herself, it never even occurred to me that she might be-' Megan faltered and wiped her eyes.

'What happened next?'

'We got to Frances's house and Amelia ran upstairs whilst I went into...' She looked away. 'There was so much blood,' she said, her voice barely a whisper.

'Please, Ms Parkinson,' Jenny urged gently.

Megan took a deep breath. 'I went into the living room and that's when I saw her. I don't really remember what happened next, but I must have screamed because Amelia came barrelling downstairs and pushed past me. Then she started screaming as well. That's when I rang 999.'

'OK, I think we have everything that we need. Thank you for your time.' Jenny switched off the recorder, put it in her jacket pocket, and along with George, made to leave.

'Do you have any suspects?' Megan called after them.

Jenny paused, then turned to face her. 'I can't discuss the details of an ongoing case, I'm afraid.'

'Have you spoken to *her* yet?' Megan asked.

'We have already spoken to Ms Simpson-'

'No, not Amelia. *Her*, the other florist. Kirstie.' She practically spat the name.

'No, why? Should we?' Jenny asked carefully, her attention fully on Megan again.

'She didn't tell you, did she?' Megan rolled her eyes.

'Why don't you tell us, then,' said Jenny, a hint of impatience in her voice.

'Kirstie runs the flower shop just down from Amelia's. She's been targeting Amelia for the past year, and you lot haven't done anything about it.' Megan folded her arms across her chest.

'Targeting Amelia how?' George asked.

'Well, only a couple of days ago Kirstie threw a stone

through the front window of the shop. She's thrown paint at the front of the shop and slashed the tyres on Amelia's delivery van. Amelia's reported it all to you lot, and nothing.'

'I promise you, Ms Parkinson, I will personally look into this,' Jenny assured her, and the two detectives left.

'We need to find out what the hell is going on with this other florist,' Jenny said to George as they walked back to the car. 'And that's not all: there's definitely something Megan isn't telling us about the boyfriend,' she added as she unlocked the car and they both climbed in.

Chapter 9

Back at the station, Jenny grabbed a coffee from the kitchenette and called the team into the briefing room to get a rundown of what they had learned. They had some ideas and some leads, but far too many open questions. Hopefully the rest of her team would be able to fill in some of the gaps.

The team started to file in, some taking seats whilst others leaned against the walls, some talking animatedly amongst themselves. Jenny entered the room and walked to one of the whiteboards at the front, where she pinned up a picture of the deceased, Frances Lowes.

'Right, people, settle down,' she called out over the general murmur of the briefing room. The chatter died down as everyone focused on her. 'So, what have we all found out?' she asked. 'Emma, why don't you start us off?'

All heads swivelled towards the detective sergeant leaning against the door frame, her eyes slightly glazed, a coffee steaming in her hand. Jenny understood her pain; rooting through hours of CCTV and ANPR footage took its toll even on the best of them.

'Unfortunately, we haven't identified anybody suspicious

in the vicinity of the victim's house around the approximate time of death. They could have come in via Pellhurst Road, though. We don't have any cameras at that end of Argyll Street, so they could have come and gone unrecorded,' Emma said with more than a hint of frustration.

'OK, well, that's a shame; I didn't expect we'd get that lucky-'

'We did get something, though,' Emma continued. 'The camera at the east end of the street captured Amelia and Sam entering Argyll Street at just before eight pm. The same camera shows Sam leaving at 20:37.'

'By himself, or alone?' someone asked.

'Alone,' Emma replied. 'It then shows Amelia leaving the street roughly twelve minutes later.'

'That matches what she told us,' Jenny muttered. 'DC Michaels, any luck with the door-to-door enquiries?'

'I'm afraid not. A few people think they may have seen Sam and Amelia heading towards the house together, or leaving separately, but that's it. Most people were in bed at the time of the murder, and those who weren't don't remember seeing or hearing anything out of the ordinary.'

'No independent CCTV, no doorbell cams?' Jenny asked.

'Afraid not.'

'What about you, Claire?' she asked the young DC sitting at the front.

Claire flipped open her notebook. 'I've put a request through for the phone records, but it'll be a day or two before we get them back-'

'That reminds me,' said Jenny. 'Frances's granddaughter has given us the access codes for both the recovered mobile phone and the tablet.' Jenny read out the code and Claire scribbled it down. 'Now, what about social media?'

'Yes, actually,' said Claire, 'she had profiles on both Facebook and Instagram. Nothing much to report on the latter: mostly photos of baking and Amelia. She was active on a couple of local Facebook groups, but nothing sinister. I've got a list of friends from both platforms and we're going through them to see if any jump out.' She smiled. 'We did find something worth noting in her financial records, though. She owned her house outright and had quite a bit put away in savings – upwards of two hundred thousand pounds. No sign of any debts, and she appeared to live a fairly frugal lifestyle.'

'Interesting,' commented Jenny.

'What did you learn from Amelia and Megan?' said Emma.

'Much the same as we did at the hospital: apparently she was much-loved throughout the community. Amelia also described her as street smart; she said that there was no way her gran would have opened the door to someone she didn't know, and would always verify any ID.'

'Did she elaborate on the argument with the boyfriend, Sam?'

'She did,' said Jenny. 'Sam and Amelia hadn't been at the house long before Sam and Frances began needling each other. There has never been much love lost between those two, though Amelia has kept trying to build bridges. Apparently, Frances said that Sam was a loser and Sam swore at her. It was at that point that Frances kicked him out. After that, Frances and Amelia continued the argument; Frances accused Amelia of wasting her life with Sam and thought she could be doing more than running a flower shop. She accused her of playing it safe since her parents died. Amelia stormed out and that was the last time she saw her grandmother alive.' Jenny surveyed the attentive faces.

'We also spoke to Ms Parkinson. She confirmed that Frances and Sam didn't like each other very much. She said that he does love Amelia, but she thinks he also loves the easy life he has with her. And that's not all. According to Ms Parkinson, Amelia is being harassed by the woman who owns the flower shop just down the road from hers.'

'What kind of harassment?' asked DC Michaels.

'Apparently, over the last twelve months, she's thrown paint at Amelia's shop, slashed her delivery van's tyres and earlier this week she threw a rock through the shop window. More disturbingly, Megan claims that Amelia had reported some of these incidents to us and that nothing ever came of it. Simon, I want you to look into these reports right away and find out if they were ever followed up.'

'Yes, ma'am.'

On the whiteboard, below the picture of Frances, Jenny wrote and underlined the word 'Timeline'. Below that she wrote 'May 5th' and '11pm-1am: expected time of death'. 'Right, this is what we know so far,' she said. 'Mrs Frances Lowes was murdered in her own home between eleven pm on the fifth of May and one am on the sixth of May.' She tapped her pen against the date. 'We know the last person to see her alive was her granddaughter, Amelia Simpson, who went round with her boyfriend, Samuel Jones, for her usual Thursday visit at eight pm that evening. Not long after that, we know that Mrs Lowes and Sam Jones got into an argument and he stormed out of the house, shortly followed by Amelia at 20:49. Next, we know that an intruder somehow gained entry into Mrs Lowes's house, though for what purpose we don't know, picked up a kitchen knife and stabbed her to death. Any questions so far?'

'Motive?' one of the detectives called from near the back.

Jenny wrote the word on the whiteboard, next to the picture. 'That's something we're still not sure about,' she admitted. 'Initially it seemed like a robbery gone wrong, but we just don't know yet. Ms Simpson is going to have a look through the house and will let us know if anything is missing.'

'Financial gain?' Claire asked from her seat at the front. 'The victim was clearly not short of a few quid and she owned her house outright. As her only living relative, the granddaughter is likely to inherit all of this. Maybe she got tired of waiting for nature to take its course?'

'It's certainly true that she stands to inherit a lot from this but her grief does seem pretty genuine,' Jenny told the detective. She turned back to the whiteboard, her brow wrinkling in concentration. *She does stand to gain a lot from this, but can I really picture her stabbing her own grandmother to death?* Jenny absentmindedly rubbed her tired eyes with her thumb and index finger.

'What about Sam?' Emma asked. 'If Amelia is due to come into a lot of money then so is he, indirectly. As we already know, there wasn't any love lost between him and the victim.' A general murmur of agreement rippled through the room.

Jenny wrote 'Suspects', underlined it, and wrote Sam's name beneath. 'I agree. We need to dig deeper with both Amelia and Sam. Claire, get a warrant and pull the financial records for both of them, and for the flower shop as well. Let's see what we can uncover.'

[2]

London, May 2013

The tube carriages shook slightly as the train made its way through the dark tunnel. It was a Saturday afternoon, and the Central Line tube was full of people. There were a number of tourists, easily identifiable as they glanced nervously around the carriage tightly clutching their maps of the underground, noses wrinkling at the smell of stale urine and sweat that normal Londoners didn't even notice anymore. At the far end was a group of young lads all wearing Blackpool football shirts. They were talking loudly and animatedly about the previous day's football match, and how next year was finally going to be *their* year. At the opposite end to the football fans, the group of four girls appeared not to notice them, too preoccupied with their own conversation.

'So what are we going to do tonight, then?' Erica asked, gazing at the others.

'You could come round mine? We could watch a film?' suggested Katie.

'I want to go out in my new dress!' said Samantha. The girls had spent a pleasant day wandering around Portobello Market and were clutching several bags of new clothes, except for Ashley.

'What do you want to do, Ash?' Katie asked.

'Sam's right – let's get dressed up and head into the city,' Ashley said with a smile.

The others looked apprehensive.

'Come on,' Ashley continued, undaunted. 'If we all dress up, we're bound to find a couple of bars that'll serve us.'

'I'm up for that,' said Samantha, earning a smile from Ashley. After a little more persuasion, the other two girls were convinced as well.

The group hopped off the tube at Mile End and agreed to meet later at Erica's. She lived nearest to the tube station and her mum would be at work all evening – and was fairly relaxed about the girls helping themselves to drinks providing they didn't get carried away.

Ashley turned onto Hewlett Road and had to step off the pavement to get past the mob of twenty-something blokes gathered outside the fried chicken shop, kebabs in hand, already smelling strongly of alcohol. Ashley smiled at the sight; she did love London. She reached her house, pushed the gate open, unlocked the door and stepped inside.

'Hi Mum,' she shouted as she pushed the front door shut, swearing quietly as it stuck and shoving it hard to close it. *When will she get this fixed?*

Silence. Ashley frowned.

'Mum?' She glanced into the kitchen – maybe her mum had just popped out for a forgotten ingredient – but the kitchen was empty and the hob bare. No sign that dinner had even been thought about, let alone started.

I'm sure she's not working today, and she didn't say she was going out, thought Ashley with a touch of irritation. She pulled out her phone and dialled her mum's number. It connected, and a moment later she heard the familiar ringtone coming from the empty living room. Ashley's frown deepened, then eased as she decided there must be an obvious explanation which was eluding her.

Ashley dumped her bag on the floor, opened the freezer, and smiled in triumph as she pulled out a frozen pizza. She switched the oven on and put the pizza straight in. In her opinion, people had better things to do with their lives than preheat ovens. Like choosing what to wear tonight.

She went upstairs, laid out all the possibilities on her bed and scrutinised them before picking out a short black skirt and a tight white top. The more the bouncers were admiring her body, the less they would think about her non-existent ID, she reckoned.

With her outfit sorted, Ashley checked on her dinner and went to grab a quick shower. She flicked between songs on her phone as she pushed open the door to the bathroom. Then she looked up. Her phone dropped from her hand and clattered loudly on the tiled floor, but Ashley didn't hear it. She stared in horror at the scene in front of her.

Her mother lay in the bath, her pale blue eyes open but unseeing; the water a deep crimson red. One arm was submerged, the other hanging over the side of the bath. Deep cuts ran down the length of her forearm, and her blood had pooled on the floor. A razor blade gleamed on the grey bath mat having dropped from her lifeless fingers.

Chapter 10

Jenny and Emma pulled up outside St Mary's Hospital and made for the main entrance, a summer breeze whipping their jackets, the morning sun creeping over the top of the building. They went downstairs to Pathology, pushed through the double doors, and headed to the small reception desk, manned by a bored-looking young woman. She was scrolling through her phone, but put it down hurriedly when she saw them.

'DI Stone and DS Marie here to see Dr Rahman,' Jenny said, and she and Emma flashed their warrant cards.

'Yes, of course. Let me see if he's available,' the receptionist told them, a model of professionalism as she disappeared down the corridor, leaving the detectives standing there.

A couple of minutes later, she returned and ushered them to a room at the end of the corridor. Dr Rahman stood up from behind his desk as they entered, and shook hands. Jenny glanced around the room. One wall was full of shelves holding medical textbooks. On another wall was a whiteboard with a list of bays, two-thirds of which had names allocated; a quick scan told Jenny that Frances Lowes was in bay three. The only other feature was a desk, on which sat a computer and a couple of neat stacks of files.

'I've finished my initial investigation for Mrs Lowes,' said Dr Rahman, dispensing with the formalities.

'What can you tell us?' Jenny asked him, as directly.

'The cause of death was blood loss, resulting from a single stab wound to the abdomen. The murder weapon was a knife of at least six inches in length, slightly serrated-'

'The knife found at the scene,' said Emma.

'I would say so, yes. Time of death would have been between eleven pm and midnight on the fifth.'

'Have you found any other injuries?' Jenny asked as she scribbled in her notebook.

'No. An external examination identified no bruising, no obvious defensive wounds, no sign of sexual assault and no skin cells or other forms of DNA. Sorry.'

Both detectives looked disappointed. 'What else can you tell us?' Emma asked.

'For her age, she was in quite good health, with no underlying health conditions.'

'So not about to drop down dead, then?' Emma remarked.

'I don't think so, no,' he replied with a small smile.

'OK, thank you for your time, Dr Rahman. Call me if you find anything else,' Jenny said, and handed him a business card.

'Sorry I couldn't be more help.'

'No signs of any defensive wounds,' Emma said as they walked down the corridor. They glanced at the receptionist, who was scrolling through her phone again.

'To me, that suggests Frances was either caught unawares, or she knew her assailant and that they were able to get close enough to her to attack without drawing suspicion,' Jenny replied.

* * *

Amelia ducked under the crime scene tape and walked down the path. Just being at the house brought everything rushing back. Her stomach lurched and her vision blurred. She leant against the wall of the house and took slow, deep breaths. Gradually, the feeling of nausea passed.

'You don't have to do this now, you know.'

She turned to face Sam as he followed her down the path and saw curtains twitching across the road. *More people who can't mind their own damn business!* Her hand tightened on the keys, but she took another deep breath and pushed the thought away. She'd had already had several reporters ringing both her home and mobile number, and she'd told them all to get lost.

'I have to,' she told Sam. 'The police need to know if anything is missing. They said it was important.'

'I'm sure it wouldn't matter if we came back tomorrow,' Sam grumbled, but moved to join Amelia. Amelia unlocked the front door and they made their way inside.

Amelia looked around the house she had once loved, wrapped her arms round herself, and shivered in spite of the warm day. She had spent many a summer here as a girl with her mother, and plenty of time since she had moved to be near her gran. Now, it felt alien. Everything looked the same as always, but now there was a grey filter over everything. It was the same but different, like *Alice Through the Looking Glass*. Just being there made her feel sick.

'Let's start upstairs.' She took a couple of deep breaths to steady herself and immediately wished she hadn't: the coppery smell still lingered.

In the main bedroom, the duvet was still thrown back. Amelia pulled it straight and sat down. She picked up one of the pillows, held it to her face and took a deep breath. The fragrance of her grandmother's perfume was still there. She put the pillow back and wiped away a tear. *I need to be strong,* she thought as she picked up a framed photo from beside the bed. *I owe it to Gran. This could help the police find the person who killed her, and when they do, I'll kill the bastard.*

She stared at the photo. It was of her and Frances, taken a couple of years ago on Ryde beach, with the castle visible in the background: her gran's favourite spot. She put the photo down and began her search.

'You spot anything?' Sam asked, trying and failing to keep the boredom out of his voice.

'No. Her watch and rings are still here and none of her drawers look like they've been touched.'

They both went to leave the bedroom but Amelia stopped short. 'I should have been here. If we hadn't argued...'

'If you hadn't argued, you still wouldn't have been here,' Sam replied. 'You heard what the detective said: it happened between eleven and one. Even if you'd had a great night, all laughter and jokes, you'd still have been home by ten.' He walked over, put his hands on Amelia's shoulders and looked her in the eyes. 'You can't keep beating yourself up over this.' Amelia nodded sadly.

Back downstairs, Amelia headed into the kitchen, unable to bring herself to go into the living room yet. Everywhere she looked brought back memories. *This is too soon. Maybe Sam was right; I should have left it longer. I'm not ready for this.*

Finding nothing amiss in the kitchen, she steeled herself and headed into the living room. Refusing to look at the carpet, she carried out a quick, cursory scan, turned and left the room, not wanting to be in there a moment longer than she had to.

'You done?' Sam called from his position by the front door, glancing up from his phone.

'Yeah. I don't want to be here any longer,' Amelia replied.

She opened the front door and was about to step outside when she froze, frowning. She turned and headed back to the living room.

'What's going on?' Sam called, but Amelia didn't answer. Instead, she went straight over to the fireplace.

'Sam, you haven't touched anything in here, have you?'

Sam appeared in the doorway. 'No, why would I?'

'You haven't taken a photo off the mantelpiece?' she said, concern in her voice.

'I said I hadn't touched anything, didn't I?' Sam said tersely. 'Why?'

'The photo of me, Mum and Gran is missing.'

* * *

The main door of the police station flew open, which made the desk sergeant spill his coffee onto the keyboard. 'Crap,' he muttered, and looked around for something to mop it up as Amelia stormed to the front desk, Sam following in behind her. 'Can I help you, madam?' he asked, his search temporarily on hold.

'Is Detective Inspector Stone around?' she asked, glancing around as if the DI ought to be in the room.

'That depends,' he replied. 'What's it about?'

'It's about my grandmother's murder!' she replied, her voice rising.

'Amelia, calm down,' Sam soothed. He placed a hand on her shoulder, which was immediately shaken off.

'Hold on,' said the sergeant told her, and disappeared into the station.

Amelia paced, unable to settle down. She stopped, took a breath, and picked up a leaflet on Neighbourhood Watch. She tried to read it, then gave up and slapped it back on the counter.

The inner door opened and the desk sergeant came in, followed by DC Bancroft. 'Ms Simpson, the sergeant says you have some information regarding your grandmother's case?'

'I wanted to speak to DI Stone,' she said, glaring at the sergeant.

'DI Stone is busy at the moment. Maybe I can be of some help?'

'Something's missing!' she cried.

'What's missing? From where?' he replied, his eyebrows knitting together.

'My gran's favourite picture: the one of her, Mum and me. It's gone!'

George led Amelia and Sam down to interview room three and instructed a uniformed officer to fetch them both a coffee, then vanished. Amelia glanced around the room. It was a soulless space with cheap carpet tiles on the floor, worn and in dire need of being replaced. The walls were the same dull green as the briefing room. The only furniture was a small table with audio recording equipment on one side and four plastic chairs placed around it.

'Are you sure this is wise?' Sam asked Amelia, who was pacing the small room, too agitated to sit.

'You know what she told us,' she snapped. 'Report anything we think of, no matter how small!'

Sam gave up and stared out of the small window at the car park beyond. He gave the wire mesh a small, experimental shake, but it refused to budge. Bored, he decided to sit down.

Nearly five minutes later, the door to the interview room opened and the young uniformed officer entered, carrying two coffees. Close behind was George, followed by Jenny.

Jenny and George took seats on one side of the table and Jenny gestured at the free seat opposite. 'George says you wanted to see me, Amelia? That you've found something missing in Frances Lowes's house?'

'Yes, her favourite photo. The one of me, her and Mum at the beach when I was six. It's always been in the centre of the mantelpiece for as long as I can remember.'

'Are you sure she didn't move it, or put it away somewhere?' Jenny gazed at her, her tone level.

'No,' Amelia replied. 'Even if she had, I would have found it somewhere else in the house.'

'Did you find anything else missing? Jewellery, electronics, valuables?' Jenny asked.

'No, that was it.'

'OK. Thank you for letting me know.' Jenny stood up and walked towards the door.

'Is that it?' Amelia cried.

Jenny turned to face her. 'I am very busy trying to find your grandmother's killer. If you think of anything further, please ring the number I gave you.'

'Why haven't you arrested anyone yet?' Amelia shouted, her voice cracking. Tears ran down her cheeks.

'These investigations take time. It may not seem like it, but we are moving forward. That's all I can say for now, but I will be in touch with any new developments,' she told Amelia, her voice still calm. She left the interview room and asked a uniformed officer to show Amelia and Sam out.

'That was a little harsh, wasn't it?' said George, once the pair had gone. 'She just wanted some information on the case.'

'I can't make false promises to her about catching this killer, George. You know that.' Jenny turned to face him. 'And I'm not about to divulge details of a murder investigation to someone I haven't ruled out as a suspect.'

* * *

Jenny parked in front of their cosy three-bed bungalow and rubbed her aching shoulders. She was looking forward to at least an hour in the bath, with nothing but her Kindle and a glass of red wine for company.

She had only taken a couple of steps when the front door was thrown open and her eight-year-old daughter Sophie came charging out, her blonde hair still wet from her bath. 'Mum, Mum! Guess what?' she shouted, bobbing up and down.

'What is it, sweetheart?' Jenny asked, squatting down to Sophie's level. Greg was standing in the doorway, smiling.

'Annabelle has had to drop out of the school play, and Mrs Singh has asked me to take her place!' she told her mum excitedly, all smiles and wide blue eyes.

'That's excellent! Well done!'

'You will come and see it, won't you?' Sophie asked, and the uncertainty in her voice sent a wave of guilt flooding through Jenny.

'I wouldn't miss it for the world.' Jenny took her daughter's hand and they walked into the house.

Jenny closed the front door and took off her jacket. The house was warm, and she could smell something cooking in the kitchen which made her stomach rumble. Greg ushered Sophie to the bathroom to clean her teeth, then joined Jenny in the kitchen. She had already fetched a bottle of wine and was in the middle of removing the cork. 'Want one?' she asked.

'In a bit.'

Jenny poured a generous glass and set the bottle down on the worktop. She took a sip and sighed contentedly.

'Rough day?' he asked, sitting down at the breakfast bar opposite her.

'Yeah. This case is proving to be a pain in the ass. Edwards wants it solving quickly because he's afraid of a PR disaster. He's more concerned about possible damage to his career than the fact that there's a killer on the loose.'

Sophie bounced into the kitchen before Jenny could elaborate further. 'Done my teeth!' she declared, with a wide, toothy smile in case they didn't believe her. Jenny laughed.

'Good girl,' said Greg. 'Now say goodnight to your mum and pick what stories you want. I'll be through in a couple of minutes.'

Sophie kissed Jenny and said goodnight, then bounded off towards her bedroom. Greg looked at Jenny. 'She's really excited about this play. You will go, won't you?'

'Of course I will. I told her I would, didn't I?'

Greg held her gaze. 'It wouldn't be the first school event you've missed.'

'You know what my job's like,' Jenny snapped. 'Unfortunately, I don't get to pick and choose when crimes happen, they don't consult me about my schedule first.'

'For fuck's sake, Jenny,' Greg muttered. 'I'm going to go and put our daughter to bed.' He got up and left the kitchen. Jenny watched him go, then took a gulp of her wine, trying to stave off her annoyance.

Chapter 11

Jenny and Emma opened the front door of Frances's house, stepped in, and closed the door behind them, wrinkling their noses at the smell of detergent and bleach. Even though the house had been cleaned up, the coppery smell of blood still lingered.

'So, what do we know?' Jenny asked, looking around the hallway.

'At around eight pm Amelia comes for her usual visit, only this time she drags Sam along with her,' Emma replied.

They walked through the house to the living room, Jenny's gaze finding the watercolour of Ryde beach that they now knew was painted by Megan. 'We know they sat in here,' she said. 'They exchanged small talk for approximately thirty minutes before an argument broke out between the victim, Frances Lowes, and Amelia's boyfriend, Samuel Jones. Shortly afterwards Frances kicked him out, and a separate argument broke out between her and Amelia before Amelia also left the premises.'

'We can confirm these timings based on CCTV footage from the bottom end of the road,' said Emma.

'This is where it gets fuzzy.' Jenny left the living room and headed upstairs, and she and Emma entered the main bedroom.

'At some point between ten to nine and midnight, Frances cleaned up and went to bed,' said Emma. 'The state of the bed suggested that she had been lying in it. Whether she was asleep and was woken, or she was sitting up reading-'

'Something made her go downstairs,' said Jenny. 'A noise from inside the house, or perhaps someone knocking at the front door.'

They left the bedroom and went downstairs again. 'At this point the suspect, who has somehow gained entry into the house, picks up a kitchen knife and stabs Frances before dropping the knife and leaving.' Jenny's forehead wrinkled in confusion.

'And they take the picture from the mantelpiece,' Emma reminded her.

Jenny wandered over to the mantelpiece. There were pictures at either end: one of Amelia on the right, and an old photo of a much younger Frances, standing with a young man that Jenny guessed was her husband. 'The layout does suggest that something is missing. Are we sure the picture hasn't simply been moved?'

'Our search of the house hasn't turned up a photo that matches the description Amelia gave us,' Emma said, shrugging.

Jenny sighed. 'More and more, I'm moving away from the idea that this was a robbery gone wrong. The knife left on the floor feels as if it was left deliberately. Then there's the lack of forced entry, and the fact that they appear to have taken a trophy. It feels as if Frances herself was targeted.'

'But why?' asked Emma. 'From everything that we've found out, Frances was a much-loved member of the local community. Nobody has a bad word to say about her.'

'What we do know is that she has a fair bit of money stashed away, and according to Dr Rahman, she was in good health.'

Emma scrutinised her. 'So you think it's all about the money?'

'That's the only motivating factor I can see in this case,' said Jenny. 'Let's be honest, it usually comes down to one of three things: money, sex or power. In this instance, the victim had money.'

'You really think it could have been Amelia?' Emma's tone was sceptical.

'She stands to gain a lot from her grandmother's death. And it also answers another question.' Jenny smiled.

'Which is?' Emma asked, intrigued in spite of herself.

'How the perpetrator gained entry. We've found no signs of forced entry and we know Amelia has a key. She could have let herself in, or if she knocked on the door there's no doubt that Frances would have let her in. Her guard would have been down as well, which accounts for the lack of defensive wounds.' Jenny folded her arms.

'But if Amelia had access to a key then so did Sam,' Emma countered. 'Or he could have knocked on the front door, claiming that there was something wrong with Amelia. Frances would have let him in, no questions asked. And there's another thing to consider.'

'Which is?' asked Jenny.

'Power. That evening, Frances had goaded Sam by calling him a loser and tried to undermine his relationship with Amelia. According to Megan Parkinson, it isn't the first time she's done this, either. Maybe Sam feared that his easy life with Amelia might come to an end, or he wanted revenge for being made to feel weak. Maybe the money is just a nice little perk.'

'Unfortunately, this is all just speculation. Right now, what we need is a solid motive,' Jenny said, frowning.

'We need to get back to the station and see how Claire is getting on with those financial records, see if we can't find one.'

* * *

Jenny and Emma pushed through the grey double doors into the main control room. There were dozens of officers and civilian staff sitting at desks. Whatever the time of day, this room was always busy, and now was no exception.

Emma spied Claire at the far end of the room with George, both hunched over a computer screen. They arrived at the desk to find George typing a report. A steaming mug of coffee sat next to the keyboard, and Jenny eyed it longingly. 'Hands off,' said George, without looking round.

'Have you had any luck digging into Amelia and Sam's finances?' Jenny asked, casting one final look at the coffee, wishing she'd thought to stop by the kitchenette on the way in.

'Yeah,' said Claire. George tapped a few keys on the computer to bring up a summary.

'So what do we know?' Emma asked impatiently.

'Well,' said George, 'Sam has some savings, just shy of eight grand, and his only debt appears to be a few hundred on a credit card – nothing to write home about. He doesn't earn much, but also doesn't appear to have many outgoings.' He paused. 'Amelia, on the other hand, is interesting.' A small smile played across his face.

'Well?' Jenny prompted.

'Amelia is doing very well for herself.'

Jenny frowned. 'How well?'

'She has upwards of four hundred grand in the bank.'

'Wow! I wasn't expecting that,' Jenny exclaimed.

'And it appears that she owns her flat outright,' George continued.

'I should have been a florist,' Emma muttered.

'That can't all be down to a small flower shop in Ryde, surely?' Jenny asked, eyes wide.

'No,' said Claire. 'The shop does make a little, but it's nowhere nearly profitable enough to allow someone her age to own their property outright, let alone have enough savings to buy it twice over.'

'So where has it all come from?' Emma asked, frowning.

'Inheritance,' said George. 'Her mother – Frances's daughter – and her father were killed in a car crash in London back in 2011. She was a housewife, and he was a consultant heart surgeon at Royal London Hospital. As their only child, Amelia inherited the lot.'

'Damn,' said Jenny.

Claire stared at her. 'Ma'am?'

'We had a theory that either Sam or Amelia might have been involved in Frances's death, but we thought the motive was financial. This kinda blows it out of the water.'

'It doesn't rule out Sam, though,' Emma pointed out. 'If anything, it makes the case stronger. He could have been looking to shut her up, not wanting to risk losing a free home and a comfortable life.'

'True,' Jenny conceded.

'Ma'am!' came a shout from the other side of the room. DC Simon Michaels was heading over to them.

'What can I do for you, Simon?' Jenny asked, a touch wearily; the news about Sam and Amelia's finances had dampened her earlier enthusiasm.

'I've been looking into the complaints made by Ms Simpson regarding the neighbouring florist.'

'What have you found out?' Emma asked, leaning forward.

Simon grimaced. 'Amelia had made a number of complaints about harassment and threatening behaviour from a Ms Kirstie Williams, owner and manager of Flowers by Kirstie, which is less than one hundred metres from Amelia's shop.'

'What kind of complaints?' Jenny asked.

'It's like her friend said. Complaints that her delivery van tyres were slashed, that paint was thrown at her shop and abuse was spray-painted on her door.'

'That's a new one,' said Jenny. 'What was our response?'

'A couple of uniforms went to speak to Kirstie and she denied all knowledge. She claimed that Amelia was making it all up and that Amelia had been harassing *her*. There was no proof either way, so nothing came of it.'

'Good work, everyone,' said Jenny. 'I think we should pay a visit to Flowers by Kirstie.'

* * *

Jenny and Emma drove down Dover Street. The Solent and Portsmouth showed in the distance, the spring sun an early promise of the summer yet to come. Halfway down they turned on to Melville Street and continued towards Flowers by Kirstie.

'Park here,' Jenny told Emma, who obediently pulled into a nearby space.

'What's the matter?' Emma asked as they climbed out of the car.

'Amelia's shop is open. I want to take a look inside.'

They crossed the road, Jenny frowning at the chipboard covering the bottom half of the shop window. They pushed the pale-blue door open, a bell announcing their arrival. The shop had a handful of customers: a couple browsing and one at the counter, deep in conversation with a grey-haired woman in her late fifties or early sixties.

Eventually the shop cleared and Jenny and Emma approached the assistant. 'Can I help you ladies with anything?' she asked with a broad smile, a badge on her tunic identifying her as Maria.

'Detective Inspector Stone and Detective Sergeant Marie,' Jenny said, by way of introduction, and both women flashed their warrant cards.

Maria's smile faltered for a moment, but quickly reasserted itself. 'How can I help you both?' she asked, her tone pleasant but guarded.

'Is Ms Simpson around?' Jenny asked.

'No. She's still off after…' Her voice cracked a little and she wiped her eyes with a tissue she dug out from her tunic pocket. 'You have to catch the monster who did it.'

'We will do our best,' Emma assured her, and Maria nodded.

'What can you tell us about Kirstie Williams?' Jenny asked.

Maria's smile disappeared and her eyes narrowed. 'Don't get me started on that woman,' she spat. 'It's about time your lot took some action against her after all she's put poor Amelia through.'

Clearly more than a normal employee / employer relationship here, Jenny thought. *Interesting.*

'So there's been some animosity between the two of them?' Emma asked.

'Hardly,' Maria replied. Jenny and Emma exchanged glances. 'What I mean is that nasty piece of work down *there*,' - she jerked her finger in the direction of the other shop - 'has had a vendetta against poor Amelia ever since she opened her shop a year ago. Amelia has done nothing. We were here

94

first, for God's sake! If she doesn't like competition, she should have opened her shop elsewhere.'

'So you would describe the hostility as one-way, then?' Emma asked.

'Amelia wouldn't hurt a fly.'

'I think that's all for now,' said Jenny. 'Thank you for your time, Maria.' Both detectives headed towards the door.

'Wait! Do you think she was involved with what happened to Frances?' Maria called out.

'We just want to talk to her, that's all,' Jenny replied. 'At this time there's nothing to suggest she had any involvement.' Maria stared as she closed the door.

Emma and Jenny continued down the street, the sun warming their faces. 'No love lost there,' Emma commented wryly as they reached the second flower shop. From the window, they could see two women standing by the counter. Both wore purple polo shirts, and were huddled over a single mobile phone, laughing over something on the screen. The detectives pushed open the door and headed inside.

The two women looked up at their approach. The older of the two, a woman who looked in her late twenties with shoulder-length brown hair, put down the phone and came over, smiling. 'Hi!' she said brightly. 'Are you looking for anything specific, or just browsing?'

'Are you Kirstie Williams?' Jenny asked, and flashed her warrant card.

The smile vanished. 'Yeah, that's me. What's all this about?'

'We'd like to talk to you about Amelia Simpson,' Emma said curtly.

'And you are?'

'Detective Sergeant Marie,' Emma answered, reaching for her own warrant card.

'Why don't you go across the road and get us some

coffees,' she said to the second woman, who nodded and quickly left the shop.

Kirstie folded her arms and stared at the two detectives.

'Do you know anything about the vandalism that occurred last week at Flowers by the Beach?' Jenny asked, matching her glare for glare.

'A detective inspector and a detective sergeant, just to ask about a broken window? Don't you lot have anything better to do?' Kirstie snorted.

'Just answer the question, please.'

'No, I don't know anything about the vandalism.'

'Your name has been given to us by a couple of people as the person responsible,' Emma told her.

'Oh, has it? Well, they're wrong. If anything, it's the other way round,' she fired back.

'In what way?' Jenny asked, her voice still calm.

'She's been harassing me ever since I opened this shop! She's obviously afraid of the competition. I actually went round there when I first opened, because I wanted us to be friends, and she all but laughed in my face and threw me out!'

'Can anyone vouch for any of this?' asked Jenny.

'Yeah. Bethany, my assistant.'

Jenny regarded her for a moment, then smiled. 'I will be sure to speak to her in due course.' She turned and left, Emma right behind her.

Jenny and Emma were heading to their desks, having remembered to grab coffee first, when George and Claire hurried over. 'How did that go?' George asked eagerly.

'We met Amelia's assistant, Maria. She looked like she

wanted to claw Kirstie's eyes out as soon as we mentioned her name,' Emma told them.

'Yeah, and Kirstie told us that it was the other way round, that it was Amelia who had been harassing her,' Jenny added. 'There was something not quite right about her; I find it hard to believe she's the victim in all this—'

'DI Stone, do you have a moment?' The shout came from DCI Edwards, who then disappeared into his office. Jenny raised her eyebrows at the others.

When Jenny walked into the office, DCI Edwards was already seated and gestured towards an empty chair. Jenny pulled it out and sat down, familiar with the routine now.

'How's the case going? Are you any closer to making an arrest?' he asked, leaning forward to rest his elbows on his desk.

Jenny brought her boss up to speed on what they had learned so far.

'Interesting,' DCI Edwards commented.

'That's not all. We've discovered that the florist down the road from Amelia seems to hold a bit of a grudge against her. Over the past year, Amelia has lodged a number of complaints for harassment and vandalism, naming her.'

'Do you think she could have done it?'

'I don't know. I certainly wouldn't put it past her, she does come across as pretty nasty, but it's quite a jump to go from vandalism and harassment to murder.'

'Keep me updated,' he said, sighing and rubbing his eyes tiredly. 'I want this wrapped up soon, OK?'

'Yes, sir.'

Chapter 12

Amelia stood in the main entrance to her building. She was holding a small metal dish which she tapped with the nails of her free hand, the soft metallic sound echoing around the hall and out to the driveway. She looked better than she had done in days, having finally managed to shower and change. The previous night was the first night she'd slept all the way through since her grandmother's murder, and although she'd never admit it, she had felt better for it when she had woken that morning. But now she was worried.

'James?' she shouted as she scanned the driveway, but the tabby-and-white cat was nowhere to be seen.

It was a pleasant evening, coming on for eight thirty, and the sun was setting. A faint chill was in the air and Amelia rubbed her arms.

'Look, I'm sorry, OK? The door was only open for a moment,' Sam said wearily from behind Amelia.

She flashed him an icy glare and returned to her search of the driveway and road beyond. 'You know he's an indoor cat,' she fumed. 'He was gone for days the last time he got out.'

'I didn't do it on purpose. You shouldn't keep a cat locked up all day, anyway.'

Amelia ignored this last comment and continued her survey of the driveway.

'He's probably just found himself a little friend and he's having a bit of fun. He'll be back by the morning. Come on, let's go in. I want to watch telly.'

'We have to go out and look for him,' said Amelia.

'Oh, for God's sake, do we have to? It's only a sodding cat.' Amelia shot Sam a look that caused any further complaints to go unspoken. 'He doesn't bloody like me anyway,' he muttered.

A figure appeared at the bottom of the driveway. It was Megan, her mousey-blonde hair tied back in a loose ponytail.

'Have you both been standing there waiting for me? Don't get me wrong, I'm touched, but maybe you need to get yourselves a hobby.' Megan's smile faltered when she saw the look on Amelia's face. 'What's happened?' she asked cautiously.

'James got out.'

Megan groaned. 'How did that happen?'

'*Someone* left the front door open when they went to get the mail this morning.' Amelia's tone was still frosty. 'We were just about to go and look for him.'

'I'll help if you want? I fancy a walk,' Megan said, pointedly ignoring the look of relief on Sam's face.

'Great, I'm going back in then,' he announced, and bounded upstairs before Amelia could object.

'Come on then.' Megan linked her arm through Amelia's. 'I'm sure he won't be far away.'

They reached the driveway and turned onto Castle Street, the salty smell of the Solent thick in the air. The gulls cried and the traffic sped along the seafront just behind the houses to their right as Amelia called out for James.

'How are you doing?' Megan asked, after they had been walking for a bit. She glanced at Amelia, who was chewing her lip as she considered her response.

'A little better,' she admitted, her face flushing guiltily.

'Sleeping?'

'I did last night, thankfully. You?'

'Yeah, but that was probably due to the bottle of wine.' Megan smiled sheepishly.

They walked to the end of the street and turned into the next, Amelia still calling for James. 'I can't believe Sam was stupid enough to leave the door open,' Amelia snapped, gripping the food bowl tighter.

'Can I ask you something?'

'Sure.'

A pause. 'Do you ever wonder if Frances might have been right?'

'What do you mean?' Amelia asked, frowning.

'About Sam. Don't get me wrong, I love Sam, but don't you wonder if you couldn't perhaps do better? After all, you're young, pretty, successful. You're quite a catch. And Sam is, well, Sam.'

'Where has this come from?' Amelia asked, her expression guarded.

'Nowhere. Look, forget it; it's really none of my business. Now, where's that damn cat of yours?'

* * *

The following morning, Amelia switched off her alarm clock and gazed through bleary eyes at the time. Six am. She groaned, rubbed her eyes with the palms of her hands and stifled a yawn. It took every ounce of her willpower not to roll over and go back to sleep.

Perhaps today wasn't the best day to go back to work, she

thought. The look Maria had given her yesterday, when she told her she was planning to come in the next day, had nearly turned her to stone. Maria had insisted that she could handle the shop by herself and Amelia should stay home and rest, but Amelia was adamant. Besides, if she stayed home any longer then daytime TV would probably finish her off.

Decision made, Amelia climbed out of bed, being careful not to disturb Sam, pulled her slippers on, and grabbed her pink dressing gown from the hook behind the bedroom door. She pulled it on and belted it before padding out of the door towards the kitchen, coffee being the first order of the day.

Coffee made, Amelia dug out the box of kibble from the cupboard next to the sink and went to fill the empty bowl sitting by the door, but stopped short as she remembered that James still hadn't come home. She and Megan had roamed the streets of Ryde for hours the night before, but there had been no sign of him. If he still hadn't returned by the evening, then she'd have to put up posters. Sam could bloody well help, and he'd be covering any reward that they offered.

She pulled open the front door of the flat – perhaps James was sitting outside the building, waiting to be let in – but stopped short. On the mat sat a small box. It was cream with a padded fabric covering, about five centimetres on all sides. It was held shut with a brass clasp, and tied with a cream ribbon.

Amelia picked it up and smiled. *He must have wrapped this up last night and sneaked out early this morning to leave it for me.*

She glanced towards the bedroom and smiled before carrying the box through to the living room. She pulled at the ribbon, which came away easily, and lifted the lid. Inside was a note, on top of something wrapped in cream tissue paper. Amelia unfolded it and frowned. Instead of a note apologising and proclaiming Sam's love, all she found was a date printed on one side: 23rd May. Amelia checked both sides, put the note down, and tore open the tissue paper.

She stared in disbelief at the contents, her eyes wide. Inside the paper was James's collar, stained with what looked like blood.

Chapter 13

Sam opened the door to find Jenny and George standing there. At the sight of them, he absentmindedly ran a hand through his unkempt hair in an effort to get it under some sort of control.

'May we come in?' Jenny asked.

Sam nodded, and led them through the house. He looked as if he could have done with at least a couple more hours' sleep; his eyes were bloodshot and there were dark bags underneath them. *Definitely not a morning person,* Jenny thought.

He led them through to the kitchen, where Amelia sat on a stool by the breakfast bar, nursing a cup of coffee. Her hair was a mess and she had been crying; there were several wadded tissues on the breakfast bar and Jenny could see the traces of tears on her cheeks. Amelia started to raise the coffee to her lips, but her hand shook so violently that it started to spill onto the counter. She put it down with a faint curse.

'How are you, Ms Simpson?' George asked, but the look Amelia shot him made him blush.

'Can you tell us what happened?' Jenny asked.

Amelia took a couple of moments to steady herself. 'I got up this morning to get ready for work, opened the front door to check for James, and that was when I found the box.'

'What time was this?'

'My alarm went off at six. I got up, made coffee and then went to the front door.'

'Can we have a look at the box, please?'

Amelia led them reluctantly through to the living room. The curtains were open and sunlight was streaming in. The box was sitting on the coffee table, the lid now closed, its contents lying next to it with the tissue paper. Amelia stared at the box warily, and stayed in the doorway as Jenny and George approached it, pulling on latex gloves.

'Have either one of you touched this?' Jenny asked with a frown.

'I did this morning, but...' Amelia shuddered. 'I haven't even been able to go into the living room since.'

'What about you?' George asked Sam. He shook his head.

Jenny gently picked up the note, sniffed it and examined both sides. 'Does the twenty-third of May mean anything to you?' she asked Amelia, who shook her head, arms wrapped around her body.

'Nothing?'

'No.'

'A forensic team will arrive shortly to take the box and note away,' Jenny told them both. 'Until then, please don't touch it. We need to try to preserve any forensic evidence.' Amelia gave a little nod.

'Is that it?' Sam asked angrily as the two detectives moved towards the door.

'What were you expecting?' Jenny replied.

'I don't know. More than this, though.'

'A forensic team is on their way, and we will be making enquiries. As soon as we have something, we'll be in touch. In the meantime, have a long, hard think about that date. Both of you. It has to mean something.'

Sam frowned but said no more. With a nod to Amelia, the detectives left.

* * *

'Emma, Claire, Simon. Briefing room, five minutes,' Jenny called as she pushed through the double doors into the control room. Instead of going to her desk, she made a beeline for the kitchenette. The call from the duty sergeant had come through while she was getting ready to leave the house that morning, and she'd yet to have her first cup of coffee and was in danger of getting cranky.

Caffeine craving partially sated, her half-empty coffee cup clutched in her hand, Jenny went through to the briefing room and found George filling in the other detectives on the events of the morning thus far.

Jenny cleared her throat and they all turned to face her. 'Right, as I'm sure you're now all aware,' she began, glancing at George, 'at approximately six am this morning Amelia Simpson opened her front door to find a cream box on her doorstep. Inside was a bloodstained collar that Amelia claims belongs to her cat, and a note which was blank except for a date: the twenty-third of May.'

'Does the date mean anything to either Amelia or Sam?' asked Simon.

'They claim not. Nothing that immediately sprang to mind, anyway.' George replied.

'Have we been able to get anything from the box or its contents?' Claire asked.

'Not yet. Sunil and his team were just pulling up as we left. I've asked him to let me know what they find ASAP.'

'I don't like this development,' said Simon. 'This suggests someone is targeting Amelia, and to me, a date implies there's more to come.'

'Are we now thinking that this could be tied in with the grandmother's murder? That she was targeted because of her relationship to Amelia?' George asked.

'We don't know that, and we shouldn't jump to conclusions,' Jenny reminded them. 'But it's a hell of a coincidence if they aren't related. And elements of the murder scene – the photo taken – feel personal.'

'So what's our way forward?' said Emma.

'Simon, George, I want you to find out if there are any cameras in the area around Amelia's flat. This box was left by somebody, and I want to see who it was.' The two detectives nodded. 'Claire, see if you can find out anything about the date. Look into both Amelia and Frances. The date didn't mean anything to Amelia but there must be a reason for it. It wasn't plucked out of thin air.'

'What do you want me to do, boss?' Emma asked.

'So far, the only person we've uncovered with a grudge against Amelia is Kirstie Williams. We need to have a proper chat with her.'

* * *

Jenny and Emma pulled up outside Ellie's and got out of the car. They darted through a gap in the traffic and went into Kirstie's shop. Inside, Kirstie was serving a middle-aged woman. She glanced up at the sound of the door and did an almost imperceptible double take at the sight of the two detectives. Then her smile returned as quickly as it had slipped. The customer took her bouquet and left the shop, smiling politely at the detectives as she passed.

'Don't you lot have anything better to do?' Kirstie asked, leaning on the counter.

'We would like you to come down to the station,' said Jenny. 'We have a few questions to ask you.'

'Are you arresting me? On what grounds?' Kirstie stammered, brown eyes wide with shock.

'Not at this time,' Jenny replied calmly. 'We simply want to talk to you.'

'When?'

'The sooner the better,' said Emma. 'But if you prefer, you can come in after the shop has closed.'

'No,' she said, reaching behind her to untie her apron. 'I'd rather get this out of the way now, if it's all the same to you.' Kirstie turned and shouted towards the backroom. 'I need to pop out for a bit Beth, can you look after the shop?' She turned around and glared at the two detectives. 'I won't be long,' she said pointedly.

She grabbed her bag and keys and followed the detectives out of the shop.

* * *

The interview room was small and square, with a frosted-glass window and a plastic table in the middle for the recording equipment.

Jenny and Emma took a seat opposite Kirstie and her solicitor, a balding man in his late forties wearing a cheap grey suit. Jenny pressed record on the equipment, introduced herself and Emma, and prompted Kirstie and her solicitor, then stated the time and date. 'Thank you for coming in today, Ms Williams.'

'My client would like to know why she has been dragged

here in the middle of the day,' the solicitor began, staring at Jenny with barely concealed hostility.

'For a start, your client wasn't dragged in, as you claim, but is here of her own accord,' Jenny retorted. 'As for why, we will get to that in a moment.'

'Where were you yesterday?' Emma asked, her gaze boring into Kirstie.

'At the shop. Working,' she stated, looking Emma straight in the eye.

'Can anyone verify that?' asked Jenny.

'My assistant Bethany was at the shop with me all day.'

Emma scribbled in her notebook. 'What about the evening?'

'I wasn't feeling great so I had a night in.'

'Can anyone confirm this?' Emma asked.

'No… I live alone,' Kirstie replied, her voice faltering.

'So no one can confirm you were there?'

'My client has just said that she was alone,' snapped the solicitor. 'This interview will take twice as long if you insist on repeating every question.'

'What about on the fifth of May? That's a Thursday.'

'I would have been at the shop; that's where I am every day during the week.'

'What about that evening?' Jenny asked, eyeing the florist intently.

'I don't know. Who remembers what they did on a random night nearly two weeks ago?' Kirstie sighed. 'I think I was home that night.'

'Anyone able to confirm that?' Jenny pressed.

'No. Look, what is all this about?'

'On the night of the fifth of May, someone broke into the house of Amelia Simpson's grandmother, Mrs Frances Lowes, and stabbed her to death. And at some point between ten am yesterday morning and six am today, someone snatched

Amelia's cat and sent his bloodstained collar back to her gift-wrapped.'

'You don't think I had anything to do with either of those things, surely?' Kirstie asked incredulously, her mouth hanging open.

Jenny and Emma looked at her, their expressions unreadable.

'I had nothing to do with either! As I told you when you first came to my shop, Amelia's been harassing me, not the other way around!'

'Then how do you explain the complaints of harassment that have been filed against you?' Jenny asked.

'They were nothing to do with me. She probably did the things herself, to frame me. She's been trying to ruin me ever since I opened!'

'How so?' Emma asked.

'She' been spreading rumours that my shop is over-priced, that we're often late with deliveries or the order is wrong.'

'Gossiping is hardly a crime,' Emma pointed out.

'It damages my business! But it's not just that; over the last year my front window has been smashed and glue has been poured into my locks.'

'How do you know it was Amelia?' asked Jenny.

'Who else would it be? She has a competing business just down from mine, she's trying to drive me off.'

Jenny stared at Kirstie for a minute before continuing. 'If she has been harassing you, why haven't you reported it? We checked, and there's no record of you having made any complaints against Amelia.'

Kirstie shifted in her seat and looked uncomfortable. Eventually, she spoke. 'I didn't report it because I didn't want to waste your time. I thought that if I just ignored her then she would stop.'

'Very convenient,' Emma replied.

'If you had any real evidence tying my client to either of the recent events, you would have charged her by now,' said Kirstie's solicitor. 'The same applies to the alleged harassment. Now, my client has come in of her own free will to cooperate with your investigation, so either you charge her, or this interview is over.' He slammed his folder shut.

Jenny looked furious, but knew that she was beaten for now. She ended the interview and Kirstie departed, a smug grin on her face.

* * *

'How did it go?' George asked Jenny and Emma as they entered the office. Behind Jenny, Emma shook her head at him in a silent warning.

Jenny ignored his question. 'What have you found out?'

'We've had the forensics back from this morning,' Claire told them. 'The only prints on the note were Amelia's, the paper was bog-standard printer paper which could have been bought from any stationery shop or supermarket on the island, and they haven't been able to recover anything useful from the collar, they've confirmed that it is cat blood but that's it.'

'And the box itself?'

'No markings to show where it was bought from. I've got some uniformed officers searching online to see if they can find anywhere that sells something similar, but nothing yet.'

'We do have something, though,' Simon told her with a small smile.

'What?'

'We have recovered this footage.' Simon clicked a file on his computer and the screen filled with a grainy black-and-white video. It was dark, but the sky was just starting to lighten, and the clock at the bottom of the recording showed the time as 5:03am that morning. About thirty seconds in, a person walked by on the other side of the road dressed in dark loose trousers and a hoodie, their face obscured by a baseball cap with the hood pulled over the top. They were wearing black gloves and in their left hand was what looked like a box the same size and shape as the one that had been delivered to Amelia. After a moment, the person slipped it into the middle pocket of the hoodie, hiding it from view.

'It's a shame the quality isn't better,' Claire complained.

'Where was this footage taken?' Jenny asked, still staring at the screen.

'Just down the road from Amelia's: number sixteen.'

'How tall do you estimate them to be?'

'We think between five foot seven and six foot tall. It's hard to say whether they're male or female; I'm guessing that's why they wore that clothing.'

'How tall is Kirstie, roughly?' asked George.

'About five foot eight,' Emma replied with a predatory smile.

'I want you to go back over the footage we have from the area around Frances's house, and see if we have anyone on it who matches this description.'

The duty sergeant came over. 'Sorry, ma'am, but DCI Edwards wanted to see you when you came out of your interview.'

Jenny thanked the sergeant and made her way to the DCI's office, leaving the others poring over the footage for any clues that they may have missed on the first pass. For once the door was closed, which made Jenny pause. Before she could knock, her mobile started to vibrate in her pocket. She glanced at the screen. *Greg.*

Her thumb hovered between the accept and decline icons for a moment, and she hit Decline. *I'll ring him back in a minute,* she thought, and switched the phone to silent.

She knocked and a voice inside beckoned her in.

'Ah, Jennifer, excellent timing,' DCI Edwards said as she entered.

Instead of his normal position behind the desk, DCI Edwards was sitting on one of the chesterfield sofas on the opposite side of the room. With him was an older gentleman, mid-fifties, with greying blond hair and a trim figure. 'Jennifer, you've met Detective Chief Superintendent Wilson before?'

'Once or twice. It's good to see you again, sir.'

'How is the case going, Inspector?'

'We're making progress. We've got a suspect with a clear grudge against the granddaughter of the victim, and she can't provide an alibi for either the time of the murder or the incident this morning. We've also uncovered footage that shows someone of the same approximate height approaching Ms Simpson's residence with a similar-sized package early this morning.'

'Sounds like it's progressing well. Good work.'

'Thank you, sir.'

'Jennifer, every couple of weeks a few of the senior commanders meet for a drink and a catch up, and our next one is tonight. I know it's short notice, but would you like to join us? DCI Edwards here tells me you've recently passed the promotion board for advancement to Chief Inspector. It would be a good way of getting your name out there, meet some of the other execs.'

Jenny paused. She knew she should head home and spend the evening with Greg and Sophie, especially given how much time she had spent at work recently, but it was too good an opportunity to turn down.

'That would be good, thanks sir.'

* * *

The taxi pulled up outside her bungalow. Jenny paid and made her way down the drive, a little unsteady on her feet. Just as she had found her keys in the bottom of her bag, an angry-looking Greg opened the front door.

'And just where the hell have you been?' he demanded. 'Didn't you see any of my messages?'

Jenny cursed herself as she realised that she had forgotten to switch her phone from silent mode. She took it out from inside her bag. Seven missed calls from Greg, and two voicemails. 'Sorry, my phone was on silent. Was it important?'

'What was this afternoon?'

Jenny thought, but came up blank. 'Remind me,' she told him, a little testily, not really in the mood for these games.

'It was Sophie's school play. You know, the one you promised you wouldn't miss.'

'Oh, shit.' Jenny could feel the blood draining from her face. 'Where is she?'

'In her room. She hasn't stopped crying and she doesn't want to see you. I told her something important came up at work and you really wanted to be there, but couldn't. I don't think she believed me, and I'm not going to lie to her again. You need to figure out what's more important: your career or your family.'

Greg turned and walked into the house, and Jenny stormed after him. 'Something *did* come up with work,' she protested when she caught up with him in the kitchen.

'Was there an incident that required your attention in the pub? I can smell alcohol on you.'

Jenny winced. 'I'm sorry, OK? I was invited out at the last minute for a drink with some of the senior officers, and I thought it would be a good chance to network. I genuinely didn't see your calls until just now.'

'I shouldn't need to remind you about your own

daughter's school play! Sophie was so excited when she came on stage. She was looking for us in the audience, and her face when she saw the empty seat is something I won't forget for a long time.' He paused, studying her. 'I'll go and check on her.'

Jenny stared after him, feeling absolutely wretched.

Chapter 14

Sam returned to the table with a tray full of drinks and set it down carefully. He put the bottle of Sauvignon Blanc and two wine glasses in front of Amelia and Megan, and took a swig from his pint.

All around them was the noise of people celebrating the end of the working week. To one side, a small group of lads burst out laughing at some shared joke. Judging by their volume, and the empty bottles and glasses around them, they'd been in the pub for a while, and were showing no signs of slowing. There were also a number of couples, all entwined fingers and flirty smiles. Some other patrons were a few of the older, more seasoned drinkers, perched on 'their' stool drinking pints of something dark you could cut with a knife. The pub was fairly typical of any high street in any town, with a couple of young, harassed-looking bar staff trying to keep track of who was next in an ever-growing sea of customers, the pub getting busier by the minute.

Whilst the general atmosphere was upbeat, that couldn't be said for the table in the corner.

'I'm sorry, guys,' said Amelia with a sigh. 'I know you meant well, but I'm not great company tonight.'

'Nonsense,' said Megan as she topped up their glasses.

'Yeah. The whole point of tonight is to cheer you up, so that's what we're going to do.' Sam reached over and rubbed Amelia's hand before drinking more beer.

Despite Megan and Sam's initial enthusiasm the conversation stalled. Amelia sat morosely flicking through photos of James on her phone, Sam watched the football match on the screen at the end of the bar, and Megan scrolled through Instagram, occasionally looking up to show Amelia an image uploaded by the latest influencer she was following.

'This was a bad idea; I shouldn't have suggested it,' she said. 'Maybe we should just call it a night and try again another time.' Then her expression switched from tired resignation to anger.

Momentarily distracted from pictures of her cat, Amelia followed Megan's gaze: Kirstie had walked into the pub with two friends. They headed straight to the bar, laughing and chatting, oblivious to the small group at the corner table.

'I bet she had something to do with it!' Megan snarled. Her eyes narrowed and her hands formed fists on the table. 'I'm going over there.'

'No, please don't!' Amelia cried, grabbing at her forearm. 'We don't know that.'

With a twist of her arm Megan shook herself free, then drained her glass and stormed over to where Kirstie and her friends were standing, a twenty in hand, trying to catch the barman's eye. Kirstie, alerted by the change in her friends' expressions, turned and saw Megan.

'Don't think we don't know it was you!' Megan shouted, and shoved Kirstie hard causing her to stagger backwards. 'I'm not letting you get away with it!'

Kirstie recovered quickly and shoved Megan back, but

Megan responded with a punch that connected solidly with the left side of Kirstie's face. Before she could say or do anything further, two bouncers grabbed Megan and marched her out, with Sam and Amelia hurrying behind.

Amelia and Sam piled into the street to find Megan laughing and rubbing her knuckles in the orange glow of a streetlight. 'Did you see her face? It was an absolute picture!'

'What did you do that for?' Amelia cried angrily.

'What? She had it coming!'

Amelia looked at Sam for support, but he stood there with a barely suppressed grin on his face. 'Don't encourage her!'

'Come on, Amelia, Meg's right. She did have it coming, and the look on her face was absolutely priceless.'

'It was funny,' Amelia reluctantly admitted, after a moment's hesitation. Megan laughed and slipped her arm through Amelia's and they made their way down the hill towards Union Street, their collective mood now lighter, the night young once again.

They sauntered past a couple more bars. The late-evening sea air was fresh, which added to the alcohol they had already drunk and made Amelia's head swim. The street was filled with like-minded people, all looking to have a few drinks and enjoy themselves.

They came across an upmarket bar about halfway down the hill, and went in. Unlike the previous pub, this place was full of the island's young and trendy. Expensive wallpaper lined the walls, hung with antique, but fashionable, mirrors. The bar itself was set back against the side wall with about a dozen steel-and-chrome pumps. Wooden tables and high-backed chairs were dotted about, but unfortunately it was standing room only at this time on a Friday.

'It's my round, guys, same again?' Megan pushed her way

through the throng of people to the bar, while Amelia and Sam cut through the crowd and found a space near the back.

Just as Megan returned with their drinks, Amelia felt a tap on her shoulder. She turned around to see a woman in her early thirties, with long brown hair and pale-blue eyes, staring at her with a big smile on her face.

'Dawn?' Amelia asked with a look of surprise, her smile growing to match the woman's. Without waiting for an answer, Amelia threw her arms around her, while Megan and Sam exchanged curious glances.

Eventually pulling back from the hug, Amelia gazed at the woman. 'What are you doing here?'

'I'm here on business for a few days.'

'Really? What kind of business?'

'I own a small graphic design company based in Shepherd's Bush, and we have a big client on the island.'

'Wow, that's excellent.'

'What about you? Are you in the business too?'

'No, I own a flower shop in town. Anyway, what have you done to your hair? It used to be blonde, didn't it?'

'This is my original colour: I went through the whole "reinvent yourself at uni" thing you know. I'm over it now, though.'

Before they could say anything further, they were interrupted by a small cough. Amelia blushed as she belatedly remembered Megan and Sam. 'Sorry, guys,' she said as she turned to face them. 'Dawn, this is my best friend Megan and my boyfriend Sam. Guys, this is Dawn.'

'Hey,' Sam offered and Megan gave her a little wave.

'So how do you know our Amelia?' Megan asked, with a smile.

'We met at Brighton University: I was a struggling first year when Amelia was doing her master's. One of my lecturers put me in touch with her, and she helped me through a difficult first couple of months. If it hadn't been for her, I would probably have dropped out and gone home with my tail between my legs. I got the hang of it after that, but I spent the remainder of that year hanging around with her and her housemates; she was the cool postgrad, you know. I was a bit starry-eyed.'

'Check you out!' Megan told Amelia, giving her a friendly punch on the arm. Behind them, Sam rolled his eyes. 'So what was Amelia like at uni, then?'

'So much fun! I was so gutted when you, Jodie and Paul graduated and left. You don't still hear from either of them, do you?'

'I kinda lost touch with everyone when I left.'

'That's a shame. Say, you guys don't mind if I join you, do you? I'm here by myself, and you can only scroll through your phone so much.'

'Of course not, the more the merrier! Besides, I want to hear all about little Amelia at university,' Megan put her arm around Amelia.

'You don't mind, do you, Sam?' Amelia asked brightly.

'Do what you want,' he replied gruffly.

'Do you remember that crappy nightclub we always went to on Saturday nights?' Dawn asked.

'Tonic, wasn't it?'

'Yeah. God, what a dive. I can't believe we went religiously every Saturday for the whole year!'

'Well, the drink was cheap and the music was good. What more do you need?' Amelia said with a shrug.

From there the three women spent the rest of the evening swapping stories. Megan told Dawn about the time she and Amelia went back to her shop with a couple of bottles of wine after a night out, as neither could be bothered to walk all the way home. They were woken the next day by Maria, who found them both passed out in the back room. She was mad as hell and didn't let either of them live it down for weeks. In turn, Dawn told the group about the time when she, Amelia and her flatmates got dressed up for Halloween. Jodie went as a slutty vampire, Paul as a zombie Smurf, and she and Amelia went as the twins from *The Shining*: pale skin, matching pale-blue dresses, wigs and white knee socks, the whole nine yards.

Over the next couple of hours, the three women got progressively more drunk and rambunctious while Sam sat there and played on his phone, a childish pout on his face. Before they even realised that time was getting away from them, the main lights came on in the bar announcing that it was time to go.

'Bloody hell, is it two am already?' Dawn asked, her voice slurred.

'Shit, I've got to get up for work in four hours,' Amelia replied, the blood draining from her face. She could see her future, and it involved a serious hangover.

'You're the boss, have a lie-in. Let Maria open up,' Megan suggested.

'I can't, she's got the day off.' Amelia groaned and put her head in her hands, already dreading the day ahead.

'Rather you than me, I'm afraid. I intend to spend the day in bed!' Megan told her with a smile. Amelia gave her a little shove and called her a cow in return.

'It's been great to meet you, Megan, and I've loved catching up again, Amelia,' said Dawn. 'Do you fancy meeting up for lunch before I have to go back?'

'Sounds good to me.' The girls swapped numbers before going their separate ways.

* * *

The alarm beside Amelia's bed started buzzing loudly. She hit it with a groan, rolled over and went back to sleep. Ten minutes later, the alarm on her phone went off. Amelia groaned again and groped around her bedside table to silence that one as well, but she couldn't find it.

'Shut that bloody thing off, would you?' Sam muttered from beside her.

'I'm trying.'

Eventually awake enough to process things properly, Amelia realised why she couldn't find her phone. It was on the floor by the entrance to the en suite, instead of on her bedside cabinet as usual. In a flash, she remembered that in her drunken state last night she had thought it a good idea to put her phone on the other side of the room, so that she had no choice but to get up and switch it off. She rolled out of bed, padded across the room, and swiped at the phone, silencing 'Dreaming of You' by The Coral halfway through the second play-through.

Coffee made and dry toast consumed, Amelia headed back to the en suite and took a long hot shower to try to ease the thumping headache behind her eyes. *It always seems such a good idea at the time,* she thought, thinking back to the previous night. *Still, hangovers aren't so bad if you had a good night earning it; it's the hangovers after a rubbish night that are the worst.*

Amelia stepped out into the early morning sun, squinting, her head hurting all the more. After stopping off to grab another coffee from Ellie's, she arrived at her shop, unlocked the door and went in.

She froze at the sight that awaited her, and her newly bought coffee slipped from her hand and fell to the floor.

Chapter 15

The bell above the shop door jangled, and Amelia looked up as DC Bancroft and DS Marie walked in. They stopped short as they took in the scene. The usually vibrant shop looked like a scene from a flower-based apocalypse film. All the once-colourful blooms hung down, their colours muted and dull, leaves curling and brittle to the touch.

'OK, no need to ask why we're here,' George said as he looked around.

'When did you discover this?' Emma asked, her notepad and pen already out.

'I got here just after seven thirty this morning and found it like this.' Amelia gestured to the mess in front of her before returning her head to her hands.

'Are you OK, Ms Simpson?' George asked, concerned.

'No. I've got a raging hangover and I've only had four hours' sleep. I had hoped to sit here all morning drinking coffee and feeling sorry for myself, but I guess that's not going to happen.'

'Was the door locked when you turned up this morning?' George asked whilst Emma continued to make notes.

'Yeah.'

'Does that work?' Emma asked, pointing towards a CCTV camera mounted in the back left corner of the shop.

'Yeah, it records to a computer in the back. I had it installed last year after paint was thrown at the shop window.'

Amelia led the detectives through to the back room, cleared some paperwork off an old desktop and switched on the monitor. After a few moments, she pulled up the relevant folder, then frowned.

'What's the matter?' Emma asked, noticing the expression on Amelia's face.

'There's nothing here. Look.' She gestured at the screen. 'This is the file where the recordings are saved. The last five days are here, but there's nothing from last night.' She clicked on the recycle bin, but that too was empty.

'So whoever did this also knew you had a camera, and had the presence of mind to delete the recording. Interesting,' Emma remarked.

'How did they access the files? Didn't you have a password?' George asked frowning.

'Yes but-' Amelia began before her voice trailed off and she looked away, her face turning pink.

'What is it?' Emma asked.

'The password was on a post-it note next to the computer. Maria could never remember it,' Amelia quickly added as Emma rolled her eyes.

'George, get on the phone to Sunil; I want a team down to check for prints and signs of forced entry. We'll need to take the computer with us. Maybe our forensic tech guys can recover the deleted file.'

George pulled out his phone while Emma went to the door and looked down the street. The front door at Flowers by Kirstie was open.

'They're on their way,' said George, putting the phone back in his pocket.

'Shall we take a walk down the road?' Emma asked him, nodding at the other flower shop.

* * *

'This is harassment! I haven't done anything!' Kirstie glared as Emma and George made their way through the open front door.

'Good to see you too, Ms Williams.' Emma replied with a smile.

'What do you want now?' Kirstie demanded.

'There's been another attack on Ms Simpson's shop,' Emma told her, watching for any kind of reaction.

'So? What's that got to do with me?'

'Where were you last night?' Emma continued.

'Out in town with a couple of friends.'

'And they'll verify that, will they?'

'No need – you can go ask *her*. It was that thug mate of hers who gave me this!' She pointed at a partially concealed red and purple bruise on her left cheek.

'How long did you stay out?' George added and Kirstie turned and glared at him.

'I went home not long after I was assaulted, at about ten fifteen. Funnily enough, being punched in the face for no reason rather ruins your night. And, before you ask, no one can verify that I went straight home. I went by myself.'

'Which bar was this?'

'The Red Lion, at the bottom of the high street.'

'Why did she attack you?' Emma asked.

'I don't know, I'd only just got there. I was planning on a couple of quiet drinks with my friends, and the next thing I knew, she hit me.'

'OK, thank you, Ms Williams,' said Emma and turned towards to the door.

Kirstie stared at them. 'That's it? Aren't you going to go round and speak to her? She hit me for no reason, for God's sake!'

'If you want to report her for assault then you'll need to file a complaint at the station,' Emma said, turning back to face Kirstie.

'Don't worry, I will.'

* * *

Once the forensic team had finished and taken a number of dead flowers away for further investigation, Amelia began the sad task of clearing up. She was dumping the dead flowers into the green recycling bin she had wheeled into the shop when the bell above the door jangled. Amelia looked up to see Dawn, holding a couple of takeaway cups.

'What happened here?' she asked, stopping short.

'I don't know. I arrived this morning and found everything dead.'

'Shit.'

'Yeah.'

'Is there anything I can do?'

'No, the police have been already. I'm just clearing up now. How are you feeling today?'

'Rough. I only intended to pop out for a couple. I haven't drunk like that in years. You?'

'Same. I was hoping to have a nice quiet day, but instead I came in to this,' Amelia sighed. 'Anyway, you didn't come here to hear about my problems. What's up?'

'I actually wanted to talk to you about something. Are you free for lunch? My treat.'

* * *

Amelia and Dawn pulled up a couple of chairs and sat down. 'This is nice,' Dawn remarked, looking around.

When Dawn had suggested popping out for lunch Amelia had pulled down the shutters and locked up, welcoming the excuse for a break. Yet as much as she wanted to forget all about it and go back home to bed, she knew she had to get the shop cleared out that afternoon and new stock ordered, so she had told Dawn that she needed to keep it local. That was why they now found themselves sitting in Ellie's, looking over the sandwich menu. Amelia had pointedly chosen a seat facing away from the window, not wanting to be put off her food every time she glanced up and saw Kirstie and her shop. The young waitress came and took their orders with a big smile, greeting Amelia like a long-lost friend.

'You said that you wanted to talk about something?' Amelia asked, once she had gone.

Dawn took a deep breath and fidgeted in her seat. 'I want you to come and work for me,' she said, eventually.

'What?' Amelia replied, her eyes widening.

'You're the best graphic designer I've ever worked with, and I could really use someone like you on my team. I hate to think of you wasting your abilities. Surely you must want to do more than potter around in a shop?'

'Why does everyone think I'm wasting my life? I like my shop.' Amelia sighed deeply and glanced up at the ceiling.

'I'm sorry, I didn't mean any offence. I just want you to know that the offer's there, and I'd love to have you on board. You don't have to decide right away; take some time, think about it. You can even work from home if you don't want to move. I know the rest of the team would love you.'

Their coffees arrived and the topic of conversation switched back to their time in Brighton. They spent an enjoyable hour laughing about old times before Dawn paid their bill and they parted company, Amelia promising to give her offer serious thought and call her soon with an answer.

Back at the shop, Amelia continued dumping her dead stock in the green bin, but gave up after about twenty minutes, unable to get Dawn's offer out of her head. She grabbed her phone from beside the till, scrolled down to Sam's name and hit Call. The phone rang for a few moments before Sam answered. 'Hey.'

'Hi. Can I talk to you about something?' Amelia chewed on her lower lip nervously.

A pause. 'Sure, what's up?'

'Dawn came by the shop earlier and we went out for lunch. She's asked me to come and work for her as a graphic designer.'

'Doesn't she work in London? I don't want to move. This is my home: my family's here.'

'She said I could work from home if I didn't want to move. What do you think?'

'What's wrong with your shop? OK, it doesn't make that much money, but we don't need much, do we? We're happy, aren't we?'

'Yeah...'

'So I don't see any reason to change anything. You know the old saying: if it ain't broke don't fix it, or something like that.'

Amelia told Sam she would see him later, and went back to clearing up the shop. After another hour she gave up, deciding that it would be much easier on Monday, when Maria was back and could help her. She decided to go for a walk to think things through.

The sun was shining, and as it was a Saturday, the seafront was packed with parents giving their kids a run out on the beach, people looking to get an early start on their summer tans, and couples walking their dogs. Amelia loved this part of Ryde, with its small seafront castle that no one ever knew what it was originally built for, the pitch and putt with the ridiculously steep hill either side, and her favourite, mile after mile of golden sand. While she could happily while away an afternoon sunbathing or reading a good book, especially if Lisa Gardner had just released one, she actually preferred the beach at night. She had lost count of the nights she and Megan had spent sitting there with a bottle of wine and a couple of plastic cups, discussing anything and everything. The smell of sea air and the peace and quiet made for an almost cathartic experience. She loved staring at the bright lights of Portsmouth in the distance, her own little slice of paradise.

Except today, she was still troubled. She knew that what Sam had said made sense. She loved her life and her shop, so why even consider rocking that particular boat? And she didn't like the fact that Dawn also thought she might be wasting her life. *Why am I having so much trouble with this?*

With her mind still going round in circles, she pulled her phone out of her bag and dialled Megan. Even though it had only been less than twelve hours since she had seen her last, it felt as if she had lots to tell her.

The phone connected and Amelia listened to it ringing for twenty seconds before it switched to voicemail. *I bet that lazy cow is still in bed,* she thought before hitting Redial. The phone went to voicemail once again.

'I'm coming round so you had better be up – I've been up since six! Something has just happened and I need to talk to you so stick the kettle on. Love you.' She hung up and returned her phone to her bag.

Forty-five minutes later, Amelia arrived outside Megan's mid-terrace house. She wiped her brow and, not for the first time, cursed Ryde for its hills and the day's relentless sunshine.

She walked down the path and knocked. 'Megan, are you there? It's me.'

No answer.

She knocked again, but there was still no answer. Amelia tried the door handle and, to her surprise, the door opened. She stepped inside.

'You'd better not still be in bed,' she called out as she walked through the hall, heading towards the kitchen to get herself a drink of water.

As she passed the partially closed living room door, she caught sight of something in her peripheral vision and stopped. She pushed open the door and cried out, then dropped her bag and ran to her best friend, calling her name. She dropped to her knees and cradled her friend's body against her own, desperately fumbling with her phone as she dialled for an ambulance, but even as she did, a small part of her recognised the futility of it. Megan, her glassy, unseeing eyes still open, was dead.

[3]

London, June 2013

It doesn't feel like nearly two years since I was here last, Ashley thought bitterly. She stared at the coffin and wiped the tears from her eyes.

The day was warm and muggy, with dark clouds covering the summer sky. The air was humid and a strong breeze was blowing through the trees, making the branches sway violently. *A storm is coming* she thought idly.

Ashley glanced around her as the wind whipped her plain black dress, her long, dark-brown hair dancing in the breeze. There was a small gathering of mourners: a few nurses from her mother's work, some of her friends from school, and a couple of people she recognised from their neighbourhood, but that was it.

No, not the same kind of turnout for a woman who takes her own life and leaves a teenager to fend for herself. She remembered the size of the crowd the last time she had stood here, and anger bubbled up inside her. She clenched her fists and forced it back down.

At least me and Mum are centre stage this time, she thought, and a small laugh escaped before she could stop it. A couple of mourners were giving her sympathetic looks, and that just made the pain and anger worse. She turned her head away, uncertain what she might do if she didn't.

The vicar was saying a prayer but Ashley wasn't listening; she was still thinking about that terrible afternoon just over two weeks ago.

She wasn't sure how long she had sat in the bathroom next to her mum, tears flowing freely as she held tightly on to her cold, stiff fingers. The next thing she was aware of was when two firefighters burst through the bathroom door. The pizza she had put in the oven had burned to a crisp, and a conscientious neighbour had smelt smoke and raised the alarm. The firefighters had called an ambulance, but it was obvious to all present that her mum was far beyond any medical intervention.

The vicar finished his prayer, and the coffin was lowered into its final resting place.

This shouldn't have happened. I told her she was working too hard, working too many hours, but she wouldn't listen. I should have realised, maybe offered to quit my A-levels and get a job – even a Saturday job – to take the pressure off a bit – but I didn't want to see. I was too busy hanging around with my mates. Perhaps if I'd spent more time focusing on someone other than myself, she might still be alive.

The service finished and the small collection of mourners began to disperse. A few came over with words of sympathy for Ashley, but she either didn't hear or simply ignored them. She remained at the graveside as the clouds finally gave way and the rain started to fall, slowly at first, then growing heavier until her hair was plastered to her head and her dress soaked through. But still she stayed, the only sounds those of rain beating against the coffin, the rustle of leaves and the far-off rumble of thunder. Despite this, she remained rooted to the spot, unwilling or unable to leave her mother's side, realising for the first time that she was truly alone in the world.

This wouldn't have happened if Dad was still alive. Mum would have still been happy and she wouldn't have had to work so hard. She wouldn't have felt that there was no way out, no way back from the dark place she was in. She continued to stare at the coffin, now completely alone, all of the mourners having fled at the start of the downpour.

That's two parents she's cost me, she thought, hands clenched at her sides, her expression hard and grim. *I will find her, and she is going to pay.*

The rain continued to fall.

Chapter 16

Jenny leaned against the doorway and smiled a wide, exhausted smile. Greg came over and stood next to her, a similar expression on his face. In front of them, a large group of eight and nine year olds were running, shouting and screaming. A small boy dressed as Iron Man, complete with tiger face paint, ran up and asked where the toilet was. Jenny pointed him in the right direction and he ran into the house, a look of urgency on his face.

The face-painter had been Greg's idea, and it had certainly been a popular one. There were a handful of tigers, a couple of pirates, and the remainder were unicorns. Each year they vowed this would be the last party, that it was too much work and stress, and each year they caved at the look in Sophie's eyes when they began to say no. She certainly seemed to be enjoying herself, bouncing around the large trampoline with a couple of her friends, all laughing away. As much as Jenny hated the trampoline, thinking it an eyesore that took over the garden, the kids certainly liked it: Sophie was never off the thing.

'I think she's had a good birthday,' said Greg.

'I still can't believe she's nine. She was a baby only last week, wasn't she?'

'It soon goes.'

Above the excited cries of over-sugared children, Jenny's mobile started to play 'The Pretender' by Foo Fighters, her current ringtone. She frowned and stepped into the kitchen. 'DI Stone,' she said, trying and failing to keep the annoyance out of her voice.

'Jenny, it's me,' said DS Marie. 'I'm sorry, I know it's Sophie's birthday and you don't want to be disturbed, but it's important. There's been another murder.'

Jenny's eyes widened. 'What?'

'The call's just come through. Megan Parkinson's been found dead at her home.'

'Shit.'

'That's not all. Amelia's shop was vandalised last night. Someone got in.'

'*Shit* shit.'

'We can handle things here. I'll keep you updated but I thought you should know.'

'I'm leaving now. I'll meet you at the scene.' Jenny ended the call.

'You're leaving now, are you? Have you forgotten it's your daughter's ninth birthday and her party is in full swing?' Greg stood in the doorway, arms folded.

'I have to go. There's been another murder.'

'For fuck's sake, Jenny, first you miss Sophie's play and now this? Can't it wait until after the party? Or, better still, can't somebody else take care of it?'

'It's my case and there's been another murder; I *have* to be there. Surely you can understand that?'

'I can, but there's somebody else who won't and she deserves better.'

Pain crossed Jenny's face as she looked out to the garden,

where her daughter was talking animatedly to a couple of her best friends. She walked out of the kitchen towards them, her feet heavy. Sophie saw her and ran over, her wide eyes and beaming smile causing Jenny's heart to break all over again. 'Mum, Mum, can we do the presents now?' she shouted, bouncing up and down with excitement.

'Sophie, sweetie...' Jenny began, taking her small hands and crouching so that their eyes were level.

Sophie stopped bouncing, her expression changing from excitement to wariness, the start of this conversation all too familiar.

'Something serious has come up at work.'

'You're leaving, aren't you?' Sophie asked, her voice flat. Her shoulders drooped and Jenny saw the sparkle of tears forming.

'I have to, sweetie, it's important. I'm so sorry. I'll make it up to you, I promise.'

Sophie pulled her hands away, turned her head and gave a little nod, her eyes shining with tears. Feeling absolutely wretched, Jenny kissed her on the cheek, straightened up, and started towards the house. As she reached the door she turned back and saw Sophie crying, her arms wrapped around Greg, as all her friends looked on.

I'm going to catch the bastard responsible and make them pay for this, she thought, her knuckles white as she gripped her car keys.

* * *

Jenny manoeuvred her car down the narrow street, sounding her horn to get the gathering people out of her way and receiving some dirty looks in return.

She abandoned her car next to a couple of patrol cars and angrily slammed the door, the drive in having done nothing to dissipate her bad mood. The sight of her nine-year-old daughter crying in her husband's arms still stung. She knew she was right to come, that she needed to be here, but it didn't make her feel any less guilty, and telling herself that Sophie would understand when she was older felt trite and hollow.

Jenny pushed through the onlookers and made her way to Megan's house. Thankfully someone had had the foresight to close the road, as between her car, numerous patrol cars, and the blue and white forensic tent taking up the pavement and half the road, nothing would get through any time soon. She made her way to the blue and white crime-scene tape marking a large perimeter around the house and spotted the PCSO controlling entry. She was just about to dig out her warrant card when the PCSO gave her a nod and said, 'Ma'am.' Jenny realised it was the PCSO from the first murder scene. She returned her nod and ducked under the tape.

Forensic suit and gloves donned, she entered the property. As before, the scene was already a hive of activity. She could see white-suited members of Sunil's team going in and out of the living room. She spotted Emma and went over to her. 'What have we got?'

'The victim is Megan Parkinson, found dead in her living room at 16:05 this afternoon by Amelia Simpson. Sunil and his team are preserving and cataloguing the scene, and Dr Rahman is examining the body.'

'Where's Amelia?'

'Upstairs. George is with her.'

'Good. I want a statement from her ASAP.'

Jenny walked carefully down the hallway and gazed into the living room. Sunil and a couple of forensic photographers were recording the positions of key items. Jenny could make out a hammer lying on the floor near the body, with blood and mousy-blonde hair on its head. *The murder weapon.* The body was lying face up on the floor, eyes open and glassy, hair matted with dark, dried blood. Jenny waited in the doorway, not wanting to disrupt anyone's train of thought.

Eventually, Dr Rahman spotted Jenny and came over to join her. 'Inspector,' he said, with a nod.

'What do you know?'

'This appears to be the death scene, and based on the temperature of the body I would place the time of death between two and three am this morning. I won't be able to confirm this until I can perform a proper examination, but I assume the cause of death is blunt force trauma to the back of the head.'

'Do you think that's the murder weapon?' Jenny nodded her head in the direction of the hammer.

'The pattern of injuries is consistent with blows from an object of that size, but-'

'You won't be able to confirm that till you can do a proper examination. OK, thanks doc.'

Sunil came over to join them. 'How are you getting on, Sunil?' Jenny asked.

'Slow. No prints from the hammer, I'm afraid, and we haven't found any signs of forced entry. We've recovered a good number of fibres and hairs from the body, but given that when the first officers arrived, Ms Simpson was cradling her friend-'

'Shit,' Jenny muttered under her breath.

'So for all we know, most of those came from her.'

'We'll need her clothing as well, then.'

'Already taken care of; you can thank DS Marie for her quick thinking on that one. We have also recovered a laptop, a tablet and a mobile phone, and our tech guys will get straight on to them as soon as they're back at the station.'

'OK, thanks. Let me know if you find anything else of interest.'

Jenny joined Emma and they went upstairs. The first floor had a small landing leading to three doors. Jenny could see an outdated bathroom through a partially opened door, and another door revealed what appeared to be the master bedroom. The bed was made, with a pale-green duvet, and a small teddy bear leaned against the pillow. On the bedside cabinet was a small well-thumbed paperback.

Ignoring both of those rooms for now, Jenny opened the door to the last room. At first glance it appeared that Megan must have been in the middle of decorating, but on closer inspection Jenny realised that it was an art studio of sorts. The walls were covered with paint of various colours and there were a couple of work-in-progress paintings dotted around. One wall was covered with torn-out pictures from magazines, showing various landscapes. There was also a desk and a small sofa, and on that sat George and Amelia, both dressed in forensic suits.

George stood up when Jenny entered, while Amelia remained seated, staring unseeing at the wall in front of her. Jenny had seen that expression all too often during her time working on violent crimes back in the Met. She thought back to one particular case in which a drug dealer had tried to move into another's territory and had paid for it with his life. His girlfriend had discovered his mutilated body and Jenny had seen the same kind of expression on her. Jenny had been one of the first uniformed officers on the scene. She had found the young woman slumped on the ground as far as she could get from the remains of her boyfriend, a vacant, unseeing look in her eyes. She often thought about the poor girl, and wondered what had become of her.

Jenny nodded at George, then squatted down so that she was in Amelia's eye-line. 'Amelia, are you OK to talk?'

Nothing.

'Amelia?' Jenny asked again, her tone a little sharper. Amelia's eyes refocused, seemingly realising for the first time that Jenny was there. 'We need a statement from you, and the sooner the better. Are you OK to come down to the station?'

Amelia nodded, but before she could say anything more Jenny heard raised voices outside the house. She hurried out to find Sam struggling with the PCSO and another uniformed officer whom Jenny recognised as PC Richard Gordons. 'What's going on?' she asked them.

'Ma'am, this individual claims to know the victim and is demanding to come in,' the young PC told her, still trying to hold back an agitated Sam.

'Mr Jones, if you don't settle down you will be arrested,' Jenny said, aware of all the eyes staring intently at her. That and the cameras of their mobile phones.

'What's going on? Where's Amelia? I want to see her right now!'

Before Jenny could respond there was a noise from behind her, and she turned to see Amelia pushing her way outside. Before Jenny could stop her, Amelia ran up to Sam and threw her arms around him, tears streaming down her face. 'She's dead, Sam,' Amelia cried.

'Who is?' Sam asked carefully, his gaze flitting from Jenny to the other officers nearby.

'Megan.'

Chapter 17

Jenny led Amelia through to interview room six, a soulless cube identical to the one Amelia had been in only days before. She helped Amelia sit down and sent a uniformed officer for a couple of coffees. A few moment later, he reappeared holding two steaming cups and put them on the table. Amelia cupped it in her hands and gave him a weak smile of thanks.

Jenny switched on the tape, introduced herself and asked Amelia to do the same. 'Thank you for coming down to give a statement, Ms Simpson; I appreciate how difficult this must be. In your own words, can you tell me what happened today?' Jenny asked gently.

'I tried to get hold of Megan a couple of times this afternoon. I assumed that she was just sleeping off last night's hangover, so I went round. When she didn't answer I tried the door. It was unlocked so I let myself in, and that was when I...' Fresh tears ran down her cheeks, and she put her face in her hands.

'Take as much time as you need,' Jenny prompted kindly.

Amelia took a deep, shuddering breath before continuing.

'I went in and called out to her; I thought she was still in bed or something. I went through to the kitchen to get a drink of water, and that was when I found her.'

'What did you do then?'

'I can't really remember, it's all a bit hazy. I know I must have called 999, as the next thing I remember was when the police turned up.'

'When did you last see Ms Parkinson?'

'Last night.' Amelia wiped her eyes. 'We went out for a drink in Ryde.'

'Was it just the two of you?'

'No, Sam was with us as well. It was Megan's idea; they were trying to cheer me up. No, wait, it wasn't just the three of us. We ran into an old friend of mine from uni and she joined us, we spent most of the night down Union Street, in Bohemia drinking together.'

'Who was your friend?' Jenny asked, her eyes narrowing imperceptibly.

'Her name's Dawn. Um, Dawn Coombes.'

'What did you all talk about?'

'Nothing really, we just traded stories and caught up. I hadn't seen Dawn since I finished my master's.'

'You hadn't seen her since uni? Quite a coincidence that you happened to run into her last night, then.' Jenny folded her arms.

'She owns a graphic design firm in London. She said she had a meeting with a client down here.'

'What time did you leave last night?'

'We were there till the lights came on, so probably about two am.'

'Then what did you do?'

'We went our separate ways. Me and Sam went home, Megan went off towards hers and Dawn headed towards the seafront.'

'Can you think of anyone who might wish to harm Megan?'

'No, no one.' Fresh tears formed in her eyes and Amelia took a sip of her drink, her hands shaking, and a little coffee spilled on the table.

'OK, thank you, Ms Simpson,' said Jenny, standing up and reaching to switch off the tape. 'If you think of anyth-'

'Wait, there's something else,' said Amelia, her eyes wide.

'Go on.' Jenny sat back down.

'Kirstie. Megan had a run-in with her last night.'

'What do you mean by a run-in?'

'Before we went down to Bohemia, we were in the Red Lion. Kirstie came in with a couple of friends and before I could stop her Megan stormed over and punched her in the face.'

'Why did she do that?'

'She thought Kirstie was responsible for what happened to my cat James.'

'Do you think she was responsible?'

Amelia considered her response for a minute before answering. 'No. Maybe. I don't know.'

'OK, I think that's all I need for now. If you think of anything in the meantime, please don't hesitate to call me.'

* * *

'Briefing room, now,' Jenny called as she walked into the office.

Despite it being a Saturday, the station was bustling. Normally busy anyway, it was a sea of activity now.

Jenny was already at the front of the briefing room, tapping her foot impatiently, as the whole team began to file in. She watched them take up positions around the room. Some appeared annoyed which she understood, no one wanted to give up their weekend off, while some looked focused, but they all had an energy about them.

'Right,' Jenny shouted above the general murmur. The room quietened as everyone focused on her. 'At 16:05 today we received a call from a very distressed Amelia Simpson. She had gone round to see Megan Parkinson and found her dead on her living-room floor.'

'Cause of death?' asked a uniformed officer near the front.

'We won't know for certain till the forensic examiner can carry out a full examination, but we believe it to be blunt force trauma to the back of the head. A hammer was found at the scene; we believe this to be the murder weapon.'

'How long had she been there?'

'The FE estimates time of death as between two and three am this morning.' Jenny replied.

'That's two murders of people related to or close to Amelia Simpson. That can't be a coincidence,' Claire said with a frown.

'Don't forget the cat,' DC Simon Michaels added.

'Cat?' the uniformed officer asked, with a look of confusion on his face.

'Yesterday morning Amelia found a gift box outside her flat. Inside was a bloodstained collar that she says belonged to her missing cat. More worryingly, though, there was a note with a date printed on it: the twenty-third of May, just over a week away. And that's not all. Last night, Amelia's shop was vandalised. When she opened up this morning she found all her stock dead.' Jenny paused and looked around at the team.

'Shit,' muttered someone near the back.

'Do we have any suspects?' asked Simon.

'One: Kirstie Williams. We know from Amelia's statement that Megan had a run-in with her in the hours before she was murdered. There's also clear animosity between her and

Amelia, and she hasn't been able to provide an alibi for the night that Frances Lowes was killed.'

'What about the boyfriend?'

'No motive that we can see; the three of them were on good terms. Plus Amelia said that Sam went home with her.'

The room went quiet as the officers absorbed the new information.

'Assignments,' called Jenny. 'George, Emma, I want you to track down any witnesses to last night's altercation between Kirstie and Megan. Claire, I want you and Steve to see if you can find any witnesses or CCTV near Megan's house. Simon, pull Megan's financial records and chase up the forensic analysis on the shop – and the box and note from the earlier scene.'

* * *

Emma and George pulled up down the road from the Red Lion and hurried through a light summer shower to the now-deserted bar. Emma gazed in and cursed. 'Locked up.'

They walked round the building and found a back door just off an alley. It was a lot less flashy: dull grey with a tarnished brass handle. Emma tried the door, which opened smoothly. 'Hello? Is anyone about?' she called.

A man in his early thirties with close-cropped dark-brown hair, wearing an expensive-looking black suit, came out of a room halfway down the hallway. 'Can I help you?' he asked, his expression curious.

'Police,' Emma announced as she and George flashed their warrant cards. 'Can we have a word, please?'

He took them to the room he had emerged from, which was in stark contrast to the drab hallway. There was an expensive leather chair behind an equally expensive-looking desk, on which sat a brand new iMac. The man, who introduced himself as Darren Holmes, owner and manager, gestured towards a black leather sofa and the detectives sat down, refusing his offer of a drink.

'How can I help you both?' he asked, taking a seat across from them.

'We're looking for some information. There was a fight in here last night at about ten pm. What can you tell us about it?' asked Emma.

'Not too much, I'm afraid: I was back here. I only heard about it later from Ben.'

'Ben?' George asked.

'One of our bartenders. He said that some woman started on another one, seemingly with no provocation.'

'You don't seem too concerned,' Emma replied with a frown.

He shrugged. 'It happens, comes with the territory. Sometimes tempers flare after a few drinks. That's why we pay for bouncers.'

'I'll need a list of names and numbers for the bar and the door staff,' George added.

'Sure, no problem.' He pressed a few buttons on his iMac and a nearby printer whirred into life. Moments later, he picked up two sheets of warm printer paper and handed them to the detectives.

'Do you have cameras that cover the bar area?' Emma asked, indicating towards a camera on the wall above them.

Darren clicked a few more keys and beckoned them over. On the monitor a remarkably clear video appeared of what Emma assumed was the main bar. Darren fast-forwarded to a couple of minutes before ten.

'There's Amelia, Megan and Sam,' George said, pointing at the corner of the screen.

After about a minute, the front door opened and in strode Kirstie with two other people. About fifteen seconds later,

Megan stormed over and they shoved each other before Megan punched Kirstie. Then two door staff grabbed Megan and escorted her out, followed by Amelia and Sam. A barman came over and handed Kirstie something in a cloth which she held to her cheek.

'Do you know when that woman left?' George asked, and nodded towards Kirstie.

Darren clicked a few buttons and the recording started to play at several times the normal speed. After about two minutes, Kirstie vanished. Darren rewound a little, then played the recording at normal speed. They saw Kirstie pick up her bag and leave, and the time on the recording said 10:12pm.

'We'll need a copy of this,' Emma told Darren.

* * *

Back at the station, Jenny reached Simon's desk just as he put down the phone. 'What do we know?'

'The techs are still working on the electronics recovered at the murder scene, but they've completed their analysis of the plants recovered from Ms Simpson's business. They were all killed by a concentrated solution of a chemical compound called glyphosate, a common weedkiller available from most garden centres. They haven't been able to recover anything from either the collar or the box: whoever planted it knew what they were doing. Likewise, the note hasn't offered up anything.'

'The person doing this certainly knows how to cover their tracks.'

'Yeah, we need a lucky break,' Simon agreed.

The main door to the office swung open and George and Emma came in. They spotted Jenny and made for her.

'Did you manage to find any witnesses?' Jenny asked.

'Even better: we've got footage of the incident itself,' Emma announced with a smile. 'We'll still need to speak to the bar staff and doormen to find out what was said, but from the footage it does appear that Megan attacked Kirstie for no reason. Kirstie had only been in the bar for a matter of moments before Megan was on her.'

'Good work, but I want to know what was said,' replied Jenny.

'Boss!' called Claire from the far end of the office. 'Come and look at this.'

The four detectives went over to where Claire was sitting, a satisfied grin on her face. 'We might have something. I've been working through the traffic cams and CCTV from the area around Megan's house, focusing on the hour before and after the expected time of death. Given the time of night, there are plenty of people on the streets – mostly party-goers heading home – and a reasonable number of taxis out, but I spotted this on the corner of Star Street, about forty metres from Megan's road.'

Claire pressed Play on the recording and they all leaned in. The time on the recording said 2:26am. In the background they could just see the corner of the local cinema; Jenny had visited with Sophie and Greg only a couple of weeks ago to watch the latest Pixar movie. The rest of the view showed a deserted street, all the houses dark and shut up for the night, the occupants no doubt fast asleep. Nothing happened for the first fifteen seconds except for a taxi driving past, but then a figure rounded the corner, weaving erratically.

'Megan Parkinson,' George observed before being shushed by Jenny.

The figure disappeared from view and Claire paused the recording. 'Unfortunately, this is the closest I could get to Megan's house, but as it's only a couple of minutes from here to her house, we have a pretty good idea of when she got home.' She skipped ahead ten minutes and hit Play again. 'Look: same camera. I nearly missed this person because they're doing quite a good job of sticking to the shadows, which could just be someone tipsy making their way home, but look at what they're wearing.'

The detectives stared at the image on the screen. The figure wore loose-fitting trousers and a hoodie, with the hood up and the peak of a baseball cap protruding from under it.

'The person who dropped the box at Amelia's wore that outfit,' Emma observed.

'That's what I thought. Another thing to note is the way they're walking. You'd expect anyone out at this time of night on a Friday to have been drinking. They seem perfectly sober.'

The figure on camera walked in the same direction as Megan before disappearing from view.

Claire regarded the others. 'I think this is our killer.'

Chapter 18

'Let's review what we know so far,' said Jenny. 'One: Megan Parkinson and Frances Lowes were both killed in their own homes, with no sign of forced entry. Therefore they either knew their assailants and let them in, or the assailants gained access to the property in a way that we've yet to uncover.' Jenny stared at the whiteboard in the briefing room, a deep frown on her face.

'Two: they were killed in different ways but the murder weapon was left at each scene,' George added. Jenny made another note on the board.

'Three: they targeted Amelia's cat and left a note that implied there was more to come.' Jenny finished writing on the whiteboard and turned to face the rest of the team, tapping the marker against her open palm.

'So far, the only person we've identified with any kind of grudge against Amelia Simpson is Kirstie Williams,' said Emma. 'She can't provide an alibi for the night of Frances's murder or the night that Amelia's cat was killed. And she was involved in an altercation with Megan on the night she was murdered.'

'Plus she fits the profile of our mystery person in the two recordings,' Claire added.

'Let's bring her in,' said Jenny. 'Emma, George, you go to the shop. Claire, you're with me, we'll take the house.'

* * *

The afternoon was quiet and the sky overcast as Jenny and Claire pulled up opposite Kirstie's dated terraced house. They got out, crossed the road and pushed open the iron gate. Jenny knocked loudly on the front door and waited. When this failed to elicit a response, she knocked again. 'Ms Williams, can you come to the door, please? It's the police; we would like to have a word with you.'

Still no response.

Frustrated, Jenny peered through the frosted glass of the front door but couldn't see anything. She went over to the front window, but the net curtains hid the interior of the house. 'Shit.'

Her phone rang in her pocket. She reached for it and retreated to the street, Claire right behind her. 'Emma, give me some good news.'

'Sorry, boss, the shop is shut up tight.'

'*Shit!*' Jenny said again.

'I take it that means you've had similar luck, then?'

'Yeah, no signs of life here either.'

Jenny glanced up at a noise from the neighbouring property, which, with empty wine bottles in the overgrown front garden, an overturned bin and a cracked window, made Kirstie's house look positively doted upon. The front door opened and a woman emerged. She looked to be in her early fifties, and her blonde hair showed about three inches of brown roots. She eyed the two detectives with thinly veiled suspicion.

'Excuse me,' Jenny called, 'we're looking for Ms Williams. Have you seen her today, or do you know where she might be?'

She stared at Jenny. 'Who's asking?'

'Police,' Jenny answered, pulling out her warrant card.

'Dunno where she is, but I saw her getting into a taxi this morning, about ten. She had a suitcase with her.'

'Damn it,' Claire muttered from behind Jenny.

'Do you know which firm it was?' Jenny asked.

'Not sure, think it was one of the local ones.'

Jenny thanked the woman, who retreated inside her house without another word, then pulled her phone back out and dialled a number. 'Simon,' she said without preamble as soon as he answered, 'Kirstie isn't here and it looks like she left this morning in a hurry. The good news is that she left in a taxi at around ten am. I want you to get on to all the local firms to find out if they picked her up, and more importantly, where they took her.'

'On it.'

Jenny ended the call and ran over to her car.

Jenny burst through the double doors into the office with Claire close behind and headed straight to Simon's desk. He was on the phone. She leant against his desk and he gestured that he'd only be a second. A moment later, though it felt longer to Jenny, Simon hung up and turned to face them.

'What have you found out?' Jenny asked.

'She was taken to the ferry terminal at the top of Ryde pier.'

'Dammit, Portsmouth train terminal is at the other end, so she could be anywhere by now. Get a warrant and check her financial records. I want to know if she bought any train tickets, and if so, where she went.'

'Already requested; that was who I was on the phone to,' Simon replied.

'Good work. Keep on it; tell them this is a priority. Also, speak to the taxi driver; find out if she let anything slip about her destination. Claire, I want you to get hold of the CCTV from both the ferry terminal and the train station. We can see if she got on a train at the other end, and where it was going.' She turned and made for the door. 'When Emma gets back, have her chase up the forensics on Megan's place. I want to know what they've found.'

'Will do. Where are you going now?' asked Claire.

'I'm going to get an update from Dr Rahman.'

* * *

Jenny pulled into the car park of St Mary's Hospital and parked in the first available space. Even though it was Sunday afternoon, the hospital was still busy. Jenny nodded to the woman behind the reception desk before heading down to the forensic examiner's office.

As Jenny pushed through the double doors, the same bored receptionist as before started to rise, but Jenny stopped her with a raised hand. 'Don't worry, I know the way,' she said, as she strode towards the office like a woman on a mission.

Jenny reached the office, knocked twice, and entered. Dr Rahman was typing on his computer. A flicker of surprise flashed across his face at the sight of the detective before being quickly replaced by his usual hard-to-read gaze. 'Inspector. I guess I'm not surprised. It's not just us doctors who get to work Sundays.'

'Should have tried harder in school, doc,' Jenny replied with a wry grin.

'If you're here for an update on our latest victim, you're too early. I've only completed my initial analysis.'

'What can you tell me?'

'My initial assumption was correct. Ms Parkinson was killed by two blows to the back of the head, and the damage to the skull consistent with that of a hammer similar to the one found at the scene.'

'Two blows?' Jenny asked, her eyes widening.

'Based on the angle of impact, I would say that the victim was standing for the first blow and below the attacker for the second.'

'So the first incapacitated her and the second finished the job,' Jenny surmised, her frown reappearing. 'It takes a special kind of psychopath to hit a woman with a hammer when they're already down. What else do you know?'

'I've narrowed my estimated time of death to between 2:30 and 3:30 am, but that's it, I'm afraid. I should have my final report ready in a day or two.'

Jenny's mobile started to ring and the display told her that it was Emma. She answered and told the sergeant to hold on a moment, then thanked Dr Rahman and made her way towards the main part of the hospital. 'Sorry, I was in with Dr Rahman.'

'What did he say?'

'Not much, unfortunately, just confirmed the cause and time of death.'

'Damn.'

'How are things going at your end?'

'Good, actually,' Emma said, but something in her tone made Jenny stop short, causing an elderly couple to nearly crash into her. They walked around her, muttering about manners and using phones in hospitals, but Jenny ignored them.

'Come on,' she said impatiently, 'spit it out!'

'A second sweep of the house has recovered a diary and the tech teams have found something interesting on Megan's computer and phone. I think you're going to like it.'

* * *

Jenny burst through the double doors and found the team talking animatedly. 'This had better be good!' she said.

'Sunil rang while you were out,' Emma told her. 'Our forensic tech guys found a large number of emails between Megan and Sam on Megan's laptop.'

Jenny stared. 'Sam? As in Amelia and Sam?'

'The very same. Not only that, but they've uncovered quite the chat history. Turns out the loyal best friend and the doting boyfriend were sleeping together.'

'You're kidding,' Jenny asked, her mouth agape. Claire and George smiled; it wasn't often that they found their detective inspector lost for words and were enjoying the sight of it.

'We're still going through the information, but it looks as if it had been going on for at least nine months. There are some fairly graphic photos, too.'

'No,' Jenny exclaimed.

'We've also been through the last month or so of the diary. Turns out that they've been arguing a lot lately. Apparently, Megan has been wracked with guilt about the affair and was planning on ending it. She told Sam that she couldn't do this to Amelia anymore and wanted to come clean.' Emma stared into the distance, a thoughtful expression on her face.

'What are you thinking, Emma?' Jenny asked.

'Amelia must spend time at Megan's house, what if she was there recently and saw something she wasn't supposed to see? Maybe Megan left her computer on or her diary laying out and Amelia couldn't resist a peek; let's call it natural curiosity. After a night of drinking, she decides to have it out with her best friend. And in a moment of madness, she loses her temper.'

'I don't think Amelia has it in her,' George said, frowning.

'That still doesn't explain the grandmother's murder, or targeting the cat,' Simon added.

The room went quiet as the team pondered these new developments. Eventually, George broke the silence. 'While I don't think Amelia is capable of such a cold-blooded act, Sam, on the other hand, is a different matter. He could have found the diary and realised that Megan was planning on ending it.'

'And if he realised that Megan was planning to end it and come clean, we're back to the losing-everything scenario,' said Emma. 'Megan more or less said as much when we spoke to her after Frances's death.'

'Plus Sam could have talked his way into both Frances's and Megan's homes relatively easily. That could explain why we haven't found signs of forced entry at either scene,' Claire said.

'We're forgetting a key point, though,' said Jenny. 'Amelia said they left at the same time and went home together.'

'They may have left together, but there's nothing to say that Sam didn't put Amelia to bed and head straight back out,' Emma interjected. 'If he hurried, he could get from the bar to his and Amelia's flat, then up to Megan's house by three am.'

The detectives thought this over. Then the control-room door opened and Sergeant Fischer stuck his head in. 'DI Stone, do you have a minute?'

'Sure, Tony, what's up?' Jenny replied, her voice weary.

'We've just had an anonymous phone call. Someone matching your suspect Mr Jones's appearance was spotted leaving the vicinity of Frances Lowes's house just before midnight on the fifth. Apparently he was in quite a hurry.'

'You're kidding,' Emma said, eyes wide.

'What else did they say?' Jenny asked.

'That was it. The caller was a woman and she didn't leave a name. She said that she'd read about the murder online, and thought she should report what she'd seen in case it was relevant.'

'I've heard enough,' said Jenny. 'Let's bring him in.'

Chapter 19

It was early morning the following day. The streets were just starting to get busy with the first of the day's commuters as Jenny and Emma parked down the street from Amelia's flat in an unmarked police car. Jenny had her phone pressed to her ear; after a minute she thanked the caller and ended the call, putting the phone back into her pocket. 'We've got the warrant, so we're good to go,' she told Emma, who gave a curt nod in return.

The tactical unit pulled in behind them as the two detectives got out of the car, full of nervous energy. Jenny loved this part of the job, when a suspect was in her sights and she was about to make an arrest. They went to meet the six-man team climbing out of the transport, all wearing the same black uniform, armoured vest and helmet.

'The suspect's name is Sam Jones. Six foot one, medium build,' Jenny told the team.

'Are we expecting any resistance?' asked the leader of the unit, a sergeant called Thomas Young.

'Not sure. The suspect has no history of violence or aggression, but has been far from friendly in most of our encounters. And given the cold-blooded nature of both murders, I don't want to take any chances.'

'Understood.' He turned to face his team, his mouth set in a grim line. 'Colin, Pete, I want you on the enforcer. Craig, you take the lead. If we can get the suspect to open up voluntarily, push on through and subdue him. If there's no answer, Colin and Pete, it's over to you.' Sergeant Young turned back to Jenny and Emma. 'Once the suspect is in handcuffs I'll radio the all-clear. Are we expecting there to be anyone else in the house?'

'No,' Jenny replied. 'The girlfriend should have left for work by now.'

Without another word, Sergeant Young and his team made their way in through the open front door and up the stairs, moving quickly but silently. They arrived outside flat five and Sergeant Young nodded to one of his team, who stepped forward and pounded on the door with his fist. 'Police! Open up!'

Ten seconds passed with no response. The officer repeated the process. Again, no answer.

'Do it,' the sergeant told Colin and Pete, who brought forward what was colloquially known as the big red key. They drew the enforcer back, then slammed it into the door. The first strike reverberated around the landing and caused the wood around the lock to splinter. The second sent the now-ruined front door inwards and the officers stormed into the flat. They reached the living room and found Sam just starting to rise from a chair, fear competing with surprise on his face. One hand held a PlayStation control pad, the other a large set of gaming headphones that he had just taken off his head.

'Police! Stay where you are!'

Sam, his grey eyes round and his mouth hanging open, stood there as an officer cuffed one of his wrists. Then shock was replaced by anger. 'What's going on?' he cried. He shook himself free of the officer's grasp and shoved him hard in the chest. The officer stumbled, but managed to stay on his feet. Before Sam could take another step, the remaining officers wrestled him to the ground, cuffing his wrists behind him. He tried to struggle but was held firm, his cries of frustration and rage muffled by the carpet.

'All clear up here,' Sergeant Young said into the radio clipped to his left breast. About thirty seconds later, Jenny strode into the room with a look of smug satisfaction. Emma, close on her heels, wore a similar expression.

'Nice to see you again, Mr Jones,' she told him as two officers lifted him to his feet.

'What's going on? What do you want?'

'Samual Jones, I'm arresting you on suspicion of the murders of Frances Lowes and Megan Parkinson. You do not have to say anything, but it may harm your defence if you don't mention when questioned something which you later rely on in court. Anything you do say may be given in evidence.'

'What? This is a wind up, right?' he cried, staring at her.

Amelia appeared in the doorway, keys in one hand and bag in the other. Her expression mirrored Sam's as she took in the chaos around her. 'What's going on?' She tried to enter the room, but was held back gently by one of the officers.

'Shit,' Jenny muttered under her breath before crossing the room. 'I'm sorry to have to tell you like this, Amelia, but we've just arrested Sam on suspicion of Frances's and Megan's murders.'

Amelia looked horrified, her mouth hanging open. 'This is a joke, right?'

'I'm afraid not.'

'I accept that Sam and Gran were hardly BFFs, but there's no way he would harm her. And as for Megan, we were all friends. Why on earth would he do something like that?' she stammered, her eyes going wide.

'New evidence has come to light.'

'What evidence?' Amelia asked crossing her arms over her chest.

Jenny gave Emma a small nod, and she led a protesting Sam out of the flat and down to the waiting car, the tactical unit with her. Jenny waited until they were alone before continuing. 'We have reason to believe that Megan and Sam have been sleeping together for at least the last nine months.'

'No, you're wrong. There's no way they would do that to me!' Amelia cried, putting her hand over her mouth.

'We've found some fairly compelling evidence. I'm sorry,' Jenny added, feeling lousy.

* * *

Jenny led Sam to the front desk of the station and booked him in. As he was being led away to a cell, the desk sergeant told her that DCI Edwards was looking for her. She thanked him and made her way upstairs. She headed to the DCI's office, knocked once and entered.

'Jennifer, good. Please take a seat,' he said, gesturing towards the empty space at the front of his desk. Jenny looked at her boss; his tie was loose and the top button of his shirt was undone. Jenny was surprised: this was probably the most dishevelled she'd ever seen him. 'How is the investigation going? Have you made any progress with the second murder?'

'We've just taken the boyfriend into custody. It turns out that he was sleeping with the second victim and she was planning on coming clean.'

Edwards smiled, leaned back in his chair and ran a hand

through his hair. 'Excellent! I won't keep you any longer, then.'

As Jenny started to leave, he spoke again. 'We need this wrapped up soon.' Jenny stopped and turned to face him. 'The local press are reporting that there may be a link between the two murders, and I've just been torn a new one by the Superintendent. The longer this goes on, the worse it looks for this department. And by extension, you and me. I'm sure neither of us want that,' he added in a low tone.

'I'm on it, sir,' she said, and opened the door.

'Make sure you are!' he called after her. Jenny's hands clenched at her sides, but she kept walking.

Jenny, still annoyed after her run-in with Edwards, walked into the interview room with Emma and took a seat opposite Sam and his publicly appointed solicitor. Sam stared at them with undisguised animosity, arms folded across his chest. He was wearing an ill-fitting grey sweatshirt and jogging bottoms, his original outfit having been confiscated and handed over to forensics.

Jenny pressed play on the audio recorder, introduced herself and Emma, then gestured for Sam and his solicitor to do the same. Formalities taken care of, Jenny settled back in her chair and looked at Sam. 'How are you today, Sam?'

'I've had better days off,' he replied drily.

'We just have a few questions for you. Hopefully we can get this whole mess sorted out, and then you can be on your way,' Jenny said.

Sam stared at her, his expression indicating that he didn't believe her for a second.

'Tell me, Sam, what's your current relationship status?'

'You know what it is.'

'Please, refresh my memory,' Jenny replied in an easy tone, a little smile playing across her lips.

'I'm Amelia's boyfriend.'

'How long have you been together?'

'I dunno. Just over six years, I think,' Sam replied with a frown.

'And what's your relationship with the deceased, Megan Parkinson?'

'She is – was – Amelia's best friend.'

'Is that all?'

'No. She was my friend as well.'

'Is that all? Just a friend?' Emma replied, one eyebrow cocked.

'That is what my client said,' cut in Sam's solicitor.

Emma opened up the folder in front of her and took out three printed-out images. One was a close-up of Megan, topless, the second was a photo of a fully naked and aroused Sam, and the third was another shot of Megan, this time fully naked as well. She placed them on the table.

'For the record, I am showing Mr Jones images 31 to 33. These images were recovered from Megan Parkinson's phone. The first and third images were sent from the phone number registered in her name, and the second one came from a number registered to you. However, it's not your main number, is it, Sam? It turns out that there are two phone numbers registered in your name. How do you explain that?'

No answer.

'Are these the types of images that friends send one another?'

Still no answer.

'These are just examples; we have recovered plenty more.' Emma's smile didn't reach her eyes.

'I would like to read you something,' Jenny told them, retrieving a stapled document from the folder. 'For the record, I am reading excerpts from the document marked RP03 in the folder which contains messages sent from the second mobile number registered to you and the number registered to Megan. The first excerpt is dated the twenty-ninth of January of this year.

I've been thinking about you all day. Are you coming round tonight?

What about Amelia?

Amelia will be at her gran's and won't be home for hours. We'd have the whole place to ourselves.

Yeah, OK. I bought some new lingerie today that I think you'll like.

I will if it's like that little outfit from last time. You looked sensational! It was all I could do to keep my hands off you till we got into the bedroom!'

Jenny looked up. 'The second conversation dates from the sixteenth of March this year.

She's nothing compared to you, you know that?

You can't say that!

Why? It's true. She's just some frigid flower seller. She's far more interested in that bloody cat than me, but you're something else entirely. When I'm in bed with you I actually feel alive.'

Jenny faced Sam. 'These are hardly the kinds of discussions friends have, so I ask you again: what was your relationship with the deceased?'

'OK, we were having an affair, but I didn't hurt her!' Sam picked up the plastic cup from the table and took a small sip of water, his hand shaking noticeably.

'We have also recovered Megan's diary.' The look on Sam's face suggested he had no idea that a diary existed, just as Jenny had hoped. 'For the record, I am reading excerpts from the document marked RP13 in the folder, which concerns Megan Parkinson's diary. This excerpt is dated the second of April of this year.

I spent the day with Amelia yesterday, just the two of us. We went out for a drink. It was only meant to be a couple and the next thing I know, I'm stumbling home after midnight properly shit-faced. It was such a laugh, though, and after the shitty week I've had at work I needed it. I need to end it with Sam; I can't do this to her anymore. I'm meant to be her best friend, and I'm shagging her boyfriend behind her back! What's wrong with me?'

Jenny turned a page. 'This diary entry is from just over two weeks ago, the second of May.

I chickened out. I was all set to end it with Sam last night, but I caved. To be honest, I'm a little worried about what Sam might do when I tell him.'

She looked at Sam. 'And this one is from the very next day.

I should just do it: tell Amelia and beg her forgiveness. I don't know if she would forgive me, but I can barely look her in the eye. I actually went round to see Sam tonight and told him I couldn't do it anymore and that I was going to tell Amelia everything. He grabbed me by the arm and pinned me against the wall. Then he said that I would regret it if I told her because he would deny everything, and who would Amelia believe anyway, me or him, her loving boyfriend of the last six years. I told him I had all the photos he'd sent me, and that if he ever touched me again I'd forward them all to Amelia. But as much as it pains me to admit it, Sam's right. If I tell Amelia the truth she'll never speak to me again, so I guess I'll have to pretend that everything is normal with Sam even though I don't want to see him ever again.

Jenny put the document on the table. 'You were terrified that Megan would tell Amelia, Amelia would throw you out, and then you'd have nothing. Let's be honest, you have a comfortable life with Amelia, don't you? She owns the house outright, and has a considerable sum in the bank. Not only that but she is due to inherit even more. That keeps you in quite a nice lifestyle, doesn't it? I think you were worried that it would all end, so you decided to silence Megan before she could confess.'

'No, you've got it all wrong. That's not what happened.'

'Then why don't you clear it up for us, Sam?'

'OK, I admit that we were sleeping together, but she came on to me. I realised that it was a mistake ages ago, and I've been trying to end it for months.'

'So what stopped you?'

'She wouldn't let me! She said that if I ended it then she would tell Amelia everything.'

'That's not how her diary reads, so one of you is lying. OK. Let's move onto the murder of Frances Lowes then, shall we? You didn't like her, did you? She kept trying to make Amelia realise that she was too good for you, that she should dump you and find someone better. Yet another threat to your comfortable little life. Frances tried again on the night she died and that was the final straw, wasn't it? After that, you decided she had to be silenced once and for all.'

'I left first that night, or had that slipped your mind?' Sam's lip curled.

'Where were you between eleven pm and midnight on the night of the fifth?'

'I was at home in bed with Amelia, asleep, as she can verify.'

'What I think happened was that you waited till Amelia was asleep, then sneaked out, went back to Frances's house, and let yourself in with Amelia's key.'

'No.'

Jenny continued as if she hadn't heard him. 'Maybe you didn't set out to kill her. Maybe you just wanted to scare her, to stop her badmouthing you to Amelia all of the time, but she was a strong-willed woman, wasn't she? Even at her age and with you towering over her, she refused to be cowed. And when she wouldn't acquiesce you lost your temper, went to the kitchen, grabbed a knife and shut her up permanently. You then panicked, dropped the knife, not before wiping your prints off it, and fled the scene. When you weren't immediately caught, it got you thinking, didn't it? It had been easy to get rid of one problem. If you could just do it again then you'd be home free, with no more threats to your comfortable life.'

'You couldn't be further from the truth.' Sam snorted contemptuously. 'At the time of both murders, I was at home in bed with my girlfriend. You're just fishing, aren't you? Hoping to trip me up somehow. You have no evidence that links me to either murder, or you'd have said so by now.'

'What if I told you we'd had a call placing someone matching your description in the vicinity of Frances's house at the time of the murder?'

'I told you I was at home in bed. You can't prove anything.'

Now it was Jenny's turn to sit back and scowl. He'd scored a direct hit: she had been hoping he'd trip himself up.

Sam glared at her. 'You should stop wasting your time with me and start interviewing the right people.'

'And just who are the right people?'

'Well, for a start, there's Amelia's old uni friend Dawn, who has just come to town. She was out with us on Friday night, and it definitely felt like there was some sizing up going on between her and Meg. Not only that, but Megan actually got into a fight with that Kirstie. You'd do better talking to either of them.'

'Don't worry, we'll be speaking to all parties in due course. I think we're done for now.' Jenny ended the interview, reached over and switched off the tape, then asked a uniformed officer to escort Sam back down to his cell. After his solicitor had left, Emma got up and made for the door, but stopped when she realised that Jenny hadn't moved from her seat.

'You OK, boss?' she asked.

'There's no way we'll be able to charge him with either murder based on what we've currently got, and he knows that. Annoyingly, he's right about one thing.'

'What's that?'

'We definitely need to locate Kirstie as soon as possible, and I think we should have a chat with this Dawn.'

Chapter 20

The sun was moving towards the horizon as George and Claire walked up to the entrance of the hotel. A young man with an expensive haircut, smiled warmly at them as he reached out and opened the door. George nodded in return and Claire smiled politely.

Inside, the hotel lobby was tastefully set out. To the left was a collection of expensive yet mismatched chairs in front of an unlit log fire. Just past this was a bar at which sat a young couple, chatting away.

'Seems like Dawn does all right for herself,' Claire muttered to George as they reached the front desk. An immaculately turned-out woman in her early thirties stood behind the reception desk talking on the phone. She flashed them a perfect smile and gestured apologetically that she'll only be a moment.

'Sorry about that,' she told the two detectives when she hung up the phone a minute later. 'How can I help you?'

'We would like to speak to a guest of yours: a Ms Dawn Coombes,' George said, and both he and Claire flashed their warrant cards.

'Ms Coombes is staying in room fifty-four,' she told them after tapping on the computer in front of her. 'Would you like me to call her room?'

'Please, but could you-'

'Omit the fact that you're police officers?' the receptionist finished with a smile.

'You got it.'

She lifted the phone to her ear and pressed a couple of buttons. After about twenty seconds, she put the phone back down. 'No answer, I'm afraid,' she told them, with another apologetic smile.

'Would someone be able to take us up there, please?'

After another couple of button presses, a man in his forties appeared at the desk. 'Mr Pritchard, this is Detective Constable Bancroft and Detective Constable Watson. They want to speak to one of our guests, a Ms Dawn Coombes in room fifty-four. I've tried to ring her and had no answer, so they would like access to the room.'

'I'll take them up, thanks, Katie.'

Outside the room, Mr Pritchard, who had since introduced himself as Thomas Pritchard, the assistant manager, knocked on the door and waited. When there was no answer, he swiped his key card over the electronic lock. A small LED light flashed green and there was a click as the lock retracted.

He opened the door a fraction. 'Ms Coombes? My name is Thomas Pritchard and I'm the assistant manager. Are you there?' When there was no reply, he pushed the door fully open and the three of them entered. A quick survey of the room confirmed that it was indeed empty.

The room itself was bright and airy, with the bulk of the space taken up by the king-size bed in the centre. Behind it was an elaborate leather headboard that ran the entire length of the room, and the far wall was one large window with stunning views of the Solent in the background. A medium-sized suitcase was propped up against the back wall, and a pair of wrinkled trousers and a cream top were slung over a nearby chair. On the bed was a small manila folder.

George, having put on a pair of latex gloves, carefully opened it. Inside the folder were several sheets of paper. The first appeared to be a printout from Amelia's business website. The next few pages were a handful of pictures, all of Amelia.

* * *

'Are you telling me that we've managed to lose two people of interest in a bloody murder investigation?' Jenny demanded, trying and failing to keep her voice level. They were all back at the station, the team clustered around the whiteboards in the briefing room.

Claire went to reply, but paused when Emma gave an almost imperceivable shake of her head. She had seen Jenny like this plenty of times before, and knew it was wiser to keep quiet.

'We're checking the CCTV from the hotel now,' said George. 'So far, we have footage of her leaving the hotel the day after the murder, but not returning. I've also applied for a warrant so that we can track activity on her debit and credit cards and put a trace on her mobile phone.'

Jenny took a deep, calming breath. 'OK, good. Now, where are we with tracking down Kirstie Williams?'

'Unfortunately she paid cash for her train ticket, but we do have footage of her getting on a train to London,' said Simon. 'We're checking CCTV footage from all the stations along the route, but it's slow going. There's been no activity on her bank cards as yet and her phone's switched off.'

'The photos we found in Dawn's hotel room were printouts from Amelia's Facebook page,' Claire added.

Jenny frowned. 'We're still missing something here. What is it about Amelia Simpson? This all seems to revolve around her, and apart from having a bit of money, she seems to be nothing more than a normal thirty-something florist. I think we need to bring her in for a chat. But in the meantime, I want to know where Kirstie Williams went!'

For the second time that day, Emma pulled up just outside the converted house that contained Amelia's flat. As she and George walked up the drive they passed a van for a local locksmith's. They reached the main door and were about to press the buzzer for flat five when the owner of the van came out of the house, nodded politely to the two detectives, and held the door for them. Emma and George climbed the stairs to Amelia's flat, and Emma knocked on the newly installed door.

Eventually, Amelia opened the door and scowled at them. 'What do you want?' she asked, hands on her hips.

'We'd like to have a chat with you,' said Emma. 'We were hoping you'd come down to the station.'

Amelia sighed. 'I just want all of this to be over.'

'The sooner we catch the person doing this, the sooner it will be over,' George told her, his tone softer than his sergeant's.

Back at the station, George led Amelia down to interview room two. He left and returned a couple of minutes later with a steaming mug of hot sweet tea which he put down in front of Amelia. She smiled in way of thanks and he turned to leave, but she stopped him. 'Do you really think Sam did it? Do you really think he killed not just Megan, but Gran too?'

'I can't comment on an ongoing case, I'm afraid,' George replied gently, then left again, telling her that Jenny wouldn't be too long.

After a further five minutes, the door opened and in walked Jenny, followed closely by Emma. They took seats opposite her. Jenny started the recording and took care of the usual formalities before sitting back and regarding Amelia, her pale-green eyes thoughtful. 'Thank you for coming in, Amelia,' she said finally.

'As I told your detectives earlier, I want this resolved as much as you do.'

'For the record, I want to point out that you're not under arrest and that you're free to leave at any time. I just have a couple of questions that I'd like answering.'

A nod.

'So, how are you doing?'

'How do you think I'm doing?' Amelia snapped. 'In the space of a couple of weeks I've lost my gran and my best friend. Then today I find out that my boyfriend was sleeping with my so-called best friend and may even have killed her. So you tell me how you think I'm doing!'

'I would be angry,' Jenny replied calmly, her gaze locked on Amelia.

'I am angry!' Amelia shouted, banging her fist on the table. Some tea spilled over the side of her mug.

'So angry you could kill?' Jenny countered, her voice still infuriatingly calm.

Amelia, in turn, looked as if she had been punched in the gut. She gaped, eyes wide. 'O-of course not!' she stammered.

'I don't know; in your shoes I might be. It would certainly be understandable, wouldn't it? Betrayed by two of the people you held most dear.'

Amelia sat back in her chair and wrapped her arms around herself.

'Tell me,' Jenny asked, 'on the night Megan died, where did you all meet?'

'I went round to hers, we had a couple of glasses of wine whilst she finished getting ready,' Amelia replied cautiously.

'Where was Sam?' Jenny asked.

'He stayed at home; he met us in town later that evening.'

'Did you always go round to Megan's before a night out?'

'No, sometimes she came to ours, other times we met at the pub.'

'What did you do whilst Megan was getting ready?' Jenny asked.

'I dunno, drank some wine, scrolled on my phone and chatted to Megan I think,' Amelia said frowning.

'Is that all?'

'Yeah, I think so. Why does it matter?'

'I'm just trying to get a clear picture of the evening's events. Let me tell you what I think happened. I think that maybe you decided to have a little snoop around, curiosity getting the better of you. Maybe the computer was switched on and logged in, or you came across her diary and you couldn't resist having a little look, thinking "what's the harm". And you ended up learning something you didn't want to know but couldn't let go of?'

'No! That's not what happened!' Amelia glanced at Emma for support but was met by the same hard stare.

She looked back at Jenny. 'I think I would like a solicitor present before I answer any more questions,' Amelia said finally.

'OK, I'm sorry,' Jenny conceded putting both her hands up. 'I'm just struggling to figure out is why all this is happening. First your grandmother is murdered, then your cat is killed, then your shop is vandalised and finally we have

Megan's murder. I find it hard to believe that all this isn't related. Someone is clearly targeting you, and I need to know why.'

'I don't know,' Amelia replied, looking tired. 'I've never hurt anyone; I've never even been in a fight before.'

'What is the twenty-third of May?'

'I don't know,' Amelia repeated. 'I'd tell you if I knew, I really would. I don't know why anyone would target me – I'm just a florist on the Isle of Wight, for God's sake – and I don't know what the relevance of that date is. I've been racking my brains since I first saw the note, and nothing has ever happened to me on that date. Maybe it's just arbitrary?'

Jenny leant back in her chair and let out a sigh of frustration. She glanced at Emma, who shook her head. 'I think that'll do for now, but we may need to speak to you again soon.' She reached across the table to switch off the tape. 'Please, if you notice anything peculiar or think of something, give me a ring.'

Amelia gave a small nod.

'I'll get George to run you home.'

* * *

Amelia unlocked the front door to her flat, walked inside and closed the door. She leaned against it and slowly slid to the floor. She started to cry as the events of the last couple of weeks finally caught up with her.

Why me? I'm a good person, aren't I? I've never done anything to hurt anyone, so why is this happening? Eventually the tears dried up and she dragged herself to her feet. She went to the kitchen, grabbed a bottle of red wine and opened it, pouring a generous measure into a wine glass. After a couple of gulps she went to the bathroom, returning with the bottle of sleeping pills which her doctor had prescribed to help her sleep after her grandmother's death. She set them down on the counter, next to her half-empty glass.

Chapter 21

Jenny arrived in work already in a bad mood. She had got home late the day before, and Greg had made a few offhand comments about Sophie never seeing her anymore which had made Jenny feel guilty.

It wasn't just that, though, it was everything about this damn case. She was sure Sam was behind both of the murders – he had reasons to want both women dead – but the lack of physical evidence troubled her. While she believed he was capable of carrying out the murders, she didn't think he would have done it quite so cleanly, leaving no trace. The interview with Amelia hadn't turned anything up, either. She didn't really think that Amelia had attacked her gran or her best friend. The shock on Amelia's face yesterday had seemed pretty genuine, either that, or she was a fantastic actress. But the date troubled Jenny most of all; she was sure it wasn't arbitrary. So, all things considered, she was in a bad mood, and she doubted that would change any time soon.

Dumping her bag at her desk, she headed straight to the kitchenette, grabbed a mug and poured herself a cup of coffee. She had barely made a dent in it when Emma came in and disturbed the peace. 'Boss, we've had the ME's office on the phone-'

'Good morning to you too, DS Marie,' Jenny replied, a little testily.

'Sorry boss, it's just that Dr Rahman's finished his examination of Megan Parkinson.'

'OK, get him to email the report over and I'll take a look.'

'He wants to speak to you personally. He says he's found something which we may find interesting.'

Jenny walked to her desk and set her coffee down. Her mood had improved a little – they desperately needed a break in this case – but she wouldn't want to be Dr Rahman if he'd got her hopes up for nothing. She picked up her phone, dialled his number, and put the phone on speaker.

The call connected on the second ring. 'Good morning, Inspector Stone,' said Dr Rahman. 'I had a feeling it might be you.'

'I believe you've got something for us?' Jenny asked, cutting to the chase, trying and failing to keep the hope from her voice.

'I've finished my examination of the latest victim, Ms Parkinson. As I told you before, the cause of death was blunt force trauma to the back of the head. The victim also had excessively high levels of alcohol in her bloodstream, which would no doubt have affected her ability to fight back. I have, however, discovered something I think you'll be interested in. I have recovered skin samples from beneath the fingernails of the right hand.'

'Enough for a DNA analysis?' Jenny asked excitedly.

'There should be, yes.'

'That's great news, doc! Can you get it analysed ASAP?'

'I've already sent it off and marked it as high priority. You should have the results back tomorrow.'

'You're an absolute star!' Jenny told the doctor. She ended

the call and turned to Emma. 'Is it too much to hope it will match with the sample we took from Sam yesterday?'

'We can hope,' Emma agreed, her grin matching Jenny's.

'We need a sample from Amelia too,' said Jenny. She looked around the office, spotted George talking to one of the PCSOs, and hurried over, cutting him off mid-sentence. 'George, I need you to get a DNA sample from Amelia Simpson right now. Tell her it's for crime scene elimination. I need her sample and Sam's processed as a matter of urgency.'

'Will do, boss. Does that mean...?'

'Yes: we've recovered a sample from Megan's body.'

George slowed down as he approached the shop. Closed, as he had expected. It was worth checking, though, given that it was only a minute or two's drive between the shop and the house. He parked up outside Amelia's building. The front door was shut, so he pressed the buzzer for flat five. No response. He tried again, with no result. Just as he was about to give up and head back to the car, a tinny sound came over the intercom, followed by Amelia's voice. 'Who is it?' She sounded tired.

'It's Detective Constable Bancroft. May I come up?'

Amelia didn't respond. Just as George was weighing up whether to ring again or come back later, a buzz came from the door. George gave it a push and it swung open.

He went upstairs and was about to knock when the flat door opened and Amelia stared out at him. Her hair was a mess, her eyes bloodshot, and judging by the bags under them, she hadn't slept much the previous night. 'What do you want?' she said, finally.

'I need to get a cheek swab from you, if that's OK.'

'What for?' she asked, her voice rising.

'It's routine; it's just to rule you out of our enquiries.'

'You'd better come in then.' Amelia turned and walked into her flat and George followed. He coughed as he was hit by an overwhelming smell of stale cigarette smoke. It took him back to Saturday mornings at university, waking up after a big night out and being able to smell his clothes from halfway across the room. In his opinion, one of the best things to come out of this century so far had been the smoking ban.

'I didn't realise you smoked,' he called out conversationally as he followed Amelia to the kitchen.

'I don't. Sam used to years ago, but quit. I was rooting through his things last night and found a packet. I guess that was another thing I didn't know about him.'

They entered the kitchen and Amelia sat at the breakfast bar. George produced the swab kit and took the sample, then sealed and pocketed it. He got up and turned to go, but stopped himself and turned back to Amelia.

'Was there something else?' she said.

George stared at her for a minute, not too sure how to ask or whether he even should. 'Are you OK?'

'I wish people would stop asking me that,' she said tiredly.

'Sorry. Stupid question, I guess.'

Amelia sighed and got up. 'Do you want a cup of tea?' George accepted gratefully.

'Only a couple of weeks ago,' Amelia said over the rising whine of the boiling kettle, 'my life felt almost perfect, you know? I still had Gran, Sam and I were happy, and I still had my best friend.' She smacked the worktop, making George jump. 'But that was all a lie, wasn't it?' she said, her expression hardening. 'The reality was that my so-called best friend and my boyfriend were shagging behind my back. They must have had a right old laugh about it. Poor, gullible

Amelia. My gran was right, wasn't she? He's a loser, and I should have kicked him to the kerb years ago. If I'd listened to her, maybe the last conversation I ever had with her wouldn't have been an argument.' She paused. 'But it was. And I have to live with that now, don't I?'

'If it's any consolation, Megan felt terrible about it and wished it hadn't happened.'

'She still did it, though,' Amelia snapped. 'You know, I'm torn. I desperately miss Megan; I would tell her when anything bad happened and she always helped me through it, either by talking or by taking me out for a drink to forget about it. But I hate her for what she's done. I've got nothing left now, no one. I'm alone.'

'It'll get better,' George told her, realising just how trite that sounded.

'It can't get any worse, can it?' she said, and a harsh laugh escaped her. 'I don't know if I've got enough energy left.'

'Whatever you're thinking, just don't, OK? I know the world seems dark at the moment, but it won't always be. You can't let this beat you.'

The look on Amelia's face suggested she was far from convinced. George pulled out a business card and scribbled on the back before handing it to Amelia. 'Look, I know this whole situation doesn't feel great and you can't see a way out, but promise me one thing. Call me if you think about doing something stupid. It doesn't matter what time of the day or night it is, I'll answer. My work number is printed on the front, and my personal mobile is on the back.'

Amelia looked at the card, then met his eyes and gave him a weak smile. George thanked her for the tea, and left.

[4]

Ashley stood outside the Georgian townhouse and wondered for a minute whether she had come to the right place. It was only when she spotted a small brass plaque with the title *Steve Walsh, MSc, DClinPsy. Clinical Psychologist* that she knew she had.

Being a therapist must pay pretty well, she thought to herself as she took in the house before her. The small front garden was immaculate, the white sash windows stood out against the sand-coloured bricks, and the black front door was framed by a fanlight and half-pillars on either side.

After a moment's hesitation, Ashley pushed open the black wrought-iron gate and made her way down the brick path. She reached the front door and knocked once.

Twenty seconds passed, and nothing. Just as Ashley was starting to consider leaving, a light came on. A few moments later the door was answered by a slim, tall man in his mid to late thirties, dressed in expensive dark blue jeans, a white shirt, and a grey jacket. Ashley, in her slim-fitting jeans, loose black hoodie and white beanie, felt positively scruffy. 'Ms Johnson?' he asked.

A curt nod.

'Good to meet you. I'm Steve.' He held out a well-manicured hand, which Ashley glanced at before turning to stare at anything other than him, her hands clenched in the front pocket of her hoodie.

Unfazed, he invited her in and led her to a medium-sized room towards the back of the house. The walls were painted teal, the large windows facing a well-maintained garden. At only five pm, the sun was still shining, making the room feel warm and cosy. A large mahogany bookcase covered one wall. While it was mostly filled with academic-looking books, there was occasionally a framed photo or a small pot plant, which made the room feel less imposing. The wall next to the bookcase featured a brick fireplace. A fire was laid but not lit, since the temperature was still in the late teens.

Ashley took a seat on the large, comfortable corner sofa by the window and Steve sat down in the small chair opposite, the only item between them an aluminium and glass coffee table.

'Would you like a drink?' he asked. 'Tea? Coffee? Water?'

She shook her head.

Another thirty seconds passed. Ashley stared at Steve, looking bored. In return, Steve stared at her intently, studying her.

Eventually, he broke the silence. 'So, Ashley,' he began, his gaze still on her. 'The school got in touch about you. They're worried about your recent behaviour; turning up late, outbursts in class, getting into fights with your fellow students, and even with your friends.'

Ashley stared at the table, her hands fidgeting in her lap,

then picking at a loose thread on her hoodie. A couple of minutes passed.

'Can you tell me what's going on? Why you're acting out in this way?' Steve picked up a small black notebook and pen from the table.

A shrug. 'They started it.'

'You've been in four fights in six weeks, Ashley. That's a lot of other people starting it. What's stopping you just walking away?'

'I'm not a coward,' Ashley replied. Her pale-blue eyes narrowed, focusing properly on Steve for the first time since they had started talking.

'I didn't suggest you were. I just asked what stops you from walking away when these people antagonise you.'

'Well, they start it, so I finish it.'

'It doesn't finish though, does it, Ashley? All it does is draw more attention to you. Now you're here, wasting your time talking to me, while they're probably out with their friends enjoying themselves.'

'It finished it then. They didn't say anything else to me.' A small smile that didn't reach her eyes played across her lips.

'That person didn't, but someone else will,' Steve told her, his voice still infuriatingly calm.

'Then I'll do the same to them. Eventually word will get around.'

'You can't fight everyone forever. I've met far bigger and tougher people than you.'

She scowled at him.

'Eventually you'll run out of road. By then, the school and any friends you still have left may well have given up on you, and then you'll truly be alone. Is that what you want?'

Ashley glared at Steve but didn't say anything, her hands clenched in her lap, her breathing a little ragged.

'Look, Ashley, I know you have to be here. It's part of the

conditions the school set when they let you off with a final warning instead of expelling you. But now that you are here, you might as well try to get something out of it.'

'Why do you want to help me? What do you get out of it?' Ashley asked, her eyes narrowing in suspicion.

'I get paid to be here. You'll only get something out of this if you talk to me,' he said, matter-of-factly.

'What can I get out of this?' Ashley asked, her head cocked to the side, intrigued in spite of herself.

'You can talk to me, and maybe you won't feel quite so angry anymore.'

'What do you want to know?'

'I want to know why you get angry at the slightest provocation. From what I hear, you're a very bright girl, and you must know that the way you've been acting of late won't help you in the long run. So what I want to know is what makes you decide to do what you do, to retaliate instead of walking away. You must realise that these people are probably only doing this to see your reaction.'

She shrugged.

'Your approach up until now has been to get angry and fight someone, and your classmates may respect you for that, but that won't work here.'

'You're the expert, so what would you suggest? How can I fix all my problems?' Ashley asked, half amused.

'The first step is to acknowledge what those problems are. Only then can we look at taking the steps needed to resolve them.'

'What my problems are? You wouldn't know the half of it, sat here in your fancy office and expensive house. You have no idea what I've been through.'

'So assume I don't know any of it, Ashley, let alone half of it.'

'You really want to know what my problems are?'

'Part of me wants to know, and part of me just doesn't want to get bored during our time together, so I may as well know.'

'Well, my dad is dead and my mum couldn't stand to be around me any longer, so she killed herself.'

She stared at Steve, waiting for his reaction. She'd seen any number of reactions to this statement – horror, sadness, pity. Of all of them, pity was the worst. However, Steve didn't appear to be fazed in the slightest.

'What do you think your dad would say if he could see you now? Would he be proud?'

Ashley paused, not liking the question. No, that wasn't it; it was the answer she didn't like. 'He would be disappointed that I had hurt someone, given what he did for a living,' she replied.

'What was his profession?'

'He was a doctor.'

'I see.' He picked up a bottle of water from the coffee table, opened it and took a sip before putting it back down. 'What kind of relationship did you have with him? Were you close?'

'I didn't see him all the time, but that made the days we did spend together better. We always did something, made it special.'

'What about your mother? What was your relationship with her like before she died?'

'We got on OK. I didn't really see her all that much – I was at school, and she was always working.'

'How did you feel when she killed herself?' he probed, his gaze fixed on her.

'Angry,' she whispered.

'Why?'

Ashley sprang up and began pacing around the office. Though the late afternoon sun was still shining into the room, she felt cold. She stopped at the bookcase and wrapped her arms around herself. Then she picked up a framed photograph from the shelf and studied it. It showed two people in full snowboarding gear standing at the top of a snow-covered slope, holding snowboards and grinning for the camera.

'Who's this? Your boyfriend?' she asked, a sly smile on her face as she waved the photo in front of her.

'My brother, if you must know.' He walked over and took the photo from her, then put it back on the shelf and returned to his seat. 'You didn't answer my question. You said you felt angry. Why?'

'Because she chose my dad over me, and now I'm here,' Ashley shouted. 'What about me? I don't have anyone now; I'm alone.' She wrapped her arms around herself again. 'Why didn't she want to stay here, with me? Why wasn't I enough?' she said, the anger gone, her voice small.

Chapter 22

'We've got the results for the DNA found under Megan Parkinson's fingernails,' Emma told Jenny as she came in the next morning. From her tone, Jenny could tell it wasn't the smoking gun she had hoped for.

'Sam Jones?' she asked, despite knowing it wouldn't be.

'I'm afraid not. No hits on the Police National Database, either.'

'Shit,' Jenny muttered. No hits meant a dead end, and this was the best lead they'd had. Without it, they were back to square one.

'There's still one possibility, though. The lab hasn't had time to process Amelia's sample yet.'

'True,' admitted Jenny. 'Although we now have to decide what to do about Sam.'

'Yes. The twenty-four hours we're allowed to hold him for are nearly up,' Emma agreed.

'And without the DNA match we don't have enough evidence to charge him, so we'll have to release him on bail. Can you take care of that, please? I can't handle his smug, arrogant face this early in the morning.'

Jenny sat at her desk and stared at her computer screen. She was rewatching the CCTV feed recovered from the night of Megan's murder. She froze the image as the mystery person came into shot and enlarged it. Unfortunately, the quality just wasn't good enough to glean any sort of information. Hell, Jenny couldn't even say for certain if the person was male or female. Even more annoyingly, this was the only shot of the mystery person that they'd been able to find so far. She banged her palm on the desk in frustration, making Simon jump at the desk behind her.

Emma sat down at her desk, beside Jenny's. 'How did that go?' Jenny asked, continuing to stare at the image in front of her. She rubbed her hands across her face wearily, wondering if it was time for another coffee yet.

'Oh, he was suitably arrogant. He flounced off with a swagger threatening to sue for wrongful arrest, you know the sort of thing.'

Jenny nodded.

'Unfortunately, I ran into DCI Edwards and he asked how we were getting on…'

Jenny groaned; she had been hoping to have a new lead before informing Edwards that they'd released Sam.

As if on cue, the main door swung open and in strode the DCI. If his expression was anything to go by, he wasn't in a good mood. 'DI Stone, a word in my office, please.'

Jenny got up reluctantly from her chair. Emma mouthed 'Sorry' as she followed her boss into his office.

Edwards was standing by the window, looking out over the car park. 'I hear you've released Samuel Jones,' he said, turning to face Jenny. 'What are you playing at?'

'The DNA recovered from the victim wasn't a match. While he is a lowlife, without a DNA match we didn't have enough evidence to hold him any longer.'

'So where does that leave the investigation?' He sighed angrily.

'The lab is still processing the swab taken from Amelia. It's been fast-tracked, so hopefully we'll get the result soon.'

'Do you think it could be her?' Edwards asked her now.

'To be honest, sir, I don't think so. While she did have a motive and an opportunity, it doesn't fit with the first murder.'

'So we're back at square one, then.' He sat down heavily at his desk.

'Not entirely, sir. We're still trying to track down the old university friend and the other florist.'

'Find them,' he told her. 'If you need any additional resources, let me know. Just get this bloody case wrapped up.'

* * *

Sam walked up the drive to the flat he shared with Amelia, the swagger still in his step. He unlocked the main door and went upstairs to the top floor. He inserted his key into the lock on the flat door, but the key refused to move. Frowning, he tried a second time, again with similar luck.

'Amelia, what's going on?' he shouted. He knocked on the door, belatedly realising that it was a new door and, by extension, a new lock. After a moment, the door opened a little. He was about to push it wider when he spotted the chain, and behind it Amelia, her expression unreadable.

'What's going on?' he demanded. 'Why doesn't my key work, and what's the deal with this?' He gestured towards the chain.

'You slept with Megan,' Amelia responded matter-of-factly.

'You're still going on about that? Look, you've got it all wrong. OK, me and Megan slept together, but it was a mistake. She came on to me, then she threatened to tell you and make out it was all me unless we carried on.'

'Did you kill her? Did you kill Gran?' she asked, her voice cracking slightly as she struggled to keep her composure.

'No! Of course not, how could you even think that? And as for your gran... OK, I admit that we didn't get on, but I know how much she meant to you; I'd never hurt her. Do you seriously think I could do something like that?' Amelia's gaze softened slightly. 'Come on, take the chain off. Let's talk inside.'

'No,' Amelia told him, the wavering in her voice gone and her shoulders squared. 'Even if you didn't hurt Gran or Megan, you still cheated on me.'

'Come on, this is my home!' Sam protested, rolling his eyes.

'I need time to figure out what I want. I'll be in touch.'

Sam reluctantly nodded, turned and headed back down to the front door, his earlier swagger now gone.

* * *

'Right, everyone, briefing room now!' Jenny called out as she closed the door to Edwards's office.

When the team entered she was already at the front of the room, whiteboard marker in her hand, staring at the information they already had and trying to work out if they'd missed anything.

'How'd it go?' Emma asked her, putting a freshly made cup of coffee in front of her, a peace offering which Jenny gratefully accepted.

'He's not happy; he wants this case wrapped up as soon

as possible. With that in mind, how's the hunt for Kirstie and Dawn going?'

'Apart from the printouts at the hotel, we haven't found anything to suggest that Dawn was involved.'

'So for all we know, she could either be responsible for all of this, or she could be another victim.'

Simon cleared his throat. 'However, I spoke to some of the employees at Creative Solutions. That's the design company she owns and runs,' he added, in response to the blank looks. 'No one has heard from her in the last week. Here's the interesting part. They don't have any clients on the Isle of Wight. As far as they knew, Dawn was just taking a few days' holiday.'

'That is interesting,' Jenny admitted. She turned to the whiteboard and under *Suspects* she added Dawn's name. Next to it she wrote: *Here under false pretences.*

'We've finished reviewing the footage from the hotel and we can't find any trace of Dawn after she left the hotel on the morning of the fifteenth,' Simon said with a grimace.

'That was four days ago.' George frowned.

'Anything on her phone or cards?' Claire asked.

'Nothing. Her phone was switched off mid-afternoon on the fifteenth, and hasn't been switched back on since. Equally, there's nothing on either of her bank cards, although that doesn't mean she hasn't been paying cash. I've got a couple of PCs going over footage from all the ferry terminals to see if we can spot her leaving, but so far nothing. And that doesn't explain why she would have left all her belongings. Unfortunately, due to the number of different ports, the sheer number of sailings each day and the amount of people on each ferry, I'm not optimistic that we'll get anywhere.'

'Keep trying anyway,' Jenny told him. 'We're due a bit of luck on this case. Where are we with locating Kirstie?'

'We've made some progress with that, actually,' Claire replied. 'We have footage from Portchester station that shows her getting off the London train and onto a train heading towards Basingstoke, but there's where the trail ends. There are no cameras on that particular train, and a couple of the smaller stations on that route don't have any either. She could have got out at any of them and gone on from there. We've reached out to the local forces, but...'

'But if she keeps a low profile she could be anywhere by now,' Jenny said. 'Shit.' She turned back to the board and stared at it, willing something to jump out that they might have missed. 'I can't believe we're being continually out-manoeuvred,' Jenny said, vocalising the same frustration that the rest were feeling. 'Every time I think we might have something, some small lead we could use to nail this bastard, it turns out to be another dead end! They always seem to be one step ahead of us.'

There was a knock on the briefing-room door and a young uniformed constable stuck her head in. 'Sorry ma'am, is now a good time?'

'Yeah, sure. What's up, Mel?' Jenny asked, her voice weary. She was definitely getting sick to death of this case.

'I've got the lab on the phone; they want to talk to you.'

Jenny dismissed the team and headed back to her desk, the beginnings of a headache forming behind her eyes. She pinched the bridge of her nose and sat down, then picked up her phone and answered the waiting call. Slowly, her lips curved and a sparkle appeared in her eyes as she listened to the person on the other end. Emma gave her a curious look and mouthed 'What?', but Jenny held up a hand. After a minute more, she thanked the person on the other end and hung up, her headache all but forgotten.

'What's going on?' Emma asked as George, Claire and Simon looked on, all wearing the same curious expression.

'That was the crime lab. They've finished their analysis of Amelia's swab and compared it with the one recovered at the scene.'

Emma stared at her. 'Don't tell me it's a match.'

'It's a partial match. Paternal. Whoever killed Megan Parkinson had the same father as Amelia.'

Chapter 23

The uniformed officer opened the interview room door and gestured Amelia towards one of the empty seats.

'You didn't have to escort me, you know. I could have found my way here on my own by now,' Amelia said, but her sarcasm was lost on him. He turned and closed the door without so much as offering a drink.

Amelia had refused at first when Jenny rang and asked her to come in, unable to believe there was anything left to ask, but she had finally relented when Jenny said that they had new information directly related to her, and that it was important.

She sat there, bored, and looked around the room. It was the same drab green colour as all the rest, with the same cheap carpet tiles. She hadn't heard from Sam since the day before, which she was a little surprised about. She guessed he had gone to stay with his parents on the other side of Ryde, which she knew he'd hate, but she didn't care. *Well, too bad. He made his bed so he can bloody well lie in it.*

Eventually, the door opened and Jenny came in with George. She spotted that Amelia didn't have a drink and sent a uniformed officer to fetch three coffees. That done, she started the tape and took care of the usual formalities. 'Thank you for coming in again, Amelia.'

'That's OK, Detective. I like nothing more than spending every damn day in this bloody station.'

Jenny chose to ignore the comment and took a sip of coffee, wincing slightly at the bitter taste. 'We'd like to ask you a few questions about Dawn Coombes.'

'Dawn?' Amelia asked, confused. 'Why would you want to talk about her? What has she got to do with anything?'

'She was out with you, Sam and Megan on the night of Megan's death; we're just trying to cover all bases. Leave no stone unturned. You know how it is.'

'What do you want to know?'

'How did you meet her?'

'It was about two months into my final year of university; I was doing my master's. One of my tutors asked me if I'd help out one of his first years. She was struggling, but he claimed he could see something in her and asked if I would take her under my wing for a bit. I helped her out with a number of tutoring sessions in those first couple of months, and we ended up becoming friends. She spent the rest of the year hanging out with me and my housemates, although we lost touch when I graduated.'

'No contact since then?' George asked.

'No, nothing. Not till I felt a tap on my shoulder last Friday night. I turned around and there she was.'

'Don't you think that was a bit odd, her appearing out of the blue like that? Just happening to be in the same bar at the same time as you, Sam and Megan?'

'Not likely, I admit, but not impossible. She said she had a meeting with a client on the island.'

Jenny and George exchanged glances and wrote in their notebooks. 'Have you heard from her since that night out?'

'Yes, actually. She came to the shop the next day; she said she wanted to talk to me about something.'

Amelia's brows knitted as she watched the sudden change in Jenny and George. Jenny's gaze intensified, while George sat up straighter in his chair.

'What did she want to talk about?' Jenny asked, her pale-green eyes boring into Amelia's.

'She wanted me to come and work for her. She came to the shop around lunchtime and we went down the road to get a sandwich. She said that she hated to think of me pottering around in the shop when I could be doing more.'

'What did you say?'

'I didn't say anything. She changed the subject, and we spent the rest of our lunch reminiscing about Brighton. That was actually why I went round to see Megan; I wanted to get her opinion.'

'How did Dawn seem to you?'

'She seemed OK. A bit hungover, but so was I. Why are you asking all this? You don't think she was involved, do you?'

'Like I said, we're just covering every angle. Have you heard from her since then?'

'No. I assume she had the meeting with her client and then went back to London.'

'Can I ask about your parents?' Jenny asked, changing the topic.

'Why?' Amelia asked, her eyes narrowing.

'Just humour me, please.'

'OK, what do you want to know?' Amelia sat back and folded her arms.

'How was your parents' marriage?'

'What do you mean?'

'Were your parents happy?'

'I think so, yeah. They had their moments, argued occasionally, but what couple doesn't?'

'Did your father ever have an affair?'

Amelia nearly choked on the mouthful of coffee she had just taken. She coughed and spluttered, then wiped her mouth on a tissue she pulled from her pocket. 'What kind of fucking question is that?' Amelia stammered, her voice rising to nearly a shout.

'Just answer it, please.'

'No. My father never cheated on my mother. He loved her.'

'We were able to recover a DNA sample from under Megan's fingernails; we think she managed to take a swipe at her attacker before she died. We've had it tested, and it came back as a partial match with the sample we took from you.'

'What? That's impossible!' Amelia cried. Her eyes widened, and the colour drained from her face.

'I assure you it isn't. The lab compared the DNA with the sample you gave us.'

'Is that why you came round? You said it was just for elimination.' Amelia glared at George, who went pink.

'It was a match on the paternal side. You share a father with this person.'

'I don't have a brother or sister, I'm an only child.'

'You don't have a brother or sister *that you're aware of*,' said Jenny.

'You're wrong. My dad was devoted to my mother; there's no way he would have cheated on her.'

Jenny opened the brown folder on the table in front of her and took out a sheet of paper. She slid it across the table to Amelia. 'This is an electropherogram.'

'It's used to plot DNA,' George added, in response to Amelia's confused look.

'The top row is your father; the middle row is the sample we took from you the other day. See how these markers match?' Jenny tapped her pen on certain points of the profile. 'This was inherited from your father. The bottom row is from the DNA we recovered under Megan's nails. See, these markers match with the top row.' She tapped another point on the chart. 'That could only have been passed down from a parent.'

Amelia picked up the sheet and stared at it, her hands trembling. Jenny sat back in her chair and took another sip of her coffee. Eventually, Amelia put the sheet down and looked up Jenny and George, her eyes wet. 'Do you know who the other woman is? The mother?' There was a slight tremble in her voice.

'Yes. Her name is Kelly Johnson. Her DNA was on the system; she was a nurse at Royal London Hospital. That was the hospital your father worked at, wasn't it?'

Amelia nodded. 'I need some air,' she said finally.

Jenny paused the recorder and George escorted Amelia out of the interview room towards the car park. The sun was shining brightly, but Amelia hugged herself and shivered. The tears that had been building up started to run down her cheeks.

'Are you OK?' George asked, offering a packet of tissues.

Amelia smiled weakly and took one. 'Sorry,' she told him, wiping her eyes.

'You've nothing to apologise for. It must have been a shock.'

She nodded, and they stood in silence for a minute.

'Look, people aren't perfect,' George said finally. 'While you, maybe, your father was a larger-than-life character incapable of doing wrong, at the end of the day he was still human, still capable of making mistakes. And maybe that's all it was? One incident he immediately regretted and spent the rest of his life trying to make up for.'

'You didn't know them. He worshipped my mum. There's no way he would have done something like that to her.'

'Unfortunately, the evidence doesn't lie. I'm sorry, I really am. And I know how you feel, if that's any kind of consolation.'

'How?'

'My mother cheated on my father when I was six; I didn't find out till I was in my twenties. All I remember from that time is them arguing a lot, but I was too young to understand why.'

'How did you find out?'

'My Uncle Paul accidentally blurted it out one night when we were down the pub. I couldn't believe it. I felt like you do; I thought my parents' marriage was perfect. It really hit me hard.'

'What did you do?'

'I talked to them about it. It was with a work colleague – such a cliché, I know. Mum told me it was rough for a while, but they got through it. Dad forgave her and in the end it actually brought them closer; it made her appreciate what she had nearly lost. My dad, for his part, admitted that he had been taking Mum for granted and in a way, he was grateful for the wake-up call.'

'At least you were able to talk to them and achieve some sort of closure. I don't have that luxury, unfortunately.'

Unsure what to say in reply, George held the door open and Amelia went back in.

In the interview room, another coffee had appeared in front of Jenny and a second was next to George's seat. Jenny asked Amelia if she'd like another but she shook her head. Jenny pressed Play on the recorder.

'We have started digging into Kelly Johnson's background. It turns out she had a daughter – Ashley, an only child. According to her birth certificate, she would be twenty-six years old now. She doesn't have a criminal record – that's why we didn't get a hit on the DNA initially – but she is wanted in connection with a murder back in 2014. She fled from the scene and hasn't been seen since.'

'And you think she's here, on the island somewhere?'

'She must have been here on the night of the 14th – there's no other way for her DNA to have got under Megan's fingernails – but unfortunately, we don't know where she is right now.'

'Why would she be targeting me?'

'That's something we're trying to find out, and we'd very much like the opportunity to ask her. We have discovered something else, though, something very relevant. Her mother, Kelly Johnson, committed suicide. She was discovered by Ashley in the bath, having cut her own wrists. The date that she died was the twenty-third of May, 2013.'

Chapter 24

Amelia got on the train and stowed her overnight bag in the rack at the end of the carriage. Though rush hour was over, the train to London was still packed with what remained of the morning's commuters and what looked like a school field trip. Thankfully, though, she managed to find an empty seat opposite a well-dressed man in his late forties who was busy reading *The Guardian* and paid her no mind.

The train slowly ambled its way out of Portsmouth. Amelia stared at the trees and fields flowing past and tried not to think about what she had learned yesterday. She still didn't believe that her dad had had an affair, let alone fathered a child with another woman, but the evidence the detectives had presented was pretty hard to ignore.

She sat leaning against the window, lulled by the rhythmic rolling of the rails, and almost managed to convince herself that it was all a mistake. That it was all just a bad dream and at any moment she would wake up and find Sam snoring gently beside her and James asleep on her feet. That Gran was alive and well.

She was shaken from her reverie by a tap on her shoulder.

Thrust painfully back to reality, she found an old man looking at her expectantly. Amelia stared at him, confusion etched on her face.

'I said, do you mind if I sit here?' he repeated, gesturing at the empty seat next to her. Well, nearly empty; Amelia's grey shoulder bag was sitting on it.

'Of course, I'm sorry,' Amelia told him, her face flushing. She snatched her bag and stashed it under her seat, then turned to stare out of the window. Before long, her mind started to wander again.

'Going anywhere nice?'

'Huh?' Amelia said, once again shaken from her thoughts.

'Sorry. I just asked if you were going anywhere nice.'

'Just up to London,' Amelia told him before turning back to the window.

'I'm sorry, I didn't mean to pry,' he told her, and pulled a dogeared paperback from his jacket pocket. He opened it about halfway and started to read.

Amelia winced slightly as she realised how she had sounded. 'I didn't mean to be rude. It's just that I've got a lot on my mind at the moment.'

'I'm happy to lend a sympathetic ear, if you like. It might make you feel better if you talk about it.' He put his book down and turned slightly so that he was facing Amelia.

'I just found out that I've got a younger sister,' she told him, after a pause. 'It turns out that my dad was living a secret life behind mine and my mum's back. That's actually why I'm going to London: I need to speak to someone and I think it'll be better to do it face-to-face. I'm hoping he can help me track down my sister.'

'What does your dad say about all of this?'

'He died a long time ago,' she said quietly.

'I'm sorry. Look, I know this is none of my business, but in my experience, families are complicated things. Becoming a parent doesn't automatically grant you wisdom or knowledge. Your dad was as equally fallible after you were born as he was before, and people make mistakes; I certainly did with my two boys. Was he a good dad?'

'Yeah,' she said with a smile, her first in days. 'He was a doctor. He worked very hard, very long hours sometimes, but he always made sure he was there for the big things like birthdays and Christmas. Even the little things like school plays and piano lessons. He was always there, even if he'd just spent twelve hours in surgery. He'd take the time to ask me how my day was, and sit for hours while I bored him half to death with tales of who'd been seen kissing whom or why I wasn't speaking to someone.'

'That's what counts, in the end. That's what you need to remember.'

The train pulled into a station on the outskirts of Guildford and the old man got up to leave, straightening his jacket and pocketing his book. He took a step toward the doors at the end of the carriage but stopped and turned back to face Amelia again.

'I really hope you find your sister,' he told her, before he ambled towards the exit.

* * *

Amelia got off the train at Waterloo station. A quick tube ride later, she checked into a small, nondescript hotel just outside Shoreditch, overlooking a small park and a budget fried-chicken shop. After a quick shower and change of clothes, she took a tube to Earl's Court and from there into Kensington.

Amelia made her way down streets she had known like the back of her hand when she was younger but hadn't seen in years. Past the old Woolworths that was now a Co-op, the halal butcher's, and The Prince of Wales pub where she'd had her first legal drink. Eventually she arrived at an apartment block in one of the more upmarket areas. There, on the intercom, was a name she hadn't heard in years. She stopped, her hand inches from the buzzer, the guilt at having not spoken to this person in over a decade weighing heavily on her. She pushed it aside; she needed answers about the woman who was supposedly her sister, and this was as good a place as any to start. If her dad had told anyone about the affair, and Ashley, then it was him. She pressed the buzzer and waited.

Just as she thought that no one was in, a man's voice came out of the speaker. 'Yes?'

'Hi, Uncle John, it's Amelia.'

A smartly dressed man in his early sixties opened the door of the fourth-floor flat. He smiled broadly when he saw Amelia and pulled her in for a big hug. He pulled back to look at her, his hands on her shoulders. 'It's so good to see you, Amy! Please, come on in.'

He took her into the living room and gestured towards one of the low-backed leather sofas before heading back the way he came. The living room was all white walls, straight lines and muted colours; it had changed a lot since she had been here last. A large TV was mounted on the main wall with two wireless speakers to either side, a chrome and glass coffee table sat between the sofas, and expensive-looking contemporary art hung on the walls, the only real splashes of colour in the whole room. *A true bachelor's pad,* she thought with a smile; her Uncle John definitely hadn't changed in the years since she'd seen him last. She called him uncle – she had since she'd been old enough to speak – but they weren't related. He had been her dad's best friend for as long as she could remember, and he felt like family to her.

After a couple of minutes, John returned with a bottle of

wine and two glasses. 'White OK? I know it's only two pm, but this is a special occasion.'

They both took a sip from their glasses and sat in a comfortable silence. Amelia's guilt and awkwardness had vanished.

'How long has it been, Amy?' John asked, at last.

'Nobody calls me Amy anymore, Uncle John, and my mum always hated it when you did!' she told him, with a smile.

'Why do you think I kept it up?' he replied with a wink and a smile of his own, eliciting a laugh from Amelia.

'I'm sorry I haven't been in touch since the funeral,' Amelia said sheepishly. 'I left London straight afterwards and this is my first time back. It was just too hard. Too many memories.'

'You don't have to apologise to me; I understand. I haven't been back to some of our old haunts, either. Even twelve years on I still struggle to believe that he and your mother are gone. I still miss them both dearly.'

'Yeah, so do I,' she told him sadly. 'It still feels like yesterday. Sometimes when my phone rings I half-expect it to be Mum ringing for a chat or Dad checking up on me.' She took a deep breath. 'I was surprised to catch you in. I didn't know whether to come here first or go straight to the hospital.'

'Just as well you didn't, I took early retirement five years ago.'

'You, retired? You were as bad as Dad! I thought they'd have to drag you out kicking and screaming.'

'What happened to your mum and dad made me realise that life's too short. It wasn't just that, though. I saw too many of my colleagues work themselves to death or keel over shortly after retirement, so I thought, to hell with it. I've worked hard and I want to enjoy my retirement. I had enough money put away, so I packed it all in and I haven't looked back! What about you? Where are you living these days?'

'After I finished university I moved down to the Isle of Wight to be near Gran.'

'God, I remember Frances. She always blamed me for leading your dad astray, when most of the time it was the other way round! How is the old bird? Still as fearsome as ever?'

Amelia looked away, still finding the words hard to say, not wanting her voice to crack in front of him. 'She died just over two weeks ago,' she said finally.

'Oh Amy, I'm so, so sorry.' John enveloped her in another hug. 'She was a remarkable woman.'

'Yeah, she was,' Amelia agreed, with a sad smile.

Another silence descended. Amelia took a gulp of her wine and looked towards the window.

'OK, onto lighter topics,' John said, and put his glass on the table. 'What are you doing with yourself these days?'

'I run a little flower shop.'

'Oh. I thought you'd be doing something in design. Your mum and dad always said how talented you were and how proud they were of you. I just assumed that's what you'd do after university.'

'I wanted to be near Gran; there weren't many opportunities for graphic design.'

He topped up both their glasses and leant back in his chair. 'So... while it's great to see you again, I suspect you haven't come all this way just to make small talk with me.'

'Actually, no. There's something I want to talk to you about.'

'Sure, go ahead. If I can help, I will.'

'Would you say that you knew my dad well?'

'I'd like to think I knew him better than most people. He was my best friend since medical school, after all. I'd say the

only person who knew him better than I did was your mum.'
He frowned. 'What's all this about?'

'Can I ask you something?'

'Of course you can,' he replied with a smile.

Amelia sat up straight. 'Do you know Ashley?'

Chapter 25

John regarded Amelia for a couple of seconds with a puzzled expression. 'Who's Ashley?' he asked, and took another sip of wine.

'You really don't know?' she said, studying him carefully.

'I can't think of anyone with a connection to your father or mother by the name of Ashley, I'm sorry.'

Amelia stared at him, trying to read his mind, but his bright-blue eyes gave nothing away. After a couple of heartbeats, she decided that he was telling the truth, that apparently there was one thing her father had kept from him through all those years of friendship. 'She's my sister.'

Any lingering suspicions she had that John was lying were banished by his expression; his mouth had dropped open and his eyes were wide. Her Uncle John, completely unflappable the whole time she had known him, looked utterly dumbfounded.

'Sister?' he said, when he was finally able to speak. 'Amy, you don't have a sister. You are, and have always been, an only child. I know your parents toyed with the idea of having a second, but it never happened.'

'Until yesterday that's what I thought too, but unfortunately it's true. I didn't believe it at first either – I refused to believe it – but the police showed me some pretty irrefutable evidence.'

'The police? What have they got to do with it?'

She told him about the events of the previous few weeks: her gran's murder, her cat's disappearance, the vandalism of her shop, and finally, Megan's murder and the DNA evidence revealing the existence of a half-sister, Ashley Johnson. As the story unfolded John stared at her with growing disbelief, hardly able to believe what he was hearing.

Once Amelia had finished he got shakily to his feet, went to a sideboard at the back of the room and took out a decanter and a couple of crystal tumblers. He set them on the table and poured a couple of generous measures of a Scottish single malt that he usually saved for special occasions. He picked up the glass nearest to him and took a large drink. 'I don't know where to begin,' he said finally. 'Your father really had another child by this Kelly Johnson? And the police told you she was a nurse at Royal London?'

'That's what they told me. Did you know anyone by that name?'

John got up and paced, holding the tumbler in his hand. 'Maybe? I don't know. It's a big hospital and there are hundreds of nurses. I don't remember anyone by that name, but that doesn't mean there wasn't. I can't believe that he cheated on your mother; he was utterly devoted to her.' He leaned on the back of the sofa opposite her as if his strength had left him completely.

'I'm still struggling to get my head around it too. It feels as if I didn't know him at all.'

'And the police think that this Ashley is behind all of it? Frances's and your friend's murders?'

'They haven't said that outright, but why else would her

DNA be under Megan's nails? And the date in the note I received was the date when her mother killed herself.'

'Then why are you trying to find her? If this nutjob really is responsible for all that's happened, surely the best course of action is to get as far away from her as possible!' He pushed himself upright and came round the sofa to Amelia, then sat down and stared at her intently, a worried expression on his face. 'I have a holiday home in Ibiza; I'll get on the phone right now and arrange a flight for first thing tomorrow. You should stay out there until the police find this woman!'

Amelia reached out, took John's hands in hers, and gave them a squeeze, more touched by his concern for her than she could put into words. 'Thank you, Uncle John. It's a very kind offer and I really am grateful, but I can't.'

'Of course you can. It isn't your job to find her.'

'I know, but I'm sick of not doing anything, and I won't do it anymore. She is targeting the people I love, for some sick and twisted reason, and someone has to stop her. The police haven't had any luck, so I want to see what I can do. After all, she is family,' she added wryly.

Amelia could tell by the look on John's face that he was far from convinced. Then he stood up abruptly. 'You're as stubborn as your old man, you know that?'

Amelia smiled and gave him a big hug. She felt tears in her eyes and blinked them away before he could see them.

'You look after yourself, you hear me,' John said as he pulled back from their embrace. 'If there's anything I can do to help, I'm only a phone call away, day or night.' He scribbled a number onto a post-it and handed it to her. Amelia smiled and pocketed it.

Amelia thanked him once again, then turned and left.

Once outside, Amelia assessed her options. She had been so sure that John would know of either Ashley or Kelly that she hadn't thought much further ahead. After deliberating a few moments longer, she decided the best next port of call would be the hospital. Surely there would be someone still working there from her father's days who could point her in the right direction.

Mind made up, Amelia walked to the nearest tube, back past the old Woolworths. The pavements were busy – they always were in London – and a couple of times Amelia nearly collided with other pedestrians, so lost in her thoughts was she.

She made it relatively unscathed to the tube station and jumped on a Circle Line train to Tower Hill before switching to the District Line. As she made her way out of Whitechapel station, the flood of nostalgia nearly threatened to overwhelm her. As difficult as it had been to walk the streets around John's home, actually seeing the hospital that her father had worked at was something else entirely. She couldn't count the number of times that her father had taken her to work for the day over various school holidays or when her mother was busy with a charity function or social event. She'd sit in his office and happily draw or read a book, or on the rare occasions that he wasn't in surgery or checking on patients she'd sometimes just sit there and watch him work. He'd look up, catch her eye, and smile the warm easy smile that he always had for her.

She went through the large revolving door and approached the reception desk. The woman behind it, who looked to be in her late sixties, smiled warmly as Amelia approached.

'Excuse me,' Amelia began, knowing how stupid this was going to sound but with no idea what else to try, 'I wonder if you could help me. I'm trying to find someone who may remember a nurse who worked here, nearly ten years ago now.'

The woman behind the reception looked a little taken aback, she was used to just being asked for directions to various departments and felt a little out of her depth at this unexpected deviation from the norm. 'Um, I don't really know what to suggest. You could try asking some of the older nurses; some of them have been here years. They may have known your friend. What department did she work in?'

'I'm afraid I don't know.'

'You could try Jane Turner up on Paediatrics; she's been here for as long as I can remember.'

Amelia thanked the woman and made her way to Paediatrics. The walls of the waiting area were painted in a variety of bright colours: yellow, pink, blue. A rainbow ran down one side and a large collection of toys was piled in the far corner. Twin boys were fighting over a small wooden train that they both seemed determined to have, their mother too busy on her phone to notice or care.

Amelia went to the desk where a young receptionist was sat frowning at a computer screen.

'Hi,' Amelia said, a little self-consciously. 'I wonder if you can help me. I'm looking for a Mrs Jane Turner.'

'Do you have an appointment?' The receptionist asked.

'No, I just need to ask her something, it won't take long.'

'Our nurses are very busy and don't have time to talk to everyone that stops by,' the receptionist said curtly.

A woman in her fifties came over and laid a hand on the receptionist's shoulder. 'It's OK Tina,' the woman told her. She turned to regard Amelia.

'I'm Jane,' she said. 'How can I help you?'

'I'm looking for someone who may have known a nurse that worked here ten years ago, and the woman on reception said I should talk to you. Her name was Kelly Johnson.'

'I'm sorry,' she replied with a frown. 'The name doesn't ring a bell.' She relented slightly when she saw the disappointed look on Amelia's face. 'You could try Clare Hastings, the head nurse. She's been here as long as I have, and she knows everything that goes on in this place. If she doesn't know her, no one will.'

'Where can I find her?'

'She has an office on the fifth floor, but at this time of day she's probably making her rounds on the trauma ward, so your best bet is be to try there.'

'Ok, thanks,' Amelia replied with a smile. Out of the corner of her eye she spotted the mother of the twins, phone forgotten, consoling one crying child whilst the second pushed the train around the play mat, oblivious.

Amelia made her way to the trauma ward and was about to head to the nursing station when she spotted a small woman in her sixties standing in front of two younger nurses.

'Excuse me,' Amelia said hesitantly as she approached the group. The woman turned and regarded Amelia thoughtfully, her head tilted slightly to one side.

'I was hoping you could help, I'm looking for Clare Hastings.'

'That's me. What can I do for you, young lady?' Her tone was firm and direct; this was a woman who was not accustomed to being interrupted.

'I'm looking for information about someone who used to work here-'

'Look, I'm a very busy woman. I don't have time to chat to everybody who comes in, I'm afraid. If you're not sick or here to visit someone then you shouldn't even be here in the first place.' She turned back to the nurses.

'My name's Amelia Simpson and I'm looking for someone who knew Kelly Johnson,' Amelia said in desperation.

Clare froze, then turned, her expression softer. 'Not little Amelia, Anthony's daughter?'

'My dad was Dr Anthony Simpson,' Amelia confirmed with a smile.

'God, it must be fifteen or twenty years since I saw you last,' Clare told her, her smile having softened her face considerably. 'It was such a terrible shame, what happened to your parents. Such a tragedy. What did you say you were here for?'

'I'm trying to find someone who might have known a nurse who worked here ten years ago. Her name was Kelly Johnson.'

Clare's face changed again, her smile fading, her eyes becoming unreadable. 'I think it's time for my break. There's a Costa on the ground floor. Let's get a proper coffee, not that machine rubbish.'

Amelia found a table while Clare bought coffees.

'Kelly Johnson is a name I haven't heard in years,' she told Amelia as she placed the drinks on the table and sat down opposite her. 'What do you want to know?'

'What can you tell me? All I know is that she died ten years ago.'

'Why are you trying to find out about her?'

'I'm actually trying to track down her daughter, Ashley. I've just found out that she's my half-sister.'

'That poor girl,' Clare said, stirring her coffee absentmindedly, her voice tinged with sadness. 'She was never the same after her mother's death.'

'In what way?' Amelia asked, leaning forward a touch.

'I only saw her once or twice after her mother's death, but she seemed so angry. Not like the funny, happy child she once was.'

'When did you last see her?'

'A couple of weeks after the funeral; she came to pick up her mother's things.'

'What was Kelly like?'

Clare smiled again. 'She was a lovely girl. Very bright, very bubbly, couldn't do enough for her patients, but one day she changed.'

'What do you mean? Changed how?'

'Just that. She went from being a happy, bubbly person to quiet and withdrawn almost overnight.'

'What happened?'

'I wish I could tell you. No one knew, or if they did, they didn't say. And a year or two later, she took her own life. It was a terrible shock to us all.'

'I'm sorry I brought all this up. I didn't mean to bring back bad memories.' Amelia stood up and made to leave.

'Actually, I might have something you'd like up in my office, if you've got five more minutes?'

They took a lift to the fifth floor and Clare led Amelia down a nondescript corridor to a small office. Inside, she rooted around in a drawer, withdrawing an old folder with a small cry of triumph. She took out some old photos, selected one, and handed it to Amelia. 'This was taken maybe twenty years ago. The previous head nurse retired, and we had a big retirement party for her here in the hospital. Do you see that woman? That's Kelly.' She pointed at a woman in her early thirties, beaming for the camera. She had her arm around a smiling child of about five or six years old.

Chapter 26

Amelia sat with her back against the suede headboard and stared at the photo. After she had finished at the Royal London, she had gone back to her hotel to regroup and work out what to do next. The problem was that too much time had passed since her dad and Kelly's time at the hospital. The world had simply moved on.

The photo itself looked old; the date written on the back told Amelia that it was taken on the 19th of August 2002. It showed a group of people smiling for the camera. Amelia supposed that it was taken before the age of digital photos, where you could take hundreds of shots and not care if many were worth keeping. In those days a little bit more thought and care had gone into each shot, the roll having only a finite number available.

This particular photo showed what appeared to be a hospital training room, decked out with streamers, balloons and a large multi-coloured banner wishing someone called Janet all the very best. Front and centre was a plump, jolly-looking woman in her sixties smiling happily for the camera, a glass of champagne in hand: the woman of the hour, Amelia guessed. To the side was the woman Clare had pointed out as Kelly Johnson. Next to her, Ashley was dressed in a dark-blue dress and matching school jumper, the collar of a white polo shirt visible, white socks and black shoes, with a school bag slung over one shoulder.

So this is my sister and the woman who led my dad astray, Amelia thought bitterly, her hands gripping the photo so tightly that her knuckles were white. She got off the bed and started pacing the room, but quickly gave it up. It was hard to pace effectively in a room barely big enough for the bed alone.

The problem was that while she had found out some more information about Ashley and her mother, none of it was helpful; a twenty-two-year-old photo was nothing much to go on. Frustrated, she picked up the phone and ordered some food from room service, then went to take a shower.

Refreshed, having washed off the day's travel, Amelia padded back through to the bedroom. A couple of minutes later there was a knock at the door, and Amelia opened it to find the member of staff who had checked her in earlier standing there with a tray. She accepted it gratefully and took it to the desk at the far end of the small room. She had been so focused on what she would do and where she would go next that she had completely forgotten to eat.

While she tucked into her Thai curry, which looked suspiciously like a supermarket-bought one she had had last week, she propped up the photo of Ashley and her mother in front of her and studied it. A detail caught her eye and she put her fork down. She picked up the photo and peered, her food momentarily forgotten. There was a school logo on Ashley's jumper; she'd seen it earlier but hadn't taken it in. She could just about make out the writing below the emblem: Mountbatten's Primary School.

Amelia dug out her phone and opened the maps app. She

quickly found the hospital and searched the area for schools. Sure enough, second on the list was Mountbatten's Primary School, complete with a link to the school website. A quick scroll through that showed that the school was closely affiliated with a nearby secondary school, St John's, complete with a link to their website. A quick check on the maps app confirmed that this school was also in the vicinity of Royal London Hospital.

Amelia clicked back to the St John's school website, growing more excited by the second as an idea formed, her dinner getting cold in front of her. She scrolled down the school homepage until she found what she was looking for: a link to a page with bios of the school staff. She scrolled down the list, but was quickly disappointed. She had hoped to track down one of Ashley's teachers, who might have been able to point her in the direction of some friends, but they had all started well after Ashley would have been a student.

Frustrated at having hit another dead end, Amelia went to close the page, but spotted something at the bottom of the screen – a link marked as *St John's Through The Years*. Amelia clicked it and the screen was filled with thumbnails of photos, some of the earlier ones in black and white. Amelia started searching through them all, a couple of hundred in total. While none of them showed anyone who looked like an older version of the girl in the photo, one detail excited Amelia. The same woman kept appearing in the later photos, the captions identifying her as *Patricia Riley, the head teacher who served the school from 1992–2017.*

She would have been the head teacher when Ashley attended the school, thought Amelia excitedly. A quick search online brought up the addresses of several Patricia Rileys living in the capital, but only one anywhere near St John's secondary school.

* * *

The following day, Amelia stepped out of the tube station at Bethnal Green and pulled her jacket tighter around her, shivering slightly at the unseasonably cold day. She glanced at the overcast sky and hurried on her way, not wanting to be caught out when the heavens inevitably opened. She turned onto a side street with townhouses on either side and trees lining the pavement.

About halfway down the street, Amelia found the house she was looking for: narrow, stucco-fronted, with steps leading up to a front door covered by a small overhang with pillars on either side. There was an intercom by the door with three buttons, suggesting that the once-grand townhouse had been redeveloped into flats by developer's looking to increase their profits. The button at the bottom had a name printed next to it: *P. Riley*. Amelia pressed it and waited.

'Yes?' came a stern-sounding voice.

'Are you Mrs Riley? The former head teacher of St John's?' Amelia asked tentatively. 'My name's Amelia Simpson. I'm trying to track down a former student of yours, Ashley Johnson, and I was hoping that you might be able to help me.'

There was no reply. Just as Amelia was about to press the button again, the buzzer sounded. She pushed the front door open and knocked twice on the adjacent flat door. After a moment, it was opened by a stout woman in her seventies. Despite her advancing years she held herself well, and still had a gaze so direct that it took Amelia straight back to her school days and her own headmistress, who had ruled with an iron fist.

'Are you with the police?' Patricia asked, her gaze never wavering.

'No. I've just found out that Ashley and I are related: she's my half-sister.'

Patricia stared at Amelia for a few moments before opening the door wider. 'You'd better come in,' she said, and led Amelia through to the living room. It was as Amelia had expected: wood-panelled, with an open fire and mahogany bookshelves. The walls were hung with old oil paintings.

Patricia gestured towards one of the brown leather chesterfields before taking the one opposite. 'You're Ashley's sister, are you?'

'Half-sister: we have the same father. I found out a couple of days ago, and thought I would try to track her down.'

'Ashley did indeed attend St John's, but I'm not sure what help I can be or even whether I should help given the circumstances.' Patricia clamped her mouth shut and blushed slightly, belatedly realising that she might have said too much.

'What was Ashley like? Who were her friends?' Amelia asked, either not picking up on Patricia's comment or choosing to ignore it.

Patricia sighed. 'When she started at St John's she was a happy, bubbly, intelligent young girl. I thought she had such a bright future ahead of her,' she said, with a touch of sadness in her voice.

'What happened?'

'Simply put, she changed. Her schoolwork didn't suffer, but she started acting out, lashing out at people, and getting into fights, even with her friends. She was just angry all the time. I tried to talk to her on more than one occasion but I couldn't get through to her. I had plenty of grounds to expel her, but I didn't want to ruin her future. I thought it was just a phase, but then her mother killed herself and things got even worse. I took it upon myself to try to save her, but I failed. In the end, I'm not sure she had any friends left.' She paused for a moment, her brows knitted. 'No,' she said, eventually, 'there was one. She and Ashley were as thick as thieves; they were never apart.'

'Do you remember her name?' Amelia asked, on the edge of her seat.

Patricia thought for a while longer, then shook her head. 'Sorry, no. My memory isn't what it once was, I'm afraid.'

Amelia looked crestfallen, but rallied quickly. 'When you answered the door and I said I was looking for Ashley, you asked if I was with the police and then mentioned that you weren't even sure you should help me find her. Why was that?'

Patricia squirmed a little and looked away, then took a sip of her tea and faced her. 'Unfortunately, Ashley is one of our more infamous students. In my attempt to help her I referred her to a psychologist who specialised in dealing with troubled youths. I had referred several students to him over the years, and I thought he would be able to help her.'

'What happened?'

'He was murdered; hit on the back of the head with an ornament from his own office. Ashley, as a client, was a suspect, but vanished before the police could ask her any questions. As far as I know, she hasn't been seen since.' She sighed. 'I should have expelled her when she started causing trouble. I should have accepted her for what she really was: rotten inside. If I had, then perhaps that poor man might still be with us. That is something that I have had to live with.'

Amelia bit her lip. 'I'm sorry this has brought up unpleasant memories.'

'It's not your fault, dear. Is there anything else I can help you with?'

'No, that's all. Thank you for your time, Mrs Riley.'

'I'm sorry I couldn't be of more use.' Patricia got up and took Amelia to the front door.

As Amelia was about to leave, she paused and turned back to face Patricia. 'You said Ashley was bright. What was her best subject?'

Patricia thought. 'She was bright generally, but she had a real talent for art. And she was especially good at graphic design.'

Chapter 27

Emma left the kitchenette carrying two mugs of coffee, one for her and one for Jenny, and used her shoulder to push open the door to the main office. She had bad news for Jenny, and she knew that it was best to come prepared.

She made her way to the inspector's desk and found Jenny frowning over the CCTV footage from the night of Megan's murder. They had tried to enhance the quality of the image of the person approaching Megan's house, but so far, it hadn't revealed anything new.

Emma put the coffee down and then leant on Jenny's desk. Jenny smiled gratefully as she picked up the hot drink but then her eyes narrowed. 'You never bring me a coffee without being badgered. What's happened?' She eyed her sergeant with obvious mistrust.

'I've been back to both the shop and her flat, and there's no sign of Amelia anywhere.'

Instead of responding, Jenny picked up her desk phone, tapped out a number, and hit the speaker button before replacing the handset. A few moments later the call connected, immediately followed by a voice. 'Hello?'

'Amelia, this is Detective Inspector Stone. Where are you?'

'Shoreditch.'

Jenny's eyes widened and Emma tensed herself, ready for the inevitable explosion.

'Shoreditch? As in London?' Jenny asked incredulously.

'Yeah.'

'This shouldn't need to be said, Amelia, but if someone is being targeted by a killer, they shouldn't just up and leave without informing the police beforehand.' She was using the strained-patience voice she normally reserved for Sophie when she refused to do as she was told. Emma managed to mask her laugh with a cough, which she only partially got away with judging by the look Jenny shot her.

Silence on the other end. 'I didn't think of that,' came the eventual, sheepish reply.

'What was so important that you had to drop everything and head to London?'

'I wanted to see if I could track down Ashley.'

'You what?' Jenny exploded. 'Are you crazy? You shouldn't actively seek out the person targeting you! Leave that to the professionals, please.'

'Well, you lot aren't exactly having much luck, are you?' Amelia snapped.

Jenny didn't reply but Emma watched her as she closed her eyes and silently counted to ten, her mouth forming the words. She took a deep breath. 'Did you find anything?'

'I spoke to Ashley's old head teacher and a nurse who knew her mother slightly; they worked together at the Royal London. At first both the mother and Ashley were happy, bubbly people. Then something happened and they both changed. Her mother withdrew and became depressed and Ashley became angry, lashing out at everyone. Her head teacher said she could have expelled her several times but she kept giving her one more chance, hoping Ashley would sort herself out. She said she was a bright girl and she'd thought she had a bright future ahead of her, so she didn't want to ruin it by expelling her. One thing she did mention was that Ashley's best subject was art and she was especially good at graphic design'

'Interesting,' Jenny muttered.

'and I've got hold of a picture of the mother and Ashley from when she was six,' Amelia continued.

Jenny was impressed in spite of herself. She glanced at Emma, who smirked at her

'OK, good, but that's enough playing Miss Marple. I need you to come back to the island now.'

'OK, I'll get on the next train. I think I've done all I can here anyway.'

'When you know what boat you'll be on, let me know. I'll send a pair of my officers to pick you up.'

'Why?'

'Because I believe that you're in danger. The twenty-third is only two days away, and I think that's when Ashley will make her move. For the time being, and certainly until the twenty-third has passed, I'm going to move you to a safe location for your own protection.'

Emma and George watched as the passenger ferry moored alongside the pier, the breeze whipping through them. Gulls circled overhead, their piercing cries drowned by the roar of the ferry. After a few minutes, a steady stream of passengers made their way down the ramp. At the back was Amelia, pulling her small suitcase behind her. She caught sight of the detectives and made her way over to join them.

'I should thank you,' Emma offered up by way of a

greeting as she led Amelia to the unmarked police car parked nearby.

'Why?' Amelia asked cautiously.

'Jenny's face when you told her that you were in London trying to track down Ashley was a picture.'

'Yeah, I'm sorry I missed that one,' George confirmed with a smile.

They reached the car and Amelia loaded her small suitcase into the boot before climbing into the back seat. The two detectives took the front.

Emma turned round in the front seat. 'Do you need anything from your flat, or are we OK to go straight to the safe house? Personally I'd prefer to go straight there, but we can swing by yours if you're quick.'

'Do you really think this is necessary?'

'Yes, and so does DI Stone. This person is clearly resourceful and more than capable of covering their tracks,' George told her.

'Fine,' Amelia replied with a sigh. 'All the clothes in my bag are dirty, so could we go via mine, please?'

Emma started the car and they drove slowly down the pier towards the seafront. A gap appeared in the mid-afternoon traffic and she pulled onto the main road. A few minutes later, they arrived at Amelia's flat. Emma parked and the three of them went upstairs. Once inside, Amelia headed straight to the bedroom while George carried out a quick check of the remaining rooms and Emma waited by the front door. She could hear cupboards and drawers being flung open.

Amelia's head poked around the door, concern clouding her face. 'Do you think Sam is in danger, too? Should we warn him?'

'I think if Ashley was going to target him she would have

done so by now,' said Emma. 'I don't think she'll risk revealing herself again before the twenty-third. To be honest, I'm surprised you care about him, given what he did to you. I'm not sure I would in your place.'

'I know I shouldn't, but it's hard not to, you know? I hate him for what he did, but a part of me still loves him in spite of what happened. It's hard to switch those emotions off; we were together for six years, after all. I don't know if I can forgive him, or if I even want to, but I don't want him or anyone else to die because of my twisted half-sister.'

'Don't worry, it won't come to that. We'll find her and we'll stop her.'

'You don't even know who she is, though. I mean, you have a name and her DNA, but you couldn't pick her out of a crowd, could you? For all I know, I sat next to her on the ferry back. Or she's someone I've known for years, just biding her time.'

Emma didn't have a good response to this, and after a moment Amelia continued with her packing. What bothered Emma most was that it was true. While they could prove that Ashley had been at the scene of at least one of the murders, they didn't know who she was, what she looked like, or, crucially, where she was right now.

Eventually Amelia reappeared with an old sports bag slung over her shoulder. She took one final look at the flat, almost as if she thought she wouldn't see it again, before following Emma back down to the car.

With Amelia safely ensconced on the back seat and her shoulder bag in the boot, Emma pulled out of the driveway and turned onto the main road, with George beside her in the front.

'Where are we going?' Amelia asked, leaning forward in her seat.

'We've got a place just outside Sandown. Don't worry, it won't take long to get there,' Emma told her.

They had just pulled onto the main road that ran from the seafront to the outskirts of Ryde when Emma frowned.

'What?' Amelia asked, her voice slightly panicked, having spotted Emma's change of expression in the rear-view mirror.

'It's probably nothing, but I'm sure the blue Citroen two back from us was at the top of the pier when I picked you up. What do you think, George?'

'Could be,' he replied, uncertainly.

'What do we do?' Amelia asked, her hands gripping the seat in front of her.

'Relax, it's probably a false alarm,' Emma replied, though her worried face suggested otherwise.

Emma took a right onto a side street and continued driving, repeatedly glancing in the rear-view mirror. Shortly afterwards the blue Citroen turned onto the street, maintaining the gap between them. 'Damn,' she cried.

Amelia glanced behind her. 'Is it her?' she asked Emma anxiously.

'I can't tell. They're too far back.'

'Hold on a second.' George snatched the radio from the centre console and thumbed the talk switch. 'Control, this is DC Bancroft. I need a registration check,' he said and listed off the number plate details.

Emma pushed the unmarked car a little faster, and the blue Citroen increased its speed to match.

The radio crackled. 'The plate belongs to a black Volkswagen Polo registered to a Mr Jason Thompson.'

'Shit,' Emma muttered. She weighed up her options. She couldn't increase her speed any further, as they were in a built-up area and already exceeding the speed limit.

She rushed past parked cars, missing their wing mirrors by inches. Without warning, Emma made a right turn, immediately followed by a left and another right, narrowly avoiding a small hatchback coming the opposite way. The driver of the hatchback slammed on the brakes and swore at her through their open window. Emma ignored it and slowed the car down to a normal speed. George kept a lookout behind them for their unwanted tail, but the road behind remained clear.

'I think we've lost them,' George announced, and a pale-faced Amelia visibly relaxed.

For the next five minutes Emma took a convoluted route around the back roads in order to shake any potential tail, but nothing looked out of the ordinary and they saw no further sign of the blue Citroen. Eventually they joined the main road out of Ryde and continued towards their original destination. A few minutes later they were back on Beaper's Shute; and passed the spot where the car crash had happened only weeks before. The only signs of it were the bunches of flowers lining the place where the young lovers had lost their lives, the wrecked car having been cleared long since.

'Are you sure we're not being followed?' Amelia asked anxiously as she glanced out of the rear and side windows.

'There's no sign of them, but I don't see any point in hanging around. Let's get you to the safe house; there's twenty-four-hour surveillance, so they won't be able to reach you.'

A flash of blue, then the sickening crunch of metal on metal as the blue Citroen shot out of a side road and slammed into the car's front wing. Amelia screamed as Emma's head hit the side window with a thud.

The glass broke and the unmarked car lurched to the left. George leant over the unconscious Emma and tried to regain control, but the tree rushed up too quickly for him to avoid it. He managed to wrench the wheel round so that the stricken car only gave the tree a glancing blow, but the car still spun, the momentum sending it into a second tree before it came to a final, shuddering stop.

[5]

London, December 2014

Ashley pushed open the gate and made her way down the brick path. She shivered and pulled her coat tightly around her, her breath fogging the air in front of her. It was only five pm but it was already dark and cold, winter having fully hit the capital. She reached the front door and knocked, returning her gloved hand to her pocket and stamping her feet to warm herself up.

After about a minute, her therapist Steve answered the door. Ashley entered the immaculate Georgian townhouse and without waiting to be invited, went to the usual room at the back of the house: the one that overlooked the garden. She entered and sighed happily. The open fire was burning and the room was lovely and warm, a pleasant contrast to the cold winter evening outside. She took off her gloves and hat and stuffed them into the pockets of her parka before hanging it on a hook beside the door. She walked over to the large grey sofa by the rear window and sat down.

'So how have you been, Ashley?' Steve asked as he sat down opposite her. He opened a bottle of water and took a sip before placing it on the coffee table between them, his brown eyes studying her.

'Yeah, OK, I suppose,' Ashley replied, not making eye contact.

'The school say you've been keeping out of trouble. No incidents at all since I saw you two weeks ago, and your schoolwork has improved. Mrs Riley is very pleased.'

A shrug.

'Have any of the other students tried to get a rise out of you? At your last session, you said that a few of them had been making comments.'

'One or two have tried.'

'How did you handle it?'

'The way you told me to. Every time I felt myself getting angry, I counted to ten and walked away to take myself out of the situation. After a while I guess they just got bored and moved onto somebody else.'

'How did it feel, walking away?'

'Difficult. I nearly didn't a couple of times.'

'But you did. That's what matters.'

Another shrug.

'Don't dismiss this as nothing. You walked away; you were the bigger person.'

Ashley didn't say anything but instead got up and paced. She went to the bookshelf, picked a book at random and idly flicked through the pages before putting it back. 'I felt weak,' she said, eventually.

'You shouldn't: it took more strength to walk away than to stay and fight. That was what they were after, and you denied them that.'

'Maybe. But it would have felt good to shut them up.'

'It might have felt good in the moment, but in the long

term you would have regretted it. That's what you really need to remember, Ashley; your short-term actions can have lasting effects. As soon as you accept that, the easier this will be for you.'

'I do try to remember that, but when I get angry my mind goes blank.'

'That's the whole point of taking a deep breath and counting to ten. It allows anger to fade to a point where you can make a more informed choice.'

'Very easy to say that, doc, not easy to actually do it.'

'As I've told you before, I'm not a doctor. I want to talk further about this anger of yours. I know I've asked this several times in our sessions, but why are you so angry?'

'Well, my dad died and my mum killed herself not long after, or had you forgotten?'

'Is that all it is? I'm not saying it wasn't incredibly painful, but plenty of people have lost family members and they don't lash out at everyone in sight.'

Ashley looked down at her jumper and started to pick at a loose thread.

'Do you blame yourself for their deaths? Is that what it is?'

'No,' she replied quietly, picking at the thread with increased fervour.

'Then what is it? You don't blame yourself, but something must be causing all this anger inside you. Until you can be honest with me and with yourself, we won't make much more progress.'

'I don't want to talk about it.'

'Why not?'

'I just don't.'

'Then I don't see what more we can achieve here. Maybe we should just end our sessions.'

Steve pushed himself to his feet and stared down at

Ashley, who was still sitting on the chair opposite. He went to the door, opened it, and looked at her expectantly. Ashley in turn, made no effort to move, but she had stopped picking at her jumper and was now matching his gaze, her blue eyes growing hard.

'I'm not wasting my time. If you don't want my help, there are other people I could be helping instead. If you want to stay, you need to start being honest with me. If you don't blame yourself, who do you blame?'

'Her,' she muttered, looking away again, her voice only just audible over the crackle of the fire.

'Her?'

'My sister.' Ashley's voice was still quiet but her hands clenched, knuckles white.

'There's nothing in your notes about a sister,' Steve said, his brow furrowing in confusion.

'She's my half-sister on my dad's side.'

'Interesting. And why do you think she's responsible for the deaths of your parents? The first was a car crash, the second was suicide.'

More pulling at the loose thread.

'Ashley, tell me why you think your sister is responsible.'

Ashley sprang up from the sofa and started to pace, then stopped at the bookshelf. She eyed the shelves before picking up a small bronze bust and studied it for a minute. It showed a stern man in his seventies. There was no nameplate to identify the mystery person, but she didn't much care. Ashley hefted it and found that it was surprisingly heavy in her small hand.

'Who's this?' she asked, her head cocked to one side, her voice light, and a small smile on her lips. She turned and held it out for Steve to see.

'Don't avoid the question.' He walked over, took the bust

from her, put it back on the shelf and turned towards his chair.

Ashley snatched up the bust and in one smooth motion, brought it down heavily on the back of Steve's head. It connected with a sickening crack and he pitched forward, then fell to his knees. He reached up to touch the back of his head, then looked at his fingers; they were covered in blood.

Ashley stepped forward and hit Steve on the back of the head for a second time. He fell and lay still, blood pooling on the polished wooden floor.

Ashley wiped her fingerprints off the statue with her jumper sleeve before returning it to the shelf. Then she stared at the body on the floor in front of her for a minute. A small part of her felt bad but it quickly passed, replaced by the anger always simmering just below the surface, a burning heat that she could never quench.

She crossed the room to the fireplace, closed her eyes, and enjoyed the feel of the intense heat against her skin. Then she picked up the decorative steel poker and used it to roll a burning log out of the fire and on to the floor. She nudged it over to the rug, then got her coat and opened the door.

The rug by the fireplace was just catching fire as Ashley put on her coat and gloves. She left the room, closing the door behind her.

Chapter 28

George groaned, lifted his head, and tried to work out what had happened. He took in the scene: the windscreen was a mess of fractured glass, the front and side airbags had deployed, and the car had come to a stop with its rear passenger wing crumpled around a tree. The smoke from the airbag deployments had started to clear, but the bitter smell still lingered in the air.

There was a second groan beside him and he looked over at Detective Sergeant Marie. She looked as bad as he felt; her long red hair was a mess and blood trickled from a cut on one side of her head. Now George remembered, and turned to look at the back of the car. He moved too quickly and his vision blurred, once again but when he could focus he saw that the rear seats were empty and the driver's-side passenger door was wide open.

'Shit, shit, shit,' he muttered as he picked up the radio from the footwell and tried it. It didn't work. He dug his mobile phone out of his jacket pocket and dialled, grateful that he had some reception.

'DI Stone.'

'Jenny,' he managed to say, his voice weak.

'George, what's happened?' Jenny asked, her voice urgent.

'We're on Beaper's Shute, about a mile in. We were ambushed on the way to the safe house. A car came out of nowhere and rammed us; it forced us off the road and into a tree.'

'Are you all OK? Is Amelia there with you?'

'I'm OK, I think. Emma hit her head, but she's conscious and the bleeding is light. But Amelia is missing.'

'Shit,' came the reply, then a muffled exchange that George couldn't make out. 'Hold tight, there's an ambulance on the way.'

'What about Amelia?'

'We'll find her, but right now I need to make sure you're both OK. Stay where you are and wait for the ambulance; I'm on my way.' The phone went dead.

'Are you OK?' George asked Emma as he carefully put away his phone.

'Nothing a couple of ibuprofen wouldn't fix, but I think this'll need stitches,' she told him, touching the side of her head and looking at her fingers, wet with blood.

George undid his seatbelt and pushed at his door. Despite the damage, it opened easily enough, and he climbed out to survey the scene. They were only a few metres off the main road, but the car looked beyond repair. The front wing was caved in, there was a big dent in the front of the car, and the rear wing was also badly crumpled. The rear door was open, and on the back seat sat a mobile phone. George took out his phone and tried Amelia's number. Sure enough, the phone flashed into life. George muttered a curse before ending the call and stuffing the phone in his pocket.

By the time Jenny arrived, the ambulance was already there. She surveyed the scene with a groan before making her way over to check on the two detectives. A paramedic was trying to clean up the cut on Emma's head, but progress was slow due to Emma's insistence that she was fine and her refusal to keep still and let them work. George was standing to one side, talking to another of the paramedics, but as soon as he spotted Jenny he hurried over to her. 'I'm sorry about this, ma'am.'

Jenny raised a hand. 'This wasn't your fault, and it wasn't Emma's. I don't know how, but Ashley knew we were planning to move Amelia, and she was waiting for us. How are you both doing?'

'I'm OK: a few bruises, but nothing more. Emma needs a couple of stitches and they want to keep her in overnight for observation, which she isn't overly happy about.'

Emma spotted Jenny and made her way over to her, still a little unsteady on her feet. 'Ma'am, permission to help with the search.'

'You should be in the ambulance,' Jenny said, gesturing to the cut on the side of her head.

'It's nothing; it looks worse than it is. A couple of stitches and I'll be fine.'

'George says they want to keep you in overnight for observation. That doesn't sound like nothing to me.'

Emma flashed George a murderous look which made him blush. 'They're fussing. It's nothing, really.'

'They're not fussing; you hit your head. You're off this case till they clear you to return to work.'

Emma looked as if she might protest further, then stalked back to the ambulance. Jenny felt sorry for the poor paramedic. Meanwhile, George filled Jenny in on the details; how Emma had thought she recognised the blue Citroen and managed to lose it, only for it to come out of nowhere and ambush them.

* * *

'Briefing room, now!' Jenny called as soon as she entered the office. She was at the front of the room when the rest of the team filed in, so agitated that it was an effort for her to stand still.

'Right,' she told them. 'For those of you who haven't heard, earlier today the car transporting Amelia Simpson to a safe house in Sandown was run off the road. Amelia Simpson is currently missing, presumed kidnapped.'

There were a few gasps, but for the most part the room was silent as the news was absorbed.

'What do we know about the attacker?' This came from one of the uniformed officers at the side of the room.

'Not much. We suspect it was Ashley, but we don't have any proof. The car was rammed from the side and veered off the road into a tree. Both DC Bancroft and DS Marie were knocked unconscious, and when they awoke Amelia was missing.'

'How can we be sure she was kidnapped?' asked Simon. 'She might have run off in a panic.'

'We don't know for sure that Amelia was kidnapped, but her mobile phone was found on the back seat. If Amelia had left voluntarily then I doubt she would have abandoned her phone, and I expect she would have tried to make contact by now.'

'What if she was injured? She might not have been thinking straight.'

'She wouldn't have made it far on foot if she was injured. The most likely scenario is that she has been kidnapped, but we will carry out a full search of the surrounding area in order to rule it out.'

'Have forensics turned up anything?'

'They're still going over the car and the scene, but so far, no. Given how little we've been able to recover from previous scenes, I'm not holding out much hope.' The room went quiet once again.

Jenny surveyed them. 'Simon, Claire, I want you to pull all the CCTV and ANPR footage from the pier to Amelia's flat and the roads leading out of Ryde. Emma thinks she spotted the car at the pier when they picked up Amelia. I want footage of it; we may be able to get a shot of the driver. And check the footage from the boat to see if anyone was watching Amelia. The rest of you are with me.'

Jenny paced impatiently as she waited for the K9 and handler team to arrive. She was back at the scene of the crash, forensics having finished and released the scene, and wanted to get the search under way as soon as possible. George was standing to one side, looking as impatient to get going as she was. Jenny had told him that he wasn't needed, they could manage without him, and he should take the rest of the day off, but he wouldn't listen. Jenny had relented and allowed him to lead one of the search teams. After all, she would have wanted to in his place, and the paramedics had cleared him for duty.

After a few more minutes the police-dog team arrived, and Jenny called everyone together. 'OK everybody, we are looking for Amelia Simpson or for some indication of what happened to her. We think she was taken forcibly from the scene, but we can't discount the fact that she might have fled on foot and may be injured. You all have radios; report anything you find. Let's get to it.'

The teams split up and entered the woods, the dogs and their handlers leading the charge. Jenny's team set off and they plunged ahead, the dog's nose to the ground.

After thirty minutes, Jenny spotted something in the trees

and called for the team to halt. She crept forward to get a better look, keeping low. From where she crouched, it looked like an old abandoned hut. Its walls were made of loose stones, the mortar long since crumbled away, and the tiles on the roof were covered in moss and dead leaves. A rusted corrugated sheet covered the doorway and the windows were boarded up.

She motioned to the others to stay where they were and crept forward. She reached the window and tried to see in, but the boards were firmly secured. She carried on towards the makeshift front door, put her head close to it and listened, but after a moment gave up; no obvious noises were coming from inside the hut, and the ambient noise of the forest drowned out any more subtle sounds.

Jenny withdrew her torch from her belt and thumbed it on. With one quick motion, she threw the tin sheet to the floor and entered, her flashlight moving quickly.

'Shit,' she said as she shone her torch around the interior of the hut. It was empty apart from a collection of old beer cans and a couple of used condoms on the floor. It looked like nothing more than a hangout for some of the local teenagers. There was no sign that it had been used recently and no sign of Amelia.

Jenny left the hut and went over to her team. 'False alarm,' she said, and they looked as disappointed as she felt. She sighed. 'This is a dead end; if there was something to find we would have found it by now. There's no way Amelia or Ashley came through here and left no trace.' She reached for her radio and checked in with the other search teams. They had nothing to report either, and Jenny could detect the same level of frustration in their voices. 'Right, I'm calling this. Back to the cars.'

The rest of the search teams had already made it back to the road by the time Jenny and her team emerged from the

241

woods. George hurried over as soon as her saw her. 'Anything?'

'No. To be honest, it was a long shot. It's much more likely that she was taken from the scene by the car that rammed you.'

Jenny's phone rang. She withdrew it from her jacket pocket and answered it.

'Jenny,' said Claire, with an excited edge to her voice, 'we've just had a hit on Kirstie's mobile phone.'

'Where?' Jenny asked, her face lighting up. The young detective constable's excitement was contagious.

'Ryde. She's at home.'

Chapter 29

Amelia opened her eyes, slowly lifted her head, then immediately wished she hadn't as a blinding pain coursed through her. She cried out and reached out to touch her forehead. It was tender, but there wasn't any blood, which she took as a good sign. She tried again more slowly and managed to sit upright.

Her memory was a blur; she could remember bits and pieces of what had happened, but it was patchy. The last thing she could remember was seeing the blue car that had followed them driving straight at them. The next thing she knew, the car was spinning, a tree loomed out of nowhere, and that was it. Up until a minute ago, when she had woken up here – wherever 'here' was.

She looked around but couldn't see a thing; there was no light except for a small window high in the far wall. As her eyes eventually adjusted to the gloom she made out a few more details. The room she was in looked about twenty feet square. The walls themselves looked old. They had once been covered by plaster which had flaked off, revealing the brickwork underneath. To her left, a short flight of concrete steps led up to the door.

'I'm in a basement,' she muttered to herself. She gingerly got to her feet and walked to the steps.

'It won't open; it's locked from the other side,' said a small voice, barely even a whisper.

Amelia spun round and as her eyes adjusted further to the dark, spotted a figure crouched in the far corner of the room. 'Who's there?' she called, inching nearer to the voice, relieved that she wasn't alone anymore.

The figure didn't answer, but began to cry quietly.

As Amelia crept forward, she could make out more of the person. They were sitting on the floor with their legs drawn up, and their arms wrapped around them. As Amelia approached, the person stopped crying and finally looked up, staring at Amelia with red-rimmed eyes. It was Dawn.

'Dawn!' Amelia cried out in relief as she squatted next to her. She looked at her friend, her hair was matted and tangled, there was a rip in her jacket and her clothes were covered in dust and dirt. 'Are you OK? What are you doing here? Where are we?'

'I don't know where we are,' Dawn said as she wiped her eyes, leaving smudges of dirt across her pale, tear-stained cheeks. 'I woke up here a week ago, or at least I think it was a week. It's hard to keep track of the time.'

'A week?' Amelia gasped. 'Do you know who brought you here?'

'No. It was a woman, but that's all I can tell you.'

'Have you seen her since?' Amelia asked urgently.

'She comes once a day to bring food and water but she never says anything. She just opens the door and leaves it on the step before closing and bolting the door again.' Dawn's voice was still barely a whisper.

'Can you describe her?'

Dawn shook her head sadly. 'No, it's all so fuzzy. Why is this happening?' she asked. Her voice cracked and she stifled a sob.

'I think it's my fault,' said Amelia, and placed her hand on Dawn's arm.

'How could it be your fault?'

'I think the woman who kidnapped us both is my sister Ashley.' Amelia looked away, but she could feel Dawn's gaze boring into her.

'I didn't think you had a sister. Didn't you say you were an only child?' Dawn asked finally.

'I am – or at least I thought I was until a couple of days ago.'

'Why has she kidnapped us?' Dawn asked weakly.

'I don't know, but she seems to have some sort of vendetta against me. She killed my gran, and she killed Megan that night when we all met up. That's how I discovered she existed. She left DNA at the scene which was a partial match with mine.'

Amelia got up and went to inspect the door. Unlike the rest of the room, it was new and solid. It was set flush to the door frame, and when Amelia pulled on the handle it didn't budge. There was no keyhole to peer through, so she guessed that Dawn's assessment was correct. Reluctantly, she made her way back down the stairs and looked at the room. It was empty apart from the double mattress she had woken up on and a medium-sized bucket in a corner. Amelia frowned at this, then understood; it was a makeshift toilet. She shuddered at the thought.

She made her way to the window. She judged that she could probably squeeze through it if she could get it open – but even stretching up as much as she was able, Amelia still couldn't reach the window ledge. 'Dawn, give me a boost up, would you?'

Dawn came over and linked her fingers. Amelia braced herself, then put her left foot into Dawn's hands, who pushed Amelia up to the window with a grunt.

'What can you see?' Dawn panted, the strain of lifting Amelia already showing.

'Not much. There's gravel in front of the window and then it's just trees. I guess we must be somewhere remote.' Amelia tried to rattle the window, but like the door it refused to move. Frustrated, she jumped down and Dawn shook out her fingers.

'Do you think you can get the window open?' Dawn said, sounding hopeful for the first time.

'I don't know; it feels pretty solid to me. You say she comes once a day to drop off food and water? Maybe we could ambush her. There's two of us now after all.'

'I don't think that'll work,' Dawn said sadly.

'It's got to be worth a try, hasn't it?'

Instead of answering, Dawn pointed to the corner that she had been sitting in, the one furthest from the door. At first, Amelia didn't understand, but then she saw it; a small red dot where the walls met the ceiling. Closer inspection revealed it to be a small closed-circuit camera, the wires running into the ceiling. 'There's another one by the door.'

'Damn it,' Amelia said in frustration and slid down the wall until she was sitting next to Dawn. They sat in silence for a few minutes before Dawn spoke.

'I need to tell you something.'

Amelia turned her head towards her old friend.

'There was no client meeting on the island. I made it up.'

'Why?' Amelia's eyes narrowed and she moved away from Dawn.

Dawn squirmed. 'I just came to see you. I looked you up online and saw you were living here.'

'You came all the way from London just to see me?' Amelia asked carefully.

'It was true what I said; I wanted you to come and work for me. I meant everything I said over lunch. You're the best designer I've ever seen, and I'd love you to be part of my team.'

'Why lie about it, though? Why didn't you just ring me or come to the shop?'

'I was going to. I intended to come to the shop the day after and say I'd spotted you, to make it look like a coincidence. I genuinely didn't expect to bump into you that first night. I wasn't even planning to go out that night, but I was bored. I know it sounds stupid. I just figured that I should be honest if we're going to die anyway.'

'Don't talk like that,' Amelia told her firmly. 'I was with a couple of police officers when I was taken, so they know I'm missing and they'll be trying to find me. In the meantime, let's keep looking for a way to escape.'

Chapter 30

Jenny climbed out of her unmarked car and hurried to where the armed unit were forming up. It was late in the day and she was equal parts tired and wired. Though it had been a long and trying day, they finally had a lead on their chief suspect. The trace on Kirstie's mobile phone showed that she had been home for the past hour and they needed to act quickly. They had lost time in obtaining the warrant and the whole team was restless; they knew they couldn't afford to let her slip through their fingers again.

Jenny got on the radio and checked in with the second team. 'Claire, how are you doing?'

'We're in place, boss,' came the prompt reply. Claire and the second armed response unit were just beyond the fence at the rear of Kirstie's garden, having gained access from the industrial site behind the property.

'Stand by,' Jenny told her, and went to check in with the tactical unit, who were ready and waiting for the order to proceed.

'Our target is Kirstie Williams,' she told them. 'We need

her in cuffs and we need that now. The second team are in place and covering the rear of the property. You have a go.'

The four-man team hurried through the gate to the front door of the terraced house. Two stepped up with the enforcer, and with one well-placed strike the door crashed inwards in a shower of splintered wood and broken glass.

'Armed police, nobody move! Stay where you are!' the sergeant yelled as the team moved in with Jenny right behind them. They moved fast, keeping low, pausing as they reached the first door. The house was silent.

The first officer swung into the living room, sighting along his rifle at each corner before yelling 'All clear'. The team split, two officers heading upstairs whilst two moved quickly forward. They entered the kitchen just in time to see Kirstie run through the back door.

'Armed police! Stay where you are!' the lead officer yelled, but Kirstie kept running. Jenny stormed in, ran past the armed officers and gave chase. Kirstie was nearly halfway across the garden before she spotted the second armed response team. She hesitated for a moment and that was all Jenny needed. She caught up and in one smooth motion tackled her to the ground.

'Kirstie Williams,' she said, taking a pair of handcuffs from a pocket and securing Kirstie's wrists, 'I am arresting you on suspicion of the murders of Frances Lowes and Megan Parkinson. You do not have to say anything, but it may harm your defence if you don't mention when questioned something which you later rely on in court. Anything you do say may be given in evidence. Do you understand?' She hauled the struggling woman to her feet.

'What are you doing? Get off me!' Kirstie protested as two of the response team led her out of the side gate and down to the waiting van.

'Good work, boss,' Claire said as she reached her.

'Thanks. I must admit, that felt good. Claire, I want you and a couple of uniforms to start searching the property. I'll accompany our guest back to the station. Let me know if you find anything.'

* * *

Jenny strode into the interview room, a smug grin on her face. Kirstie and her solicitor were already seated on one side of the table, and George was on the other. The room was just like all the other interview rooms except for one small detail; the TV monitor mounted on the wall. George was just connecting a laptop to a lead trailing from behind it.

Jenny sat down and studied their suspect, who scowled at Jenny, arms folded. Jenny smiled and matched her stare for stare. Over the course of her career she had faced gang-bangers, murderers, rapists and violent offenders, male and female, young and old, so a pissed-off florist wasn't about to get under her skin. Kirstie looked away first, making Jenny's smile broaden. First point scored. Jenny pressed Play on the recorder and introduced herself and George, who took care of the formalities.

'I must remind you that you are under caution,' George stated, and was treated to the glare Jenny had been subjected to moments before.

'So, Ms Williams, can you tell me where you've been for the past week?' Jenny began.

'If you must know, I've been at a holiday cottage in the New Forest.'

'We've already pulled your financial records and we've been tracking your credit and debit cards. You haven't used them all week, and there haven't been any significant withdrawals over the last month. If you have been on holiday for the last week, how have you paid for it?'

'I won the holiday in a competition; a ten-day cottage rental.'

'You've only been gone a week,' George pointed out.

'I got bored and cut it short. There's only so much you can do by yourself.'

'How did you pay for food and drink?' Jenny asked.

'The cottage was fully stocked when I arrived; all expenses paid.'

'Isn't that convenient,' said Jenny with a smile.

'It's true. I had an email telling me that I'd won a competition and everything would be paid for, and it was. They even supplied boat and train tickets, so I didn't need to use my cards. Saying that, I did have lunch out one day. I went for a walk and found a charming village. It was a nice day, so I had a pub lunch there.'

'Was this lunch free as well?' George asked, eyebrows raised.

'I paid cash; I had enough in my purse. And the barman was cute, so I chatted to him for a bit. I'm sure he'll remember me.'

'What was the pub's name?'

'I think it was called The Watchman's Rest. It was in a village just outside Lyndhurst.'

'Which day did you go there?'

'A couple of days ago. Wednesday, the nineteenth, I think, just before midday.'

'Tell me more about this competition. Where did you hear about it? When did you apply?'

Kirstie shifted uncomfortably in her seat. Eventually she said, sheepishly, 'I didn't actually enter it.'

Jenny and George exchanged glances and Kirstie scowled again. 'You won a competition without entering it?' said Jenny. 'You'll have to tell me how to do that.'

'What I mean is that I didn't personally enter it. It was

run by a website where people can nominate local businesses if they've received exceptional service or great value for money, and a winner is drawn at random every three months or so. I haven't been on holiday in years and I never win anything, so who was I to turn it down?'

'We'll be looking into this and checking everything that you've said,' Jenny warned her. 'I have to say, though, it sounds as if you had a really nice time. A lovely cottage in the picturesque New Forest, free food and drink, and it's been twenty degrees all week...' Kirstie regarded Jenny warily. 'So I'm sure that once our tech guys access your mobile phone there will be hundreds of photos documenting your whole week. I mean, I can't speak for anyone else here, but I would have taken loads of pictures, something nice to remember the week by. These should be more than enough to prove that what you're saying is true.'

'I don't have any,' Kirstie replied quietly, refusing to meet either detective's eyes. 'My phone was stolen the night before the holiday. I didn't have a chance to replace it before I went.'

'That's remarkably convenient, but I have a question. If your phone was stolen right before your holiday, what did we recover earlier today from your house?' Jenny asked, gazing at Kirstie intently.

'I thought it had been stolen, but it turned out that I had only misplaced it. I found it as soon as I got home.' Jenny and George raised their eyebrows again. 'It's true!' Kirstie insisted angrily.

'Let's move on for a moment, shall we? I'd like to talk about the night of the fourteenth. There was an incident with Megan Parkinson, wasn't there?'

'I already told your lot about it when they came to my shop the morning after. I went to the Red Lion with a couple of friends for a drink and a chat, and before I'd even had a chance to order, that psychopath stormed over, punched me for absolutely no reason and got thrown out.'

'People don't tend to punch people for no reason,' George pointed out.

'Normal people don't, but like I just said, she's a bloody nutter. That wasn't even the first time she had a go at me. A couple of weeks ago, she assaulted me in my own home. She barged in when I was unlocking my front door and threatened me.'

'Why haven't you mentioned this before?' Jenny asked.

'You wouldn't have done anything about it, so why waste my time,' Kirstie growled contemptuously.

'OK, so by your own admission you have had several run-ins with Megan that you claim were entirely one-sided. If that was me, I would feel pretty angry at someone targeting me for no apparent reason.'

'I was angry.'

'So angry that after the latest run-in you decided enough was enough? That she needed to be stopped once and for all?'

'No, of course not.'

'I think you lay in wait for her, watched her arrive home drunk, and decided to pay her back for embarrassing you in front of your friends.'

'No! That's not what happened. I was at home asleep.'

'Can anyone vouch for that?'

Kirstie didn't answer, which told Jenny all she needed to know. 'What about Amelia Simpson?' she asked.

'What about her?'

'You seem to have quite the grudge against her, and I can't figure out why.'

'It's her that has the problem with me, not the other way round.'

'Really? I've got something I'd like to show you, if that's

OK.' Jenny pressed Play on the laptop and a video started to play on the TV. It showed a street. The clock at the bottom of the video gave the time as 07:49, and apart from one or two delivery vans it was quiet. Just visible in the top right-hand corner was the pale-blue shop front of Flowers by the Beach. About fifteen seconds later, a figure walked into shot: Amelia, arriving for work. She reached her shop, rummaged in her bag and let herself in. Jenny moved the video on two minutes and a second person came into view. Maria reached the shop and also entered. Jenny moved the video on again. 'This is the interesting part.' Jenny told the assembled group.

On the screen, another person came into shot. While the quality wasn't perfect, it was clearly Kirstie. She stopped on the pavement opposite Amelia's shop, just over to one side, in the early-morning shadows. She glanced over her shoulder, then pulled an object out of her jacket pocket and after another quick glance drew her arm back and threw the object at the shop. Then she turned and ran.

Jenny paused the video and turned to Kirstie. 'Looks like you do have some kind of grudge against Amelia. Otherwise, how do you explain throwing a rock through her window?'

Kirstie didn't say anything. She glared at Jenny and George, her hands clenching and unclenching on the table.

'What I don't understand is why,' said Jenny. 'Amelia was there first. Her shop has been in the same location for nearly ten years, and your shop has been there about eighteen months. If you didn't like the competition, why didn't you open somewhere else?'

'You wouldn't understand,' Kirstie said finally.

'Try me.'

'Ever since I was a little girl, I've always wanted to own my own flower shop in this area. I wasn't about to let some jumped-up Londoner take that away from me.'

'So you thought you might be able to scare her off, maybe

make her reconsider her choice of location. You began a campaign of hate and intimidation which lasted over a year, and when that didn't work, you started to get desperate. I think you realised that Amelia had come to the island to be near her grandmother, and as long as she was still in the picture, Amelia wasn't going anywhere. You thought that if you removed her from the scene in as painful a way as possible, Amelia would leave and never come back. When even that failed to have the desired effect, you weren't sure what to do. That's why you attacked her cat, more out of desperation than anything else.'

'No!'

'Does the name Ashley Johnson mean anything to you?' Jenny asked carefully, studying Kirstie for any kind of tell.

'No. Should it?'

'What about the twenty-third of May?'

'Again, no. What's this about?'

Kirstie reached up to tuck a strand of hair behind her ear. As she did, the sleeve of her top rode up. George's eyes narrowed, and he frowned. Kirstie put her arm down, but not before Jenny had spotted George's expression. She gave him an inquiring look.

'Would you mind rolling up your right sleeve, please, Ms Williams,' George asked, and Kirstie fidgeted uncomfortably. Reluctantly, she pushed up the sleeve of her yellow blouse and Jenny's eyes widened. On her forearm were two parallel scratches approximately two inches in length.

'How did you get those scratches?' Jenny asked, staring at Kirstie.

'I caught my arm on a thorn bush when I was out walking a few days ago.'

'You know,' Jenny began conversationally, 'just before Megan was killed we believe that she managed to scratch her assailant; we found skin cells underneath the index and middle fingers of her right hand. What are the odds that the tissue sample we took when we brought you in will match the skin samples recovered at the scene?'

'I told you, I caught it on a bush,' Kirstie insisted, but there was no disguising the panic in her voice.

Before Jenny could reply, she was interrupted by a knock at the door. A uniformed officer opened it and leaned in. 'Excuse me, ma'am, do you have a moment?'

Jenny flashed him a look conveying that this had better be worth it or he would find himself on the wrong side of traffic duty for a month. She paused the interview and headed outside, leaving George with Kirstie and her solicitor. 'I'm in the middle of an interview!' she snapped.

'Sorry ma'am, but Detective Constable Watson is on the line and she says it's important.'

Jenny thanked the officer, who hurried away gratefully. She went to her desk, snatched up the phone and took the waiting call. 'DI Stone,' Jenny snapped.

'Ma'am, it's Claire. We've found the picture of Amelia, Frances and Amelia's mother that was missing from the first crime scene.'

'We've got her!' Jenny cried, her eyes sparkling. 'Where was it?'

'It was hidden at the bottom of a wardrobe under a pile of clothes, in an old sports bag, but that's not all. There was a sketchbook with it. I've had a look through and some of the sketches look an awful lot like paintings at Megan's house.'

'Claire, you're an absolute star. Keep looking, and let me know if you find anything else.'

Jenny put down the phone and stalked towards the interview room, a definite spring in her step. She opened the door and retook her seat. George gave her an inquisitive look but Jenny ignored him and turned to focus on Kirstie.

'Kirstie Williams, I must inform you that new evidence

has come to light. I will be seeking authority from the Crown Prosecution Service to charge you with the murders of Mrs Frances Lowes and Ms Megan Parkinson, so I suggest that it is in your best interest to start cooperating with us.'

'I've told you already that I had nothing to do with either of those deaths. Why won't you believe me?'

'If that's the way you want to play it then that's fine with me.' Jenny ended the interview and a uniformed officer led Kirstie back to her cell.

Jenny turned to George. 'Once the cheek swab has been analysed, we've got her. In the meantime, George, look into any remote premises that Kirstie may have access to. We need to find Amelia Simpson before it's too late.'

Chapter 31

Jenny was sitting at her desk, reviewing the results of the search carried out at Kirstie's house. Apart from the missing picture from the first scene and the sketchbook, they hadn't found anything further of interest. They had managed to recover prints from the sketchbook that matched Megan's, and prints from Frances and Amelia were on the photo, but that was it. Kirstie could have handled them wearing gloves, but it still troubled Jenny.

She was shaken from her thoughts by the sound of the chair next to her being pulled out. 'I hear I missed all the fun!' said Emma as she draped her jacket over the back of her chair and sat down. Despite her bravado she still looked like she had been better, her normally immaculate hair was tied back in a loose ponytail and she still looked pale, even for a redhead.

'What are you doing here?' Jenny asked her, the report momentarily forgotten.

'The docs cleared me this morning. No concussion, just this little memento,' she told Jenny, pointing to the small row of stitches just above her temple.

'You should have taken the rest of the day off; no one would have judged you.'

'I'm fine, really I am. I just want to help find Amelia and nail this bastard. I saw George on my way in, he tells me you brought Kirstie in yesterday. How did the interview go?'

'She claims she's been on holiday for the last week.'

'Can she prove it?'

'No. No photos, no activity on her cards. She claims that she won it, everything was paid for in advance, and she didn't have her phone with her. She did say that she had lunch out once, though, and that the barman would remember her.'

'Hardly a watertight alibi for the time of the kidnapping, is it.'

'No, but I've got George chasing it up. Speak of the devil,' Jenny said as George approached. 'What have you found out?'

'I've spoken to the barman who was working in the Watchman's Rest pub when Kirstie said she visited. He does remember serving someone matching Kirstie's description, but he couldn't say for certain. Apparently, given their location, they get lots of new faces in every week.'

'Any cameras in the bar?'

'Afraid not.'

'Damn. Try to track down any cameras in the vicinity of the bar. I want to know if she was there or not.'

Jenny got up and made her way towards DCI Edwards's office. The door was ajar and she could hear him talking on the phone. She knocked. Edwards glanced up, beckoned her in and gestured to the empty chair opposite him. Jenny sat down and studied her boss. He finished the phone call and returned his mobile to its usual place beside his computer.

'HR, about training budgets,' he said, by way of explanation. 'What can I do for you? I hear you have a suspect in custody and you've recovered items belonging to the victims from her house. Have you formally charged her yet?'

'Not yet, sir, that's what I wanted to talk to you about.'

'What's the problem?' he said, frowning.

'She claims to have been elsewhere for the past week. If so, she couldn't have attacked our service vehicle or kidnapped Amelia Simpson. That would mean either that she isn't guilty and she's being set up, or that she's working with someone else.'

'What evidence has she put forward to support her claim that she was elsewhere?'

'She says she had lunch out one day while she was away and the barman could vouch for it. We've spoken to him, and he remembers chatting to someone matching our suspect's description. We've sent over her custody photo and he thinks it's her but he can't be certain.'

'There you go, then. You heard what he said; he can't be certain. That means she can't prove where she was last week and by your own admission, doesn't have an alibi for either of the murders. Did you get anything from the traffic cams in the run-up to the kidnapping?'

'Nothing useful. We've got images of the car, but the occupant must have known the cameras were there as they managed to obscure their face. Plus they were wearing a baseball cap, sunglasses and had a hood up. Unfortunately, when Emma tried to lose them she turned off the main road; there aren't any traffic cameras down the side streets.'

'Damn. But you still have enough evidence to move forward; finding trophies from both scenes is fairly damning. Charge her.'

'We're still waiting on the results of the cheek swab we took yesterday, sir. If that comes back as a match, we'll have her.'

'Even without the DNA match, you have plenty of evidence to suggest she was involved. The barman is hardly a reliable witness. I want this case wrapped up.'

'Sir, if there's any chance that she's innocent then we have to keep investigating. We could end up jailing an innocent woman while there would still be a killer on the loose.'

'Then you'd better go and make sure you've got the right person. Don't let me keep you,' Edwards ground out.

Jenny left the office and stormed back to her desk. 'George, keep trying to find that CCTV footage. Emma, you're with me. We're going to have another chat with Kirstie Williams.'

'Let me guess, you're both here to apologise and tell me that I'm free to go,' Kirstie said to the detectives sitting opposite her.

'We'd like to ask you a couple more questions if that's ok,' Jenny replied.

'I told you yesterday that I didn't kidnap Amelia, and I certainly didn't kill anyone. Did you speak to the barman? He must have confirmed what I told you.'

'We have spoken to him, yes. While he remembers speaking to someone, he couldn't say for certain that it was you.'

'It *was* me! There must be some way to prove that.'

'We're still in the process of recovering and reviewing CCTV footage. We have completed the search at your house, though.' Emma selected some photographs from her folder and slid them across the table to Kirstie and her solicitor. 'Photographs labelled KW-6 to KW-10 show two items discovered at the back of the wardrobe in the main bedroom of the house. The first shows a photo including the first victim, Frances Lowes, which was reported missing from the victim's house. The other photos are of a sketchbook we have confirmed as belonging to the second victim, Megan Parkinson.'

Kirstie stared at the photos then faced the two detectives, her face pale and her eyes wide. 'I'm being set up! I've never seen these before in my life!'

'So you have no explanation for how they came to be in your wardrobe?'

'That's what I just said, isn't it? Maybe one of your lot planted them when they searched my house.'

'Do you drive, Kirstie?' Jenny asked her.

'Yes. I've got a licence, but no car at the moment. Work is within walking distance and you can do all your grocery shopping online now, so I didn't see the point in continuing to pay for something I didn't need.'

'Do you have access to any cars?'

'My friends drive. I've borrowed their cars on occasion.'

Jenny terminated the interview and the detectives left the room. Jenny headed for the kitchenette, hoping a cup of coffee would take the edge off the headache forming between her eyes. She took a sip of her drink and felt a little better, though she knew better than to think this dammed headache was solely the result of caffeine withdrawal. The more she thought about it, the less she liked Kirstie for the murders. She couldn't put her finger on it, but something just felt off. Then again, a lot pointed to Kirstie as the perpetrator.

She was still mulling it over as she returned to her desk, so lost in thought that she nearly walked into George. 'Sorry to disturb you, ma'am,' he said.

'That's OK, George, what have you got?'

'I've managed to recover footage from a camera down the street from the Watchman's Rest. You'd better have a look.'

Jenny followed George to his desk. After a couple of mouse clicks, a video began to play. 'That's the bar right there,' George announced, pointing to the top left of the screen. There were people about: a young couple pushing a pram and a few kids who looked no older than twelve or thirteen – Jenny wondered why they weren't in school. A minute later, a lone female walked onscreen, facing away from the camera. She continued up the road before stopping at the edge of the pavement opposite the bar. As the last car passed, the woman turned her head to look down the street.

George paused the video. While the quality wasn't great, the woman in the video was clearly Kirstie. 'Exactly when she said,' Jenny muttered. 'Shit.'

'Sorry, boss.'

Jenny made her way back to her desk, her headache back in full force. 'You OK, Jenny?' Emma asked as she sat down heavily.

'Kirstie was telling the truth. We've got footage of her entering the bar.'

Before Emma could respond Simon came over, and the look on his face told Jenny that her headache was about to get much worse. 'I've just had the lab on the phone; they've finished the analysis of the sample taken from Kirstie Williams. No match with the sample recovered from Megan Parkinson's house, I'm afraid.'

'Goddammit!' Jenny cried and banged her fist on the desk, causing coffee to slosh over the side of her cup. Next to her, Emma muttered a similar curse. 'We'll have to release her.'

'With respect, ma'am, I disagree,' said Emma. 'We've found items from both victims' houses stashed in her bedroom, and she can't prove her whereabouts at the time of either murder. Not to mention the grudge she has against Amelia, and she had more than enough motive for attacking Megan.'

'I agree with you, but I don't think we've got enough evidence. The CPS will never authorise charging her with anything other than harassment or vandalism. We have to release her.'

* * *

'George, have you seen Emma?' Jenny called across the office.

'Not since just before lunch, I'm afraid. She said there was something she needed to do. Can I help?'

'Yeah. Come with me.'

George followed Jenny as she made her way through the station to the cells. They were at the entrance to the custody suite when Jenny felt her mobile phone vibrate in her pocket. She withdrew it; the display showed *Greg Mobile*. It was unlike Greg to call her at work but she hit Decline and checked that the phone was still on silent. She would ring him back after she had got this hateful task out of the way.

She nodded to the duty sergeant who unlocked the cell door and opened it. Inside, Kirstie stood up, glaring at each of the officers in turn. 'Come with me,' Jenny said, and led her towards the front of the station.

'Where are we going?' Kirstie demanded. 'You can't possibly have more questions.'

They stopped by the duty sergeant's desk and Jenny turned to face her. 'You're being released on bail. That doesn't mean we won't have further questions for you, though, so no more holidays for the time being. George, see her out, please.' She turned and stalked back towards her desk, already wondering if she had made a big mistake.

On her way back to her desk, Jenny diverted to the kitchenette for a much-needed drink. Coffee in hand and feeling a little better, she reached her desk and remembered Greg's phone call. She pulled out her mobile and frowned;

according to the display, she had had five further calls from him. She unlocked her phone and hit Redial, but after six rings it switched to voicemail. Jenny ended the call and returned it to her pocket.

No sooner had Jenny picked up her coffee than her desk phone started ringing. The display indicated that it was the front desk. Jenny snatched up the receiver. 'DI Stone.'

'Jenny, it's Sergeant Fischer.'

'What can I do for you, Tony?'

'Your husband is here to see you; he says it's urgent.'

Her coffee forgotten, Jenny walked quickly to the front desk, her mind racing. She couldn't remember the last time Greg had visited her at work - not since she'd been working in Ryde - so it must be important.

'Jenny! Are you all right?' Greg asked, rushing forward and clasping her by her shoulders while a bemused Sergeant Fischer looked on.

'Yeah, of course, why wouldn't I be?'

'What about the threat against you?'

Jenny frowned. 'What threat?'

'What do you mean, what threat? If there hasn't been any threat against you, why did one of your officers pick Sophie up from school earlier on?'

Jenny felt the blood drain from her face. 'I haven't sent any officers to pick up Sophie, Greg. I need you to start from the beginning.'

'I went to pick Sophie up from her after-school club and her teacher told me that an officer had picked her up just after lunch. The officer said they'd bring her here because a threat had been made against you. The school were concerned that I didn't know anything about it.'

'That order didn't come from me, or anyone else in this station.'

Before Jenny could say any more, her phone vibrated. She

reached into her pocket and withdrew it; the display told her that she had a new text message from a number she didn't recognise. She clicked on it and started to read.

'What is it? What does it say?' asked Greg.

Wordlessly, Jenny handed the phone to her husband.

Chapter 32

As George signed the three of them in, Jenny couldn't help looking at her phone, though the words of the text message were burned into her memory.

I have your daughter Sophie. All you need to do to ensure that she is returned alive and unharmed is to forget about Amelia Simpson until after the 24th. If you continue to meddle in affairs that have nothing to do with you, you will never see her alive again.

Her expression hardened as she reread the words.

The school administrator, whose name badge gave her name as Sarah, escorted them from the reception area at the front of the school, through the main doors and straight down to the headmistress's office. She knocked and waited, her expression equal parts guilt and worry. 'Enter,' came the response. Sarah opened the door and Jenny strode in, followed by Greg, with George in their wake.

'Detective Inspector Stone, Mr Williams,' the headmistress began, rising and hurrying round from behind the desk. 'Let me once again apologise unreservedly for what has happened. I assure you that we will offer any and all support that you need to find Sophie and bring her home safe and sound.'

Jenny and Greg had met their daughter's headmistress, Caroline Hoyle, a number of times over the last few years. She had come across as a force to be reckoned with, self-assured, passionate about her work, and very protective of her pupils. It was obvious from her demeanour that this had hit her hard. Normally Jenny would have felt a pang of sympathy, but not this time.

'I want to know how someone was able to gain access to the school and walk off with one of your children,' Jenny demanded, her voice rising in volume.

'Jenny...' Greg put a hand on her arm, which she immediately shook off.

'I swear that the ID she produced looked real,' said the headmistress. 'If I'd had any doubts about it, I would never have let her go. You must believe me.'

'What can you tell us about this woman, Mrs Hoyle?' George interjected.

'The name on the badge was Detective Sergeant Marie.'

'What?' Jenny cried out, her eyes as wide as they could go. 'Are you sure?'

'That's the name on the signing-in sheet as well,' Sarah added.

'Can you describe her, please?' George asked carefully.

'She had long red hair, pale skin with a smattering of freckles across her nose, and blue eyes. I'd say she was a little taller than me, maybe about five foot six, and probably in her mid to late twenties.'

'Any accent?'

'Nothing that I could detect, I'm afraid.'

'Start from the beginning, please. Tell us what happened,' Jenny said, still struggling to keep her voice under control.

'She pressed the buzzer at the main entrance just after the year three to sixes had finished their lunch break, at around ten past one. She said that she was a police officer and needed to speak to the headmistress. I let her in and she came into the school reception,' Sarah said, and Jenny, Greg and George turned towards her. 'She showed her badge and asked to speak to Mrs Hoyle. I took her name and badge number, asked her to fill out the visitor's log, then escorted her here,' Sarah told them, George making notes as she talked.

'Did she handle anything? A door handle? The sign-in book, or a pen?'

'I don't think so, no. She took a pen out of her own pocket and I opened the door for her.'

'Then what happened?'

'I brought her straight to Mrs Hoyle's office. School policy is that no visitors are unaccompanied.'

'What did she say when she was in here?'

'She asked that someone fetch Sophie,' Mrs Hoyle continued. 'She said that a threat had been made against you and your family, and that as a precaution she had orders to take Sophie to the police station.'

'You didn't think to phone me and check this story?'

'Believe me, I wish I had. I asked to see her ID and she handed it over. It looked legitimate, so I asked Sarah to fetch Sophie; she was in her classroom with Mrs Kline at the time. Sarah brought her here and I explained to her that the officer would take her to you.'

'Is that it? Did she say or do anything else?'

'No, not really. Sophie asked if you were OK and the officer told her that you were fine and you wanted to see her, and they left. I watched her take Sophie to her car and drive off.'

'You saw her car?' Jenny asked sharply. 'You didn't happen to see the number plate, did you?'

'I'm sorry, but no. The most I can tell you was that it was light blue.'

'Where was it parked?'

Mrs Hoyle led the two detectives to the big window at the side of the room and gestured towards an area outside the main entrance. 'It was just down there.'

'That's all we can do here for the moment. If you think of anything else, no matter how small, you call me and only me,' Jenny said to the headmistress, who looked at least ten years older than usual.

Outside, Jenny stopped and looked around, trying to figure out what to do next.

'Do you really think it was Emma?' George asked her.

'The description matches her, plus no one has seen Emma since before lunch.'

'Why would she take Sophie?' Greg asked.

'I don't know,' Jenny sighed and pinched the bridge of her nose. She turned to Greg. 'I need you back at the house.'

'Why? I want to stay with you and help to find my daughter.'

'We need somebody there in case the kidnapper tries to make contact. I promise I'll let you know if I find anything.'

Greg nodded reluctantly and headed back to his car.

Before George could say anything, Jenny stalked towards the main gate of the school. She stopped and looked around, the wind blowing her blonde hair across her face. 'Over there,' she said, pointing towards a white detached house about fifty metres away, and headed towards it.

'Jenny, are you OK?' George asked, struggling to keep up.

Jenny glared at him and he flushed pink. 'We're going to find her, you know. Every police officer on the island is searching for her.'

As they approached the house, George realised what had caught her eye. Above the porch, pointing towards the school gate, was a small CCTV camera. Jenny pushed open the wrought-iron gate, went up the path to the front door, and pressed the bell.

The sound of barking was followed by the voice of someone who sounded in her eighties at least. The sounds of the dog grew distant, followed by a door slamming. Eventually, the front door was opened on a security chain. Jenny had been right: the woman staring at her was at least eighty and wore an expression of undisguised suspicion.

'Good afternoon, madam. My name is Detective Inspector Stone and this is my colleague, Detective Constable Bancroft. May we have a moment of your time, please?'

'You got any identification?' she asked, still glaring at them.

'Certainly.' Jenny and George presented their warrant cards. The front door closed and they heard the sound of the chain being removed before the door was reopened.

'Please, come on in,' the woman told them, her tone noticeably friendlier. 'Would you like a drink at all? Tea, coffee, squash?' she asked, leading the two detectives into a kitchen that apparently hadn't been decorated since the seventies.

'No thank you, Mrs...'

'Cauldwell, Muriel Cauldwell. How can I help you?'

'The camera above your front door, does it work?'

'Oh yes, my son had it installed a couple of years ago. I had trouble with the school across the road, you know. The little hooligans kept throwing rubbish into my front garden and when I told them off they started throwing stones at my windows. The camera seemed to do the trick, though - not so brave when they knew they were being recorded.'

'Is it on now?'

'It should be. I never touch it; I don't know how. My son set it up for me, you see,' she offered in way of an explanation.

'Can I have a look at some footage from this afternoon, please? It's very important.'

She led them through to a small dining room. In the corner was a tiny desk, on which stood a desktop computer. Judging by the thick layer of dust on it, it hadn't been used in some time. Muriel looked pensively at it. 'I'm not really sure...' she said, wringing her hands.

'Would you mind if I had a look?' George asked, gesturing towards the computer.

'No, of course not,' Muriel replied, looking visibly relieved and stepping back to give George access.

George fired up the antiquated computer and after a small amount of searching, found the folder he was looking for. A couple more clicks later, a video feed filled the screen. The picture quality was surprisingly clear, Jenny noted; the system itself must have cost hundreds, if not thousands.

George rolled the video back to just after one o'clock and they waited. At 13:08, a blue Ford Focus pulled into shot and drove through the main gates of the school. A figure got out and pressed a button on an intercom by the main door. A moment later they entered the main building. George wound the recording forward until they spotted the same person leaving, accompanied by a small girl with blonde hair. While the system was an expensive one, the distance was too great to make a positive ID of the driver. All they could tell at this range was that it seemed to match the description they had been given.

'Damn,' George said, frowning. 'I wonder if there's any way to enhance the image.' He glanced at Jenny, who had gone white. 'Are you OK, boss?'

'Rewind it to the beginning.'

George did as requested and pressed Play.

'Stop,' Jenny said suddenly and George clicked Pause. On the screen, the car was just turning into the school. From this viewpoint they had a better shot of the driver, and could make out the number plate of the car.

'That's Emma's car; I recognise the plate. Not only that - do you see there?' Jenny pointed to the woman driving; her face was in profile. 'That looks like a row of stitches.'

Jenny hurried out of the front door and ran towards her car, leaving George to thank a bemused-looking Muriel before hurrying after her.

Jenny unlocked the car and grabbed the radio in the centre console. 'Control, this is DI Stone. I need DS Marie detaining on sight.'

* * *

Jenny pushed open the door to the office, George trailing behind her. A few people approached to offer words of comfort or support and some called out questions, but Jenny waved them all away. 'Claire, get me a search warrant for DS Marie's house.'

'Ma'am?'

'Just do it!' Jenny growled.

Claire turned to her computer and got on with the task. There was an edge to Jenny's voice that left any further questions unasked.

'Simon, do we have Emma's DNA on file?'

'We should; we have everyone's on file for crime-scene elimination.'

'Great. Run a comparison with the DNA found at the second crime scene. I want the results as soon as the lab can get them to us.' Jenny turned to face the room. 'Everyone else, briefing room, five minutes.' With that, Jenny strode to DCI Edwards's office, knocked and entered.

'Jennifer,' Edwards said, caught off guard with his phone in one hand.

'Sir, I need to speak to you. It's important.'

DCI Edwards made his apologies down the phone and ended the call. 'Jennifer, I need to speak to you too.' He paused, unable to look her in the eye. 'There's no easy way for me to say this, but you're off the case.' Jenny glared at him and he had the good grace to look ashamed.

'What?' Jenny stepped forward and thumped her palms down on DCI Edwards's desk.

'You need to take a step back. You're too personally involved now, whether you're prepared to admit it or not. This will affect your judgement. I can't have the lead detective on a murder and kidnapping case running around half-cocked.'

'I am not stepping back from this!' Jenny shouted, her chest rising and falling rapidly. 'For God's sake, Tom, they have my fucking daughter!'

'And if something happens to her because you couldn't step back and look at the bigger picture, you'll never be able to forgive yourself!' Edwards shouted back.

Jenny paced to the window and took deep, shaky breaths. He was right. All she could think about right now was getting her hands on Ashley and Emma and choking the life out of the pair of them. She should step back and leave this to somebody else – but she couldn't.

She turned to DCI Edwards. 'You're right,' she told him. 'I should take a step back, but I can't. The reality is that there's nobody else even remotely experienced enough to take this over, especially now that Emma has…' Jenny bit out a curse before taking a deep breath and continuing. 'You could get another detective in, but there isn't time for them to get up to speed. This is due to come to a head *tomorrow!*' She looked him in the eye. 'I'll personally remove myself from the case if I think my judgement is impaired.'

Jenny and Edwards stared at each other for a minute before Edwards sighed. 'I'm not happy about this,' he told Jenny finally.

Jenny, still watching him, let out her breath.

'If you need anything, you only have to ask. Rest assured that you have all our support.'

'Thank you, sir,' Jenny replied with a tight smile. 'The first thing I need is a search warrant signed for Sergeant Marie's residence.'

'Do you really think she could be involved?'

'Yes sir, I do. I have evidence showing that she abducted Sophie from the school earlier today. A neighbouring property caught her on camera arriving at the school and leaving with my daughter shortly afterwards.'

'Shit.'

'I've got Claire raising the paperwork for the warrant and Simon is organising a comparison of the DNA found at the second murder scene with the sample on file for DS Marie. I'm just about to brief the rest of the team.'

Jenny and DCI Edwards got up and made their way to the briefing room. The rest of the team were already waiting and before Jenny even entered the room, she could hear a greater than normal level of chatter. It died down almost instantly as the two senior detectives came in. Jenny took her place at the front, while DCI Edwards stood to one side.

'By now I'm sure most of you have heard that at just after 13:00 this afternoon, my daughter Sophie Stone abducted from Town Park primary school on the outskirts of Sandown. What you may not have heard is that we have a suspect: Detective Sergeant Emma Marie.' With this, the whole room erupted into chatter.

'Quieten down!' DCI Edwards called over the noise.

'With all due respect, ma'am, how sure are we that it's one of our own?' one of the uniformed officers asked from the front row.

'We have footage that shows DS Marie arriving at the school and leaving with my daughter fifteen minutes later. A couple of hours later, I received a message from an unregistered mobile phone informing me that she was being held and that I was to step away from the Amelia Simpson case until after the twenty-fourth.'

'Something doesn't add up, ma'am. If DS Marie is Ashley Johnson, and is responsible for the recent murders, then who rammed the car she was driving and abducted Amelia?'

'We don't have an answer for that yet, but we hope to find one when we search her house.'

'You're good to go on the search warrant, ma'am,' Claire said from the doorway.

'Excellent work, Claire. Simon, Paul, Terri, start working your way through the ANPR footage from around the school; I want to know where Emma went after she left. Claire, get a warrant and put a trace on her mobile. It's almost certainly switched off, but we might get lucky. In the meantime, I'll carry out a search of her home address. George, you're with me.'

* * *

Jenny and George pulled up just down the road from Emma's two-bed terrace and got out of the car; Jenny noted that there was no sign of Emma's Ford Focus.

It was early evening, and the road was starting to fill up as people returned from work, blissfully unaware of the drama

276

unfolding nearby. As much as Jenny loved her job, sometimes she envied those people. To have a job you could just leave at the door at clocking-off time, never worrying that something you did or something you missed might end up being the difference between life and death for someone that you loved was the worst part of the job. Jenny pushed that thought from her mind as she jogged over to the tactical unit. 'I want the house secured as soon as you get through the door.'

The sergeant nodded and the four-man team hurried down the street until they were outside Emma's front door.

'Police! Open up!' the lead officer shouted, pounding on the door with a gloved hand. When no response came the sergeant nodded to the two rear officers, who moved forward with the enforcer. The uPVC door groaned on the first strike, buckled on the second and flew inwards on the third, and the tactical unit stormed in. The noise of the enforcer and the shouting of the officers had drawn a few people out of their houses into the street. 'Police! Get back in your homes!' Jenny shouted, and they dispersed.

'All clear,' came the cry from the back of the house. Jenny and George entered, stepping over the ruined front door and snapping on latex gloves.

Inside, the property looked like any young professional's home. The living room was small but neat, with a blue sofa facing a large widescreen TV, a fireplace with a mirror above it, a collection of photos on the mantelpiece. Jenny went over and picked one up. It showed Emma with a small group of friends, smiling for the camera, clearly on a night out.

George shouted from upstairs. 'Boss, you'd better come up here.'

Jenny took the stairs two at a time and found herself on a small landing with three doors leading off. George was standing by the one at the far end of the landing. His eyes met Jenny's, and she could tell she wouldn't like what she was about to see. She joined him and looked into the room. It had been converted into a study, with a bookshelf against one wall and a desk with a fairly new Apple Mac taking pride of place, but it was the far wall that had drawn the shout from George. The wall was covered in dozens of pictures of Amelia.

[6]

The canteen at St John's secondary school was a large industrial-looking space with cream walls and a large stainless-steel serving area at the far end. At ten past one, it was full of students either waiting to be served or already sitting down with their lunches. Most were chatting about the lessons they had just suffered through or what they had coming up that afternoon. Ashley and her friends had already been served, and were sitting at one of the picnic-style tables near the door.

'I honestly don't know why we bother with history,' Katie complained for the hundredth time, not noticing the other girl's' smirks and rolled eyes – they were used to hearing this complaint from Katie every Tuesday lunchtime. 'It's happened, it's in the past, let it go!'

'After all, who cares what some old guy in a stupid ruff did hundreds of years ago,' Katie and Samantha said at the same time, and Samantha and Erica burst out laughing. They laughed harder as Katie threw one of her chips at Sam in retaliation.

'You OK, Ashley?' Erica asked, when she saw that Ashley wasn't laughing along with them. She was staring intently at a group of girls and boys who were crowded around another girl. They could only make out snatches of what was being said over the noise of the canteen, but none of it sounded friendly.

'Who's that?' Ashley asked, pointing at the girl who seemed to be the focus of the group's attention.

'That's the new girl,' said Katie. They watched as one of the boys said something which made the rest of the group burst out in raucous laughter. The girl at the centre of it looked on the verge of tears.

'What's their problem?' Ashley asked, her brow creasing in a frown.

'Well,' Erica said conspiratorially, leaning in, 'according to Tom in my English class, she's just transferred from a girl's school in Walthamstow, apparently she's gay.'

'And that's why they're picking on her?' Ashley demanded through gritted teeth. Before any of them could answer, Ashley got up and stormed over to the group, pushing her way through so that she was standing beside the trembling girl.

'What the fuck do you think you're doing?' Ashley snapped at the head of the group, a boy in the year above her called Callum. He was just over six feet tall and well on his way to what could be described as stocky. He was a typical bully, with a group of hangers-on who hoped some of his reputation would rub off on them, and didn't dare have any independent thoughts of their own.

'What's it got to do with you, Johnson? She your girlfriend or something?' he replied, looking around his group with a smug grin. They all laughed obediently.

'You think you're a big man, do you? It takes, what, seven of you to belittle one girl for her sexuality? Maybe you're gay yourself and you're struggling to come to terms with it?'

One of the group laughed at this and earned himself a stern look from Callum. He immediately shut up and looked at the ground.

'You want to come round mine, I'll show you just how not gay I am,' Callum sneered.

'Please. I bet you wouldn't have a clue what to do with a real girl. If I see you hassling her again, you'll have me to deal with.'

They locked eyes for a few seconds before he looked away. 'Whatever, I've got better things to do anyway,' he muttered before storming off, his groupies following in his wake.

Ashley turned to the new girl. 'He should stay away from you now. If he doesn't, let me know, OK?'

'Why did you help me?' the girl asked.

Ashley saw her friends staring at her, mouths open and eyes wide, she suppressed a smirk at the sight. She regarded the new girl; she had long red hair and clear blue eyes not unlike her own, but something suggested there was more to her. In spite of herself, Ashley was intrigued.

'Seven people picking on one person just because of who they are, doesn't sit well with me, so I thought I should even the odds a little. Besides, I've had a couple of run-ins with that prick and he's all talk.'

'Well, thank you. They've been hassling me ever since I started here.'

'Is it true what they say? Are you a lesbian?'

The red-haired girl dropped her gaze. 'Yes,' she said, her voice not much louder than a whisper.

'Cool,' Ashley replied.

The new girl looked up sharply. 'It doesn't bother you?'

'Why should it?' Ashley asked, a puzzled look on her face.

'It bothers everyone else. Even my parents keep saying it's just a *phase* I'm going through and I'll get over it.'

'It doesn't bother me who a person is.' Ashley hesitated for a moment. 'Look, do you want to come and sit with me and my friends?'

'If you don't mind?'

Ashley led the red-haired girl over to the table where her friends were watching them with curiosity, and sat down. The red-haired girl hovered for a minute, then sat down too, tension radiating from every movement.

'Sam, Erica, Katie, this is... Shit, I haven't even asked you your name yet have I?'

'It's Emma,' the red-haired girl replied.

* * *

London, February 2013

Ashley kept her hands firmly in the pockets of her parka, removing them only to rub them together in a futile effort to warm them, as she walked from Walthamstow Central station into the cold February evening. The evenings were still dark, and all she could see as her breath fogged around her was a sea of headlights as the last rush-hour traffic crawled to wherever it was heading. She pulled up her hood and hurried on her way, narrowly avoiding a man in a dark suit and a grey peacoat as he darted into the tube station. He cast her an annoyed look, which she returned. Then she increased her pace.

A couple of minutes later she turned off the main road and trudged down Second Avenue. Emma's parents owned a small but tidy terraced house with a small front garden meticulously maintained by Emma's mother. Ashley pushed open the gate and was about to ring the bell when she paused. Even over the ambient noise of East London, she could clearly make out the sounds of raised voices.

'Why won't you listen to what I'm saying?' Emma shouted. Her voice was muffled slightly by the door but she sounded angry. 'How many times do I have to tell you? This isn't a phase I'm going through. I'm not going to *grow out of it,* as you keep insisting. I am a lesbian, Mother: gay. Do you know what that means? It means I'm attracted to girls, not boys. So in future, don't give my phone number to your friends for their sons, just because you can't deal with it!'

'But he's a nice boy, dear. If you give him a chance, I'm sure you'll like him.'

'I can't keep having this argument with you! I'm going out and I don't know when I'll be back.'

The sound of a latch being drawn back startled Ashley, but she managed to take a couple of hasty steps away before the front door was thrown open. Emma charged through it and slammed the door before abruptly stopping as she belatedly spotted that she wasn't alone.

'Sorry,' Ashley said, feeling her face grow hot at having been caught eavesdropping. 'I was just coming to see you. You OK?' she asked gently.

'They can't get their heads around the fact that I'm gay. I think it's their generation; they assume they've done something wrong, or they have to fix what's wrong with me.'

'I don't think there's anything wrong with you,' Ashley muttered quietly. It was barely audible, but Emma caught it and smiled warmly. She reached out and took Ashley's hand.

'You can come and stay at mine for a few days if you like?' Ashley said, and Emma nodded.

* * *

London, June 2013

The rain that had started two days before still beat against the darkened bedroom window, the continuous sound almost soothing. It had been two days since the funeral of Ashley's mother, and she had barely moved from her bed. Her tears had stopped the previous day, but Emma suspected that was more from dehydration than an improvement in her mental condition. She hadn't left Ashley's side since she had phoned her, near hysterical, after finding her mother dead. Emma's parents had tried to reach her a few times, but she simply told them that a friend needed her and she'd be home eventually.

Emma looked round as Ashley sat up and carefully leaned against the headboard. 'How are you doing?' Emma asked as she hurried over and sat on the edge of the bed, taking one of Ashley's hands in her own.

'Better, I think,' Ashley replied, her voice hoarse. She took a gulp from the glass of water Emma had left by the bed. Then she looked up; her eyes were bloodshot and her face gaunt.

'I've lost everything,' she said, her voice barely audible. 'First my dad, and now Mum. I don't even know how long I'll be able to stay in this house.'

'You haven't lost everything. You've still got me,' Emma told her firmly.

Ashley gave her a weak smile and squeezed her hand. 'Mum and Dad are gone though, because of her.'

Emma remained quiet, still holding Ashley's hand, her gaze unreadable.

'If it hadn't been for that *bitch*, Mum and Dad would still be here, and we'd still be a normal, happy family!' She shot out of bed and paced in the small room, her dull eyes wide and bright again, her hands clenching and unclenching at her sides.

'I bet she's oblivious to the pain she's caused me, and Mum! I'm going to kill her for this.' Ashley stopped, suddenly aware of what she'd said, and turned to Emma, her eyes searching her face.

Emma regarded Ashley intently for nearly a minute. Then she rose, crossed the room, and took Ashley's hands in hers. 'No, *we're* going to kill her for this,' she said, with a small smile on her face.

Chapter 33

Amelia continued to scrape at the mortar below the window. She had been at it for hours, and her hand was beginning to cramp. At first she and Dawn had been concerned about the CCTV cameras, sure that as soon as they started that they would be interrupted in their plan, but so far, nothing. They had concluded that if the cameras were real, they weren't being monitored continuously.

'We're getting nowhere!' Amelia cried out in frustration. She jumped down, kicked the upturned bucket across the basement and massaged her sore hand. They had both been working most of the night, and their fingers were aching painfully from gripping the makeshift masonry knife. They'd scoured the basement for anything they could use as a tool and all they had been able to find was the old mattress. After a bit of pulling and ripping they'd been able to make a small tear in one of the corners. After a little more effort, they had managed to work loose a couple of the springs. From there, Amelia had twisted the springs together and begun working at the crumbling mortar straight away.

'Don't say that; you're doing well,' Dawn said, giving Amelia an encouraging smile.

Before Amelia could respond, they heard a car engine, faint at first, then louder, and accompanied by the crunch of gravel. The sound of the engine ceased; then a car door opened and they heard a child crying. It grew louder before a door slammed and the house grew quiet once more.

'We need to hide this!' Amelia muttered, and the two women scrambled around, trying to mask their recent activities. Dawn kicked away the dust that had pooled under the window while Amelia stuffed the homemade knife back into the mattress and flipped it over to hide the damage.

They had barely finished when they heard a bolt being drawn back. The basement door opened and in walked Emma.

'Oh, thank God!' Amelia exclaimed, and turned towards Dawn. 'See, I told you they would find us!' Then she saw the look on Dawn's face: a look not of relief, but terror. Amelia turned back to Emma and saw the gun in her hand, pointing towards them both.

'Emma, what's going on?' said Amelia. But before Emma could answer, a second woman walked in and smiled at the two captives. She was about five foot six, with long brown hair.

Amelia gasped, recognising the woman instantly. 'You're the waitress from the café!' she cried.

'I was wondering if you'd remember me,' the woman said with an evil smile.

Amelia stared at her but couldn't focus on anything other than her pale-blue eyes. Even in the dim light of the basement they looked cruel and hard, like a hawk gazing down at its prey, waiting for the moment to strike. Though she was smiling, the smile didn't reach her eyes. The worst thing was that Amelia had seen eyes like them before; they were a warped, twisted version of her father's eyes, a corruption. Eyes she had once gazed at and loved with all her heart. She couldn't believe she hadn't noticed the similarity in the café. 'You're Ashley,' Amelia said finally.

'Hello, sister,' Ashley replied with a sneer.

'Why have you kidnapped us? What do you want from me?'

'It's pretty simple, really. You took everything I ever loved away from me, and now I'm evening up the score.'

'How could I have done that? I only found out you existed a few days ago.'

Ashley ignored her and walked down the concrete steps until she was standing only a few feet away from Amelia and Dawn. She looked at Amelia for a moment, then turned and regarded Dawn for the first time. 'There's no need for you to die here, you know; my grudge isn't with you,' she said, as Dawn gazed at her with wide eyes. 'You can still save yourself. I'll let you go now, completely unharmed. All you need to do is kill Amelia. You could say that it was self-defence; that she'd kidnapped you and was going to kill you.'

'What? No!' cried Dawn. 'I'm not going to kill anyone!' The blood had drained from her face, and she was shaking.

'That's fine; I didn't really think you had it in you anyway,' said Ashley. Then she turned to Amelia, an evil smile on her lips. 'You, on the other hand, are a different matter. You and me, we're more alike than you realise. After all, it's in your genes; we must get it from dear old Dad. Think about it. Can you honestly say you've never considered taking revenge on someone who's crossed you? Thought about making them pay? What about that other florist, Kirstie? She deserves it. Or maybe that cheating boyfriend of yours?'

She grinned when Amelia didn't immediately answer. 'See, I told you. We're more alike than you realise, and more alike than you'd care to admit, but I can see the truth in your eyes. Tell you what, if you kill your friend Dawn here, I'll let you go. I promise.'

Amelia turned to look at Dawn, who backed away, then turned back to her sister. 'You're wrong; we're not the same. Unlike you, I couldn't hurt an innocent person. You must have gotten your twisted side from your mother, not my father.'

Ashley stormed back up the steps and snatched the gun from Emma's hand, then strode to Amelia and aimed right between her eyes. 'Shut up!' she screamed, her breath coming in ragged bursts. Amelia flinched, but stayed still. 'Don't you dare say that about my mother! She was a wonderful, kind woman!'

After a few seconds, Ashley lowered the gun and took deep, slow breaths. 'No, not yet; tomorrow is the day,' she said, then turned and walked back to the steps.

'What about you?' Amelia called out to Emma. 'Why are you doing this? Is she blackmailing you, or has she promised you something? What is it – money?'

'You haven't got a clue, have you?' Emma sneered. 'She hasn't promised me anything; she doesn't have to. If you love someone, you do whatever you can to make them happy.'

'You're in love?' Amelia asked incredulously.

'I have loved Ashley ever since I first met her. And I had to sit there and watch as her life was torn apart because of you.'

'And what about you?' Amelia said, turning back to Ashley. 'If your mother was so sweet and innocent, what would she think of you now? Of the person you've become?'

'I'll never know what she would have thought, and that's your fault,' Ashley snapped.

'What did I do? How could it possibly be my fault?'

'If it hadn't been for you, my father would have left your

mother years ago and we would have been a proper family. He only stayed with your mother out of some sort of sense of duty towards *you*.'

'He said this, did he?' Amelia asked, folding her arms.

'No, my mother did. A couple of days after Dad died I found Mum drunk in the living room, crying. I tried to comfort her but it was no use, I started crying too. I asked her 'why did Daddy die? Why wasn't he here instead of in that car.' Mum finally told me, through the tears, all about his other life and you, about how he was consumed by the guilt. He really wanted to be here with us but he couldn't leave you. So you see, if you hadn't been in the picture, Daddy would have been with me and Mum that day. He wouldn't have got into that car; he wouldn't have been killed by that truck. Mum was never the same after he died, you know. She was devoted to my father, and when he died a large part of her died with him. He was the love of her life. It broke my heart watching her standing at the back at his funeral, ignored by everyone. She tried after his death, she really did, but life was too hard for her. She got a second job and worked all the extra shifts she could to make ends meet, but it became too much and she gave in.'

Emma put her hand on Ashley's shoulder and gave it a little squeeze. Ashley looked round, smiled the first genuine smile, that Amelia had seen her make and squeezed Emma's hand in return. Then she turned back to Amelia, her face hard and unreadable again.

'You'll never know what it's like to come home and find your mum dead, having slit her own wrists, having obviously decided that you weren't worth living for. Not many people at *her* funeral, not much sympathy for a woman who took her own life and left a teenage girl to fend for herself.'

'Look, I'm sorry about your mum, I really am, but you're wrong about my father,' said Amelia. 'There were obviously aspects of his life I didn't know about, but I do know one thing; he loved my mother with all his heart. Even if I hadn't been around, he would never have left her.'

'I'm sure you really believe that,' Ashley replied, and turned to leave.

'It was you, wasn't it?' said Amelia. 'You killed Megan, and my gran. Even my cat.'

'Maybe it was, maybe it wasn't,' Ashley said, grinning. 'Maybe it was that loser boyfriend of yours. He certainly looks like he has it in him: a real nasty piece of work. I know you're pathetic, but seriously, you must be able to do better than him. He was fucking your best friend right under your nose for months and you didn't suspect a thing. Poor little gullible Amelia. They must have had a right laugh at you when they were lying in your bed together. But that saved his sad little life. When I found out they were having an affair, I realised that his betrayal would hurt you more than if I killed him.'

'So it was you,' Amelia said quietly.

'You know,' Ashley continued, 'Frances called out for you as she died. It was so easy; the knife just slid in. That bloody friend of yours put up a fight, though, despite how drunk she was: a right little scrapper. The little bitch scratched me, which nearly fucked this whole thing up.'

'Why did you have to hurt Gran? What did she ever do to you?' Amelia cried out angrily, tears running down her face.

'You took everything from me; I'm just returning the favour!' Ashley shouted. 'I don't want you to die until you feel the pain I've lived with all these years!'

'Why were you working in the café?' Amelia asked.

'Why do you think?' Ashley sneered. 'To spy on you of course, I needed to learn how best to strike at you. It was so easy to eavesdrop, no one notices a simple waitress. You were always in, either with your gran, that friend of yours or your idiot boyfriend. It was a goldmine of information, easy to keep track of your plans and learn your routines. Better than that though, I soon realised there was an additional opportunity. Not long after that shop down from you opened, Kirstie came in complaining about you to one of her friends and I realised that I could turn that to my advantage. It didn't take much, a couple of words here and there and she was convinced that you were trying to ruin her. After that, all I had to do was continue fanning the flames and leave her to do the rest.'

'Why did we hear crying just before you came down?' asked Dawn. 'Who else is here?'

Ashley looked at Dawn, who took an involuntary step backwards, and frowned. 'That's just our little insurance policy. We wouldn't have needed it if that bloody florist had stayed put like she was meant to.'

Emma leaned forward so that her mouth was by Ashley's ear. 'Ash, we need to get going.'

'Ah yes, our way off this bloody island. Let's go.'

They turned to leave, and at the top of the stairs Ashley faced Amelia once more. 'Don't worry; this will all be over soon. After all, tomorrow is the big day. The anniversary of the day Mum died.' She slammed the basement door and they heard the bolt slide home.

Chapter 34

Jenny rubbed her eyes as she climbed out of the car and walked towards the station. She had finally admitted defeat sometime after eleven the night before, and driven home to try to get a couple of hours' sleep, but it had been no use. She had spent most of the night just lying there, worrying about Sophie.

Despite being bone tired, she just couldn't switch off, her sleep-deprived mind magnifying her fears until they seemed insurmountable. Was Sophie OK, or was she lying somewhere, cold, hungry, and frightened? Was she wondering why Mummy and Daddy hadn't rescued her yet?

Today was the twenty-third, the day when all this was meant to come to a head, and Jenny knew that if they didn't find Sophie alive today then there was a strong possibility that they wouldn't find her alive at all; that they would find her beloved daughter dumped in a shallow grave. She had seen too much during her time in the police to try to convince herself otherwise. She pushed that thought firmly from her mind and gritted her teeth. They were going to find

Sophie and Amelia and bring them both home safely. No other possibility existed.

She entered the building, the desk sergeant giving her a nod, and swiped her badge against the reader before heading into the heart of the station. She dumped her bag and jacket at her desk and made a beeline for the kitchenette. As she walked, she glanced at her colleagues, and was gratified to see that most looked as bad as she felt. She wasn't the only one burning the midnight oil on this one; this was personal for them all.

'Boss,' Simon shouted across the room, coming to join Jenny as she poured herself a large black coffee and dumped in extra sugar. 'We've had the report back from the lab. There wasn't a match between the sample recovered from the second crime scene and Emma's.'

'Shit,' Jenny muttered. 'Can you round everyone up, please. I want them in the briefing room in five minutes.' Simon nodded and left, leaving Jenny alone with her thoughts.

After finishing her first coffee and pouring herself a second, Jenny walked into the briefing room to find the atmosphere muted. She understood; everybody was still reeling from the news that they had all been fooled so completely by one of their own.

'Good morning, everyone,' Jenny said as she made her way to the front. 'As I'm sure you're all aware, today is the twenty-third: the date on the note. Today is when I expect Ashley to carry out whatever it is she has planned, so the bottom line is that we need to find and stop her today.'

'Did you find anything to indicate where Sophie or Amelia are being held while searching Emma's house, ma'am?' someone called from near the back.

'Nothing yet, no, although I am going back this morning. The main items of interest were the photos of Amelia in the back room. We also recovered a large collection of keys in an envelope taped under a desk drawer. Her personal computer has been seized, and is with our tech guys now. Simon has also heard back from the lab. The sample on file for Emma doesn't match the sample recovered from Megan's house, so we're obviously dealing with at least two people.'

'Are we sure they're working together?' asked a uniformed officer.

'Based on the collection of photos found, I would say we are,' Jenny replied.

'Any hits on her bank cards or phone?'

'No. The cards haven't been used, and Emma's personal and work mobiles have been switched off since yesterday lunchtime. Likewise, there hasn't been any action on the burner phone that was used to send me the message about Sophie.'

'What's the plan then, boss?' said Simon, who was sitting at the front.

'DC Bancroft and I will go back to Emma's; there must be something there which will give us a clue to where she's gone. We know she never went back there after she snatched Sophie, and by now she'll know that we're on to her, so I doubt she'll risk coming back. In the meantime, Simon, I want you and your team to continue searching through the traffic cameras; we need leads on where Emma went after she left the school. Claire, I want you to get a warrant and pull her financial records; see if she's made any payments lately for a second rental property or a holiday home. And comb through her social media; see if any places that could be used to stash two to three captives stand out. Radio the moment any of you have anything.' She surveyed the room. 'I'm sure I don't have to remind any of you what is at stake here.'

* * *

Jenny and George climbed out of their car and walked over to the second, unmarked patrol car. At their approach, two officers climbed out of the front seats. 'Anything?' Jenny asked the lead officer.

'Sorry, ma'am, nothing all night.'

'I can't say I'm surprised; she's smarter than that. Thanks anyway, guys.' Jenny walked to the house, ducked under the blue and white crime-scene tape and went in, pulling on latex gloves, with George following suit.

She headed upstairs and went to the back room. The collection of photos was still pinned to the wall. Jenny studied them; there were photos of Amelia with Frances, Amelia out drinking with Sam and Megan, working in her shop and even standing on the balcony of her home, holding a glass of red wine. She went into the main bedroom and frowned. There were two bedside tables, one either side of the bed, and while that wasn't especially out of the ordinary, both looked as if they were used fairly frequently. Both had an alarm clock; one had a well-thumbed paperback while the other had a Kindle. She couldn't speak for everyone, but whenever Greg was away and she had the bed to herself, she kept to the same side, never spreading out and certainly never swapping sides. Jenny went through to the en-suite. Sure enough, two toothbrushes stood in a cup above the sink.

She headed back out into the hallway. 'George,' she called, 'was Emma seeing anyone?'

'I'm not sure, to be honest,' George replied, coming up to join her. 'She never brought anyone to any of our work events and she's never mentioned anyone, but she was hardly one for volunteering personal information. Why do you ask?'

Jenny didn't answer. Instead, she pushed past him and headed downstairs to the living room. She went over to the fireplace and scanned the row of photos. One must have been taken at her police college graduation; she could make out a younger Emma in the second row, wearing full-dress uniform, beaming. She picked up the photo next to it, of Emma with a group of five or six other people, all smiling, dressed in thick coats, scarves and gloves. One of the girls was making the peace sign and another was wearing a flamboyant hat with '2022!' printed on it. It was night, and a full moon was visible in the background. Behind the group, to one side, a bonfire was roaring away.

'George, come and have a look at this,' Jenny called out, still studying the photo. As George entered, she handed him the photo. 'Do you know where this was taken?'

He studied it for a minute before shaking his head and handing it back. 'Doesn't ring any bells, I'm afraid.'

'Look at those pillars and that gate in the background. Does that look like Knighton Gorges to you?'

'What's Knighton Gorges?'

'How long have you lived here, George? It's the site of an old manor out Knighton way. If I'm not mistaken, that's the entrance.'

'Is the manor occupied?'

'It doesn't exist anymore. If I remember correctly, it was demolished in 1821 by the owner, to prevent his daughter from inheriting it after she married against his will. The whole area is supposedly haunted.'

George stared at her. 'How do you know that?'

'Greg teaches history. He started looking into the history of the island when we moved here; he was fascinated by the place.'

Jenny put the photo back and crossed the room. In the corner of the living room, next to the window, was a bookshelf. On it were a couple more photos and one or two plants, but for the most part it was full of books. Jenny scanned the titles before pulling one out. It was a book on the paranormal, and the one next to it was all about ghost hunting. Jenny flicked through the pages before putting them back on the shelf. 'Let's head back to the station.'

* * *

Jenny strode into the main office, forgoing her usual detour to the kitchenette. She continued until she was standing behind Claire, her hands resting on the back of her chair. 'How are you getting on?' she asked.

'I've got access to Emma's finances. There are no signs of any deposits paid to a holiday company, or any additional rent other than for her house, but I have found something. Over the last three months, she's withdrawn three lots of ten grand.'

'That would explain why we haven't detected any activity on her cards; she's been paying cash.'

'We've got something over here, boss,' someone shouted. Jenny and Claire looked up to find Simon beckoning them over, a smile on his face. Jenny, Claire and George headed over. 'We've had a hit on Emma's car. It was recorded heading down Morton Road, out of Sandown heading towards Ryde, at 13:30 yesterday afternoon.'

'That would be straight after she snatched Sophie,' said George.

'OK, where does she go from there?' Jenny asked.

'That's the only shot we've recovered so far. We've checked all the cameras on the way in to Ryde and Newport at the approximate times a car would have arrived there, and so far, nothing.'

'Let's regroup,' said Jenny. 'Emma's abduction of Sophie feels rushed to me. Everything Ashley or Emma have done until now has been well planned and well executed. Hell, if it hadn't been for Megan Parkinson scratching Ashley before she was killed, we wouldn't even know Ashley existed.'

She paused, looking at the group. 'So I don't think kidnapping Sophie was part of the original plan. The text sent to my phone sounds desperate. Emma must have known we would be able to identify her as soon as she snatched Sophie, which would explain why she made no effort to hide her identity. She would also know that we'd try to trace her car, so she'd get it off the road as soon as possible. There's no way she would have been able to avoid every camera and patrol car for long. Claire, can you check if we've had any reports of stolen cars from around the Morton Road area yesterday afternoon?'

Claire headed to her desk and picked up her phone. A minute later she returned, shaking her head. 'Afraid not.'

Jenny felt sure they were missing a crucial piece of the puzzle, but her sleep-deprived mind wasn't as sharp as usual. After a moment, an idea came to her, and she smiled before heading to her desk. 'George, you're with me,' she called as she grabbed her car keys and hurried to the door.

* * *

Jenny pulled onto Morton Road and spotted what she was looking for. Just in front of them, on the right hand side, was a second-hand car dealership. Jenny swung her car into the forecourt, killed the engine, and she and George climbed out. They had barely closed their doors before a salesman came out of the main showroom. He was mid-twenties, if that, and wearing a suit that Jenny guessed he would grow into eventually. 'What is it you're looking for?' he asked them both in his best sales patter.

Jenny looked at George, who was trying his best to suppress a smile. She turned back to the eager salesman and showed him her warrant card. His smile immediately vanished, replaced by the kind of fear she often saw when lay people were confronted unexpectedly by the police. 'Can we speak to your manager, please?' Jenny asked, putting away her card.

'O-of course,' the salesman replied, and led them through the door from which he had emerged. Inside, he took them into an office and gestured towards a couple of empty seats before disappearing. A minute later, he reappeared with his manager in tow.

'How can I help you, officers?' the manager asked, taking a seat on the other side of the desk and leaning forward. 'My name's Ted Parry, and I'm the manager and owner here.'

'Have you sold any cars in the last twenty-four hours?' Jenny asked.

'We've sold a couple.'

'Was one of those to a woman in her mid to late twenties, about five foot six, with pale skin and long red hair?'

'Yeah, we had a woman like that in yesterday afternoon; quite a looker, if I remember right. She came in with her daughter.' The manager's forehead creased into a frown.

'What is it?' Jenny asked.

'It was a bit odd, now I think back.'

'How so?'

'She was in a hurry; she didn't even want to test drive it. She paid cash, got in and left.'

'Do you have any CCTV here?'

'Yeah, we've got cameras covering the forecourt.' He fired up the computer, clicked away, then turned the screen around for Jenny and George and hit play. About fifteen seconds in, they saw the now-familiar Ford Focus drive past, slowing down and moving out of shot. A moment later, Emma walked into view. She stopped, crouched down in front of Sophie, and said something to her. Sophie nodded once and wiped her eyes. Obviously satisfied, Emma headed towards the showroom door, holding onto Sophie's hand, the young girl's head bowed. George glanced at Jenny. Her hands were clenched on the table, knuckles white, her lips a thin line. A vein stood out on her neck.

A salesman approached and started to talk to Emma, but there was no audio. Emma entered the building and Ted fast-forwarded the video. After twenty minutes, Emma and Sophie reappeared, climbed into a car at the edge of the forecourt and drove off, carrying on the way she had been heading.

'I need the registration and make for the car you sold them now!' Jenny barked. The manager quickly checked his records, jotted down the details, and handed them to Jenny. 'George, radio these in. We need to find this car now!' George nodded, took the details from Jenny and stepped out of the office.

'Could we speak to the salesman who sold them the car?' Jenny asked.

'Sure, give me a minute.' Ted disappeared, then returned a few minutes later with the salesman who had approached them initially. He sat down, still looking nervous.

'I'm told you sold a car to this woman,' Jenny said, gesturing towards the paused video.

'Yeah, that was me.'

'Tell me about the woman. How did she seem to you?'

'She seemed tense. She asked what cars we had available for a couple of grand. I listed a few and she said she'd take the first one. By the time I came back with the keys and the paperwork she had already counted out the cash; she didn't try to haggle or anything.'

'Why didn't you question her? Carry out some checks?' Jenny could feel her blood pressure rising, and fought to keep the anger out of her voice.

'I work on commission and a sale's a sale,' he replied, with a shrug.

'Did she show you any ID for the purchase?'

'Yeah, of course. They have to, with a part exchange.'

Jenny's eyes widened. 'A part exchange? So you still have the car?'

'Sure,' said Ted. 'We haven't had a chance to process it yet. It's still out back.'

Jenny didn't reply. Instead, she sprang out of her seat, prodding at her phone. 'Simon, we've got the car. We're at Ted's Autos, at the bottom of Morton Road in Sandown. I need a forensic team here now!'

Chapter 35

Amelia, perched on top of the upturned bucket, scratched furiously at the mortar around the window frame. Her hands were aching and bloody, but she pushed the pain from her mind. The night had come and gone, and there was still no sign of Ashley or Emma. Amelia knew that wouldn't last, though. If she and Dawn didn't escape and raise the alarm before they returned, her sister would kill them both.

Amelia flexed her tired, sore hands, trying to massage some life into them. They had made good progress since the previous afternoon, taking it in turns to work on the window, and they could now rock the whole frame in the wall, but it still refused to come away completely.

'Are you OK?' Dawn asked, her dark-brown hair covered in mortar dust, all efforts to hide their activity gone.

'Yeah, I just need a minute,' Amelia replied, shaking her hands to get the blood flowing through her aching fingers. Her hair and face were as dusty as Dawn's. She shook her head and coughed as she inhaled some dust.

Groaning, she forced herself to climb back on the bucket and continue scraping at the window. Thirty minutes later, after a lot of pulling and swearing, the window and its frame came away and crashed to the floor, the glass shattering on impact, causing Dawn to jump back with a shriek.

'You did it!' Dawn cried and rushed over to hug Amelia, shattered glass crunching underfoot.

'Dawn, if you can give me a boost up then I'll go round and unbolt the basement door.'

'What if they're in the house?'

'I don't think they can be. I haven't heard the car since they left yesterday, and I imagine they'd have come running by now with all the noise we've just made.'

'Yeah, I think you're right. OK. Give me your foot and be careful.'

Amelia stepped back onto the bucket and reached up to the hole left by the now-departed window, then put her left foot on Dawn's linked fingers. Dawn pushed upwards with a grunt and Amelia heaved herself through the narrow gap, her fingers scrabbling in the grass outside as she tried to find purchase. After a lot of swearing and wriggling, she managed to pull herself out and onto the grass.

For a moment Amelia just lay there, breathing in the cool clean air and enjoying the feel of the sun on her upturned face. She had only been in the basement for a few days, but it felt much longer. Though she wanted to lie there and rest, she didn't dare; she didn't know how much time they had left, and they couldn't afford to waste any of it. She scrambled to her feet and took in the scene; she was at the side of the house, with a strip of overgrown grass in front of her, and beyond were trees as far as she could see.

She hurried to the front of the house. Amelia guessed that the building had once been beautiful; bay windows stood either side of a double-sized front door and porch. There were three large sash windows on the first floor. The front of the house must have been covered in white render once, but like the basement, that had long since started to fall away, and what was left was covered in graffiti. Both the downstairs bay windows had been smashed, and so had most of the upstairs windows. Amelia looked behind her to a rough gravel path, littered with weeds, leading to a rusted iron gate and more trees either side, which looked to be the only way in or out of the property.

Amelia turned back to the house and hurried towards the front door. She tried the handle, and was surprised to find that it wasn't locked. She stepped inside the house and looked around.

The hall was as run-down as the exterior. To her right, a set of steps led to the first floor with a rickety, broken banister on the near side with more than half of the balusters missing or broken. To her left was a door leading to what she guessed was probably a living room. Past the stairs, there was a door to the right and a third at the end of the hall. The hall itself was wallpapered in a horrible yellow and brown floral design that Amelia assumed must have been fashionable once, but certainly not in her lifetime. The paper had faded with age and hung down in places, and a smell of damp seemed to come from the walls themselves.

Amelia moved forward cautiously and glanced into the first room. The walls were decorated with the same wallpaper as the hall, a rotting brown sofa stood by the window, and the fireplace was filled with dead leaves and rubbish. Amelia thought for a minute. If the entrance to the basement was going to be anywhere then she suspected that it would be directly off or near the kitchen.

She carried on past the living room and pushed open the door at the far end of the hall. As she had suspected, it led to the kitchen, which was in an even worse condition than the rest of the house so far. Half the cabinet doors were either lying on the floor or missing. One cabinet had fallen from the wall, taking most of the plaster with it, and the sink was filled with a murky brown liquid that Amelia didn't want to guess at or dare to get too near. In the far corner was the basement door, looking even more out of place in the ruined interior than it had in the basement, its clean, polished surface in stark contrast to its dilapidated surroundings.

Amelia ran to it. Two sturdy bolts held it closed, one at the top and one at the bottom. To Amelia's relief, neither was padlocked and they slid back smoothly. The bolts drawn, she pulled the door, which opened easily on well-oiled hinges.

'You did it, Amelia!' Dawn cried as she ran out, her face flushed with relief.

'Come on, let's get out of here.' Amelia started to run back the way she had come, Dawn following close behind.

She stopped suddenly as they reached the front door, causing Dawn to nearly crash into her. 'Do you hear that?' she asked quickly.

'Hear what?' Dawn replied, glancing around nervously.

Amelia held a hand up and they both listened. At first the only sound came from the birds in the trees, but after a moment they could hear something else as well: a faint whimpering coming from inside the house.

Dawn's eyes narrowed and she looked back towards the stairs. 'What's that?'

'The crying we heard yesterday!' Amelia said, a feeling of dread threatening to overcome her. 'Their *insurance policy*.'

She turned and cautiously climbed the rickety stairs, listening intently. After a glance at the driveway, Dawn followed.

At the top of the stairs, Amelia took in the scene. There were three doors to the left and two to the right. On the left, the nearest door was hanging precariously by one hinge and another door was missing entirely. The room at the end was intact, the door closed. To the right, both doors were intact and closed; however, the one at the end was much newer and secured with a padlock. Amelia hurried down and tried the door, but it held firm.

'Hello?' she called. 'Is anyone in there?'

The whimpering ceased, replaced by silence. Then a small, scared voice said, 'Hello?'

'My name's Amelia, and I'm going to try to get you out of there, I just need you to be brave for a few more minutes.' Amelia tried the door again, pushing it with her shoulder, but it refused to budge. She hurried back to Dawn. 'We need something sturdy!' she said in a rush.

'Why? Who's in there?'

'I don't know, but it sounds like a young girl and she's scared.' Amelia took Dawn's trembling hands in hers. 'Dawn, I need you to leave the house and raise the alarm while I look for something to break the lock.'

'I want to stay with you! Surely it'll be easier with two of us?'

'Ashley and Emma could come back at any moment. If we haven't got the door open by then, they'll pull their gun and that'll be it. If one of us escapes and raises the alarm, there's still hope. I'm not leaving without this girl. Who knows what they'll do to her.'

After a moment's hesitation, Dawn gave Amelia a small nod. 'Good luck.' She went downstairs and out of the house. As soon as her feet hit the gravel drive, she broke into a run.

As soon as Dawn had left, Amelia went to the nearest door and flung it open. Inside was a double bedroom, empty except for a broken wardrobe. She opened the wardrobe door; it was empty and Amelia slammed the door in frustration. She tried the remaining rooms; they too were empty.

Amelia hurried downstairs and paused while she considered her options. She hadn't seen anything in the first room, and the kitchen looked as sparse, so that left one option, the door under the stairs. Amelia cautiously pushed it open. Like the rest of the house, the room was in ruins. Part of the wall had collapsed, revealing the beams behind it, and glass and stones lay by the broken window. Amelia turned to leave, and as she did, spotted an old lamp tucked away in the corner. The lampshade had long since rotted away, with only the thin metal frame remaining. Amelia hefted it; while it smelt funny, it felt solid enough for her purposes.

Realising that she didn't have much else in way of options and with no time to continue the search, she ran back upstairs to the locked room. 'I'm going to try to break the lock. Stand back from the door!' she called.

She waited, and when she didn't get a reply she lifted the lamp and brought the base down hard on the wood above the lock. The crash reverberated around the whole house, sounding even louder in the silence that it had replaced.

The second and third strikes looked to have no effect, and Amelia brought the lamp down once more. She was sweating and her breathing had become laboured but she refused to quit. The fourth strike split the wood around the lock; the fifth strike separated the door from the padlock. Amelia threw down the lamp and quickly made her way inside.

She scanned the room; there was a single mattress on the floor, and in the far corner sat a small, scared-looking girl. She wore school uniform and her long blonde hair was matted and tangled. Her legs were drawn up to her chest, with her skinny arms wrapped tightly around them. She gazed at Amelia over the tops of her knees with red-rimmed eyes. Her face was grubby and there were traces of tears on her cheeks.

Amelia crossed the room and crouched in front of the girl so that their faces were level. 'I need you to come with me. We need to get out of here before the bad people come back.'

She stood up, but the girl stayed where she was, fresh tears running down her face. Amelia crouched down again. 'You don't need to be afraid anymore; I'm going to get you out of here.'

'My mum says I should never talk to strangers,' the girl replied in a small voice.

'Your mother sounds like a very smart woman, and she's right. You shouldn't, normally, but the scary woman who brought you here also brought me here, and they'll come back soon. If we're still here when they return, they'll lock us up again. You don't want that, do you?'

The girl shook her head.

'Why don't you take my hand, and we'll leave together. My name's Amelia. Can you tell me yours?'

'Sophie.'

'Well, Sophie, shall we leave this horrible room?'

'My mum says I should never go anywhere with strangers.'

'She's right about that too. She sounds like a very smart woman your mum and I would really like to get you home to her again. Why don't we go and find her together?' Amelia tried to keep her tone light, to keep the urgency threatening to overwhelm her at bay.

Just as Amelia thought she might have to carry the girl away, Sophie came to a decision. She nodded and climbed to her feet.

'Good girl,' Amelia said, relief washing over her.

Sophie clasped Amelia's outstretched hand, and they hurried down the stairs and through the front door into the sunshine. Amelia let out a small cry of triumph, but it was short-lived. A moment later, there was a sound of gravel crunching under car tyres, and a car engine growing louder.

[7]

Reading, January 2016

'Dammit!' Ashley cried in frustration as she slammed the laptop closed. She stood up from the small, cluttered desk and stalked over to the window, her expression as dark as her mood.

'Still no luck, then?' Emma asked as she came through the front door of the studio flat and dumped her backpack on the floor.

They had been living in the cramped apartment in Reading for a little over a year. Ashley was glad they didn't have much in the way of belongings as it was tiny. She could lean over from the end of the bed and touch the kitchen cupboards, and the far wall was not much further away. It was all they could afford, though, so they made do. Emma's parents had given Emma the deposit but they couldn't help further. They couldn't understand why Emma didn't just flat-share with a couple of other girls and get a proper place, but she had claimed that she needed her independence. They didn't know about her and Ashley, or that they were living together. They had a small flatscreen TV in the corner and an old, battered five-drawer tallboy that held most of their clothes, the rest hanging from a makeshift washing line. Apart from a few pots and pans and groceries, the only other items in the flat were a flat-pack desk, a lamp, and Emma's old computer.

'Still no luck,' Ashley confirmed. 'It's the damn privacy settings; unless you happen to be friends with a person then it won't show you any information, and I can't add every single Amelia Simpson in the UK. If that's even still her name. For all I know, she's managed to convince some poor sap to marry her and now she's not even a Simpson anymore.'

'Have you tried anything besides Facebook? Twitter, or a Google search?'

'Yeah. Twitter has the same kind of settings and Google throws up too many possibilities. I just have too little to go on. I don't even know what she looks like now.' Ashley sighed and sat down on their double bed. Emma kicked off her shoes, came to sit next to her and put an arm round her. Ashley leaned her head against Emma's shoulder, whose long red hair was still damp from the rain outside, and sighed again.

'Don't worry, we'll find her,' Emma said, giving her a little squeeze.

'Will we? We've been looking for months now and we've got nowhere!'

They fell silent, and for a few minutes the only sounds were the gentle patter of rain against the window and the couple two doors down arguing yet again. They had been for months, and Emma wished they would just break up and be done with it. Ashley had wanted to go round and shut them up, but she had managed to talk her out of it. Not because

Emma liked them; quite the contrary, she was fed up with them as well. But she couldn't risk causing a scene and the police catching up with Ashley.

When she'd had turned up at Emma's house and told her that she had killed Steve, Emma had been furious. Not because of the murder – she couldn't care less about some stuck-up quack – but because it wasn't been part of the plan. After all, Ashley could hardly take revenge on the woman who had ruined her life from inside a prison cell. So Emma had bundled Ashley away from her parents' house, given her enough money for a couple of nights in a cheap hotel room, and told her to buy an unregistered pay-as-you-go phone.

A few days later, Emma crept out of the house. Sure enough, in their old favourite spot just along the Hertford Union canal, she found an envelope tucked under some small rocks behind a bin. Inside was a note with a mobile phone number and the planning began, safe from prying eyes. A few weeks later, Emma started her course at Reading College and moved out of her parents' home. She'd only been in the flat a day when there was a knock at the door. When she answered, there was Ashley, a huge grin on her face.

Emma turned her head and looked down at Ashley, her head still laying against her shoulder. 'Look, I've had an idea,' she said finally.

Ashley lifted her head and looked at her, curious.

'This thing with your sister. It doesn't have to be right away, does it?'

'No. I've waited this long; what's a bit longer? As long as she's made to pay eventually, I can bide my time. What are you thinking?'

'Like you said, we've had no luck tracking her down online. We need a better means of searching, and who has the best resources for tracking people down?'

Ashley shrugged. 'You tell me.'

'The police.'

'The police?' Ashley asked, a lopsided smile on her face. 'In case you've forgotten, I'm trying to stay away from them. They'd love a little chat with me.'

'I didn't mean you. I meant me.'

'You? Join the police?' Ashley smirked and her blue eyes sparkled with amusement.

'You can't, for obvious reasons, but they're not looking for me. No one knows we're together; not my parents, or even that nosey bitch Mrs Riley. As far as they're concerned, I haven't seen or heard from you in years. We'd have to be careful, sure, but think about it. Their national computer system would be able to find her, and once we know where she is, we can plan. Best of all, once you've killed her, if I can get myself into the investigation then I could lead them in the wrong direction. And once we're done, I don't have to stay with them. I can quit, and we could find ourselves a nice little cottage somewhere far away. We could start again.'

'You'd do that for me?'

'Of course I would. I've seen how hard the last two and a half years have been: what that bitch has cost you. I want to make her pay almost as much as you do.'

Chapter 36

Jenny paced the floor of the service centre, stopping only to stare at the forensic team, who were bagging another item from Emma's car. It took all her willpower not to go and ask Sunil for another update on their progress. She'd been over to see him three times in the last twenty minutes, and his patience was wearing thin. It was only because he knew what was at stake that he hadn't asked her to leave the scene. The last thing she needed was to put him or his team off their work.

Hold on, Sophie, I'll find you, Jenny thought for the tenth time that hour. She dug out her phone and rang Greg to update him.

When she'd finished, George appeared and handed her a mug of coffee, which she accepted gratefully, continuing to watch the CSIs at work. They had been at Ted's Autos for nearly an hour. Jenny could feel the day ticking away, minute by agonising minute.

The second-hand car showroom had been closed; two patrol cars and the forensic team's van sat on the forecourt and a couple of uniformed officers had been posted to turn away potential customers or curious onlookers. Jenny had taken a statement from the salesman who'd dealt with Emma, then the rest of the staff had been sent home. Only the manager remained, staring at the unfolding action from the front office with barely concealed curiosity.

'We're going to get her back, you know,' George told Jenny as she sipped her coffee and winced at its cheap, bitter taste. Jenny nodded, and continued to stare at the forensic technicians.

Sunil broke off from the group and came over to the two detectives, lowering the hood of his white forensic suit. 'So far, we've recovered a large number of clothing fibres from the driver's seat and the rear seats, along with a few strands of hair.'

'Anything we can use to track her?' she asked anxiously.

'There was quite a lot of mud in the tyre treads and wheel arches, as well as in the footwells of the front seats.'

Jenny opened her mouth to speak but Sunil raised a hand and she closed it again. 'Before you ask, I've already sent one of my team to the lab with a sample for immediate analysis; it should be there now.'

'Thanks, Sunil,' Jenny said gratefully. He nodded and went to rejoin his team.

Jenny stood for a moment, thinking. 'I suspect the original plan was for either Kirstie or Sam to take the rap for the murders, but that plan started to unravel when Megan took a swipe at her attacker.' Jenny stared at the car, one hand resting on her hip, the other holding her coffee. 'I also think that Emma wanted us to waste our time investigating Kirstie. That's why she was so keen that we didn't release her. Emma and Ashley must have known we would be on to them almost immediately after they snatched Sophie. That's why they dumped the car straight afterwards, to slow us down. Even with a new car, though, she would have wanted to get off the road quickly, so it's not unreasonable to assume that she took Sophie somewhere nearby.'

Jenny suddenly turned and strode to the front office; George had to jog to keep up with her. 'I need to use your computer,' she told the manager, looming over him.

'Yes, of course,' he replied quickly, moving before Jenny could push him out of the way.

George went round the desk. Jenny had opened a browser and she was staring at a road map of the local area. 'We know Emma left Sandown and was heading for Newport via the back roads. That makes sense; she'd want to stay under the radar for as long as possible. She'd also want to stay away from populated areas. It would be far too risky to hold a child near other houses; too many potential witnesses, and someone would be bound to report an unknown, struggling child.'

'We've got people combing through ANPR images for the new car, but it's a long shot,' said George. 'Especially if she took the back roads, as you suspect.'

Jenny didn't reply. She continued to stare at the map, frowning.

'What are you thinking?' George asked.

'The photo from Emma's house, the one on the mantelpiece.'

'What about it?'

'Where was it taken?'

'You said it looked like Knighton Gorges.'

Jenny moved the cursor and zoomed in, then angled the screen so that George could see it better.

'Here.' She pointed at the screen. 'This is Knighton, and that-' She pointed again. 'That's the entrance to Knighton Gorges.' She zoomed out and pointed at a different place. 'And *this* is where we are,' she said, eyes sparkling.

'That isn't far,' said George, 'and it looks pretty secluded.

I wonder if there are any abandoned properties or empty holiday homes in the area?'

'You can check on the way!' Jenny cried, already running to the car.

* * *

George clutched the grab handle as Jenny took the car around a narrow bend, barely missing a grey Honda Civic coming the other way. 'Slow down!' he yelled, but his voice was drowned out by the other car's horn as they hurtled down the country lane, the passenger-side wing mirror skimming the hedge.

Jenny ignored him and gripped the steering wheel even tighter.

The radio in the centre console crackled to life and George snatched it up, telling Jenny to keep her eyes on the road. 'DC Bancroft.'

'George, it's Claire. We've had a hit on the new car registration.'

Jenny grabbed the radio. 'Claire, it's me. What have you got?'

'One of the traffic cameras recorded it turning off Braiding Down, heading towards Knighton. Where are you?'

'We think they're being held in a holiday home or an abandoned property around Knighton Gorges. We're on our way there now, ETA five minutes.'

'I'll mobilise an armed response unit, but the quickest they could be there is twenty minutes.'

'Understood.'

Jenny put down the radio and sped along the road, overtaking a Mini crawling along at ten miles an hour below the speed limit. Jenny flashed the driver an annoyed glance as she passed and received one back.

'The plan is to wait for the tactical unit, right boss?'

George asked, his eyes not leaving the road and his hand still gripping the grab handle.

Jenny didn't reply, which was answer enough for George.

'You can't do this alone. We need to wait for the armed response unit.'

'They have captives, including my daughter. I can't afford to wait. If I wait and they hurt her...' Her voice trailed off and her lips thinned.

They reached the bottom of Braiding Down and Jenny turned hard left onto the road into Knighton, the tyres screeching in protest.

'There on the left, that's Knighton Gorges,' Jenny said, pointing towards the stone pillars and gate they had seen in the background of Emma's photo.

A woman ran out into the road, waving her arms frantically. Jenny stamped on the brakes and wrenched the steering wheel to the right, causing the back end to slide. She regained control and slowed the car to a stop, narrowly missing the woman.

'Wait, isn't that-' George said, looking over his shoulder, but Jenny was already out of the car.

'Please! I need help!' Dawn sobbed as Jenny reached her.

'You're Dawn, aren't you? Amelia's friend?' Jenny asked, and Dawn recoiled from her. 'Relax,' Jenny said as she reached into her jacket and pulled out her warrant card. 'My name's Detective Inspector Jennifer Stone and I'm a police officer.'

'Oh, thank God!' Dawn cried as tears of relief streamed down her face. For a moment Jenny thought the young woman might collapse, but she managed to stay on her feet.

Jenny grasped Dawn by the shoulders and gave her a little shake, startling her into silence. 'I need you to keep it together,' Jenny told her firmly. 'Can you do that for me?'

Dawn nodded, eyes wide.

'Good. Now where are Amelia and Sophie?'

'I don't know about a Sophie, but Amelia is up there,' she replied, pointing behind her at the gravel path leading from the iron gate. 'She was trying to free a trapped little girl and she sent me to get help. We need to get back up there!'

'An armed tactical unit is on the way; they'll be here soon.'

'You don't understand!'

Jenny frowned. 'What don't I understand?'

'Their car passed me on my way down. I hid in the trees, so they didn't see me, but they'll be back at the house by now!'

'Dawn, wait here and let the rest of my team know where to go,' Jenny shouted as she ran round to the driver's side, climbed in and started the engine.

'What about the tactical unit?' George cried as he climbed back into the front seat next to her.

'We don't have time!' Jenny shouted as she put the car into gear.

Chapter 37

Amelia and Sophie had only made it a few steps from the house when the car rounded the bend and screeched to a halt. The driver's side door was flung open and Ashley jumped out, a gun already in her hand. In two quick strides, she was at the gate.

Emma opened the passenger-side door, climbed out, and leaned on the open door, a thoughtful expression on her face as she watched Amelia and the advancing Ashley.

'How did you get free?' Ashley demanded as she raised the Glock 19 pistol, racked back the slide and pointed it at Amelia's head. Amelia stopped and carefully raised her hands. 'Not that it matters, I suppose,' Ashley continued. 'I can kill you just as easily here as I could down in that basement.' Then her eyes widened and she spat out a curse. 'Where is she?' she snapped.

'Who?' Amelia replied, with an innocent expression.

'Don't give me that crap. You know who! That fucking friend of yours.'

Amelia smiled triumphantly at Ashley. 'She's gone to

raise the alarm.' She looked at Emma. 'Even as we speak, the rest of your colleagues are probably on their way.'

'Even if that's true, I'll still get the pleasure of killing you,' shouted Ashley. 'I'll go to prison happy, knowing that you died at my hands. I'll still have won.' She took a step forward, holding the gun steady. The only sound was her breathing, which was coming out in ragged, shallow bursts.

'I need you to be brave, OK,' Amelia whispered to Sophie as she pushed the girl behind her, out of sight of the gun aimed at Amelia. Ashley's finger moved to the trigger and Amelia closed her eyes, waiting for the end to come.

The silence was shattered by the sound of crunching gravel, faint at first, but quickly growing louder. Amelia's eyes snapped open. A moment later, a second car sped around the corner in a shower of dust and braked to a sudden halt. Before the dust had settled, the driver's door was flung open and Jenny was on her feet.

'Police!' she yelled. 'Drop the weapon and put your hands above your head!'

Amelia, still shielding Sophie, risked a glance towards Ashley and Emma. Ashley was still pointing the gun at her, but there was no sign of Emma. The passenger-side door was still open, but the sergeant was nowhere to be seen.

'Mum?' Sophie asked as she cautiously peeked out from behind Amelia, hope blossoming across her young face.

'Sophie, honey, I need you to stay where you are. Don't make any sudden movements,' Jenny called out.

'One more step and they're both dead!' Ashley shouted, her gun still on Amelia.

'You can still walk away from this. No one has to get hurt,' Jenny answered, fighting to keep her voice calm, trying to draw Ashley's focus towards her.

Back at the car, George carefully opened the passenger

side door and crept out, moving in the opposite direction to Jenny. He hadn't made it more than a couple of metres when a gun was pressed to the back of his head. He swore under his breath and stopped.

'Don't even think about it,' Emma said calmly and he slowly raised his hands.

'I was wondering where you were,' Jenny called out towards Emma. 'How could you do this, Emma? How could you betray your friends and colleagues, all that you stand for, like this?'

'What I stand for?' Emma replied, with a mocking laugh. 'You really don't get it, do you? This has just been a means to an end. I don't give a damn about you or the police; I'm here to make sure Ashley gets the revenge she deserves. After that, we're gone.'

'You kidnapped my little girl. I will never stop hunting you down.'

Emma shrugged. 'You can't hunt us down if you're dead.' Ashley looked at Emma and smiled, and the gun dropped slightly.

Seeing her chance, Sophie wriggled free from Amelia's grasp and ran towards Jenny, tears of fear and joy running down her face.

'Stop right there!' Ashley shouted as she spotted the movement from the corner of her eye and aimed her gun at Sophie, who was now only two or three steps away from Jenny.

'No! Don't hurt her!' Jenny cried, taking a step towards Sophie. The little girl had frozen, terror on her face as she stared at the gun pointed directly at her.

'You stay where you are as well!' Ashley screamed, and trained the gun on Jenny.

With Ashley's attention on Jenny and Sophie, Amelia saw her chance. She ran forward and launched herself at her sister, forcing the gun up and away. As the two sisters went down in a tangle of limbs, Ashley lost her grip on the gun. It went sprawling across the gravel, stopping a couple of feet from Jenny.

'Stay where you are!' Emma shouted, and switched her aim towards Jenny as she went for the gun. With the pressure on the back of his head gone, George spun round and slammed his elbow into Emma's temple. She cried out and staggered back, clutching at her head with her free hand, but before she had time to recover, George was on her. He wrenched the gun from her hand and tossed it out of reach, then cuffed her hands together behind her. Emma struggled, screaming in impotent rage, but George held her firm.

At the same time, Ashley punched Amelia hard in the face. Amelia's head hit the ground and she cried out in pain. Seeing her opportunity, Ashley quickly glanced behind her and spotted Emma's pistol. After a moment's indecision, she grabbed it just as Jenny picked up the gun that Ashley had lost in the struggle with Amelia. Ashley smiled in triumph as she quickly rose to her feet, Emma's pistol in her hand.

'Drop it!' Jenny shouted. Ashley turned, and froze; the detective was pointing a gun straight at her chest. 'Ashley Johnson, I'm arresting you for the murders of Frances Lowes and Megan Parkinson, and for the kidnapping of Amelia Simpson, Dawn Coombes and Sophie Stone. You do not have to say anything, but it may harm your defence if you don't mention when questioned something which you later rely on in court. Anything you do say may be given in evidence. Now drop the gun!'

Ashley smiled a slow smile, brought the gun up, and aimed it at the still-stunned Amelia. Her finger started to squeeze the trigger, but before she could fire, a loud crack echoed around the clearing.

Ashley stumbled and glanced down; a dark-red stain was

spreading across her pale-yellow shirt. She snarled, and her finger tightened on the trigger once again. Jenny's second shot hit just above the first. Ashley collapsed to the floor, the gun falling from her lifeless fingers.

Chapter 38

Jenny pushed open the doors to the children's ward and made for the nursing station. She carried a couple of pre-teen fashion and gossip magazines that she'd bought from the shop on the ground floor. She normally didn't approve of them – they were basically one big advert and a complete waste of money – but today Sophie could have anything she wanted. Hell, she could even have the puppy she'd been nagging her and Greg about for months.

As she waited for the nurse to finish up with another visitor, Jenny glanced around her and smiled. The walls were brightly painted in shades of blue and pink. The far wall had an undersea mural painted on it: a shipwreck, smiling fish and turtles, a mermaid, and a bright yellow submarine full of happy, smiling children. Jenny raised a hand to push her hair back, and saw it tremble. She couldn't believe how close she'd come to losing her precious daughter only hours before; seeing the gun pointed at Sophie had terrified her. She saw it every time she closed her eyes, and expected that she would for a long time to come.

'Can I help you?' the nurse asked, shaking Jenny from her thoughts.

'I'm looking for my daughter, Sophie Stone,' she replied. The nurse smiled and directed Jenny to the bed at the end of the ward. Jenny took a deep breath and made her way down.

'Mum!' Sophie cried in delight when she spotted Jenny, who ran forward and pulled her daughter into a big hug. She finally let go after nearly a minute and wiped her eyes with her sleeve. It was only then that she noticed Greg sitting beside the bed. He smiled as she looked round at him.

'How are you feeling?' Jenny asked Sophie, her brow furrowing with concern.

'I'm fine, Mum; I just want to go home. How long do I have to stay here?'

'The doctor says you only have to stay in tonight,' said Greg. 'They want to keep an eye on you to make sure you're OK. You can come home tomorrow.'

'They just want to make sure you're completely fine before they let you go,' Jenny confirmed.

Sophie looked as if she might argue for a moment, then settled back down. 'Are they for me?' she said with a smile, noticing the magazines in Jenny's hand. Jenny smiled and gave them to Sophie, who started to flip eagerly through the first one.

Greg touched Jenny's forearm and subtly nodded towards the nurse's station.

'We'll just be over here, honey,' Jenny told Sophie, but she was far too busy with her magazine to notice.

'How did it go at the station?' Greg asked in hushed tones.

'There will be an investigation by the Independent Office for Police Conduct, but that's normal in the circumstances. My federation rep says they aren't pushing for a suspension which is a good sign. If I hadn't acted when I did, Amelia

Simpson would be dead. I'm not expecting any trouble, given that there are two witnesses who can back up my version of events.'

'That's good,' Greg replied with a smile.

'How's Sophie really doing? What have the doctors said?'

'Physically she's fine; a little dehydrated, but that's about it. They're more concerned about the psychological trauma, which they say will take longer to heal. They've given me the number of a counselling service; they think it would do her good to talk about it all with someone.'

Jenny nodded and they went back into the room. Sophie was still flicking through the magazine, oblivious to the fact that they'd even left.

Jenny sat down on the hospital bed and self-consciously cleared her throat, and Sophie looked up from her magazine. 'I owe you both an apology,' she said finally. 'I know I haven't been a great mother or wife lately, and I've been far too caught up in my job, but I promise that I'll make it up to you both.' She looked down at the bed, feeling her cheeks flush, but immediately felt better when Sophie threw herself into her arms for a hug. She hugged her daughter tightly as Greg reached over and gave her hand a squeeze.

Chapter 39

Amelia was putting the finishing touches to a display of roses as the bell above the shop door jangled. She looked up as Jenny walked in.

'Jenny,' she said with a smile, taking off her gloves and putting them down on the wooden display case.

Jenny returned the smile, studying Amelia. She'd had her hair cut short into a pixie cut and she looked happier and more relaxed than Jenny had ever seen her. The intervening two weeks since the events at Knighton had been kind to her, she wasn't as gaunt as she had been when they first met, and the dark bags under her eyes had vanished completely. 'I heard that you buried Frances a few days ago. I'm sorry I couldn't attend.'

'That's OK. To be honest, I doubt we could have fitted anyone else into the church anyway; it felt as if the whole of Ryde had turned out to see her off. It helped, you know, to see how loved she was by everyone; it really helped me achieve some sort of closure on everything that's happened. She would have been embarrassed by all the fuss, of course.'

'What about Megan's funeral?'

'That's next week,' Amelia answered.

'Are you going?'

'I don't know,' Amelia said, after a pause. 'I still miss her, but I'm not sure yet if I can forgive her for what she did. Whatever I decide, I won't let it get to me anymore. Life's too short.'

'I'm glad to see you're doing well.'

'I am now. I think I'm finally starting to put this whole nightmare behind me. I even managed to sleep the whole night through last night. How's Sophie coping?'

'She's good. Thanks to you,' Jenny replied, causing Amelia to flush slightly. 'She's had a couple of sessions with a counsellor. He says that they're making good progress, but it will take time. We've got to be patient, and be there for her when she needs us.'

'She's a tough kid; she'll get through it. How's the investigation going?'

'It's progressing well. Ashley has been posthumously convicted for the murders of Frances and Megan, as well as the kidnapping of you, Dawn and Sophie.'

'And Emma?' Amelia asked.

'She's pleaded guilty to the charges, so there won't be a trial. I think she realised there was so much evidence against her that she didn't stand a chance of winning. I guess she's hoping she'll get a reduced sentence by cooperating.'

'She should rot in jail for the rest of her life, but I'm glad there won't be a trial; I wasn't looking forward to recounting this whole experience. Did you ever discover how Ashley gained access to my gran's and Megan's houses?'

'Actually, yes, we did. They had keys; we found a load hidden away in the house Emma shared with Ashley.'

'How on earth did she get those?' Amelia asked, her eyes widening.

'Emma said that she went to one of the church

meetings your gran used to attend and gave a talk on how the elderly could avoid becoming victims. She stayed after the meeting to talk to some of the members, and when Frances wasn't looking, she managed to swipe her keys and make an impression of them. That gave her your key and Frances's, so she simply let herself into your flat one day while you were here and made copies of your spare keys too, which gave her a key to the shop. As for gaining entry to Megan's, Ashley followed her home the night she died, knocked on her front door and flashed Emma's warrent card, Megan let her straight in. She also told us the cafe owner was a friend of hers, apparently Ashley had been working there cash-in-hand as a means to spy on you. The main thing we've come to realise about Ashley and Emma was that they were patient and had been planning this for ages.'

'Did Emma tell you how Gran's photo and Megan's sketchbook came to be in Kirstie's house?'

'Ashley broke in while she was away and planted them. Have you had any further trouble from Kirstie?'

'No. A few days after Ashley died I went round to her shop see her, after all, she was a victim in all of this as well. She was initially hostile, threatened to have me done for trespassing if I didn't leave immediately but I told her I wasn't there to cause trouble, that I just wanted to talk. We went for a coffee — somewhere new, I'm not too keen on Ellie's anymore — and I told her what happened, that Ashley had been manipulating both of us. In the end, I think she accepted it. Whilst I very much doubt we'll ever be friends, too much has happened for that, I think she's happy to leave what happened in the past.'

'Good.'

'Oh, I do have a little bit of good news, James is OK,' Amelia told Jenny with a wide smile.

'Your cat?' replied Jenny, her brow creasing in a frown. 'I thought Ashley killed him.'

'So did I but I got a call three days ago from a vet in Sandown, he'd been found wandering the streets and handed in. They scanned him for a microchip and rang me. I guess all Ashley managed to get hold of was his collar, it was one of those that release when caught so he must have wriggled free and escaped. He's lost a little weight and his fur is a little matted but he's his old self. He hasn't stopped following me around since I brought him home.'

Jenny smiled. 'I'm glad he's OK.'

Amelia's smiled slipped. 'Are you still under investigation for shooting Ashley?' she asked.

'No. It was ruled that there was an imminent risk to life, and my actions were justified in preventing innocent parties from being hurt or killed.'

'Good. If you hadn't acted when you did, I would be dead now and she would have won. So what's next for you?'

'I've actually been offered a promotion to chief inspector,' Jenny said, with a smile.

'Congratulations!' Amelia replied, her smile widening.

'I've turned it down.'

'What? Why?'

'The only place where they had a vacancy for a chief inspector was in Southampton. I couldn't do that to Greg and Sophie. Their lives are here, Sophie loves her school, and I can't keep putting my career first. Nearly losing her has made me realise what's important. Besides, I think I'd rather stay where I am for the time being. I like bringing in criminals, not worrying about politics and making sure the right people see the right things. The promotion can wait till I'm ready.'

Jenny paused for a moment. 'I've actually applied for temporary leave. I'm going to take a couple of months off and spend the summer with Sophie and Greg. Sophie needs to see more of me, and things are still a bit shaky between me and Greg. It's improving, but things were said that are hard to unsay. I'm hoping some proper time together as a family might help put us back on track.'

The shop fell silent, the only sounds coming from occasional cars driving past. Jenny went over to one of the display cases and admired the bouquets. Eventually, she turned to Amelia. 'Can I ask you something?'

'Yeah, of course.'

'Have you forgiven your father yet?'

Instead of answering, Amelia picked up her gloves, walked behind the counter, and put them under the till. When she looked up, her expression was thoughtful. 'I have, I think. I've thought about it a lot over the last couple of weeks, and I've come to realise that I always placed my mum and dad on a pedestal, but at the end of the day, they were only human. I don't know if what Ashley said was true, whether Dad did love her mother and stayed with Mum out of a sense of duty towards me, or whether he made a mistake and then tried to be some sort of father to Ashley. I guess I'll never know. But I've decided not to dwell upon it; instead I'm just going to remember him as a loving father and husband.'

'That sounds like a healthy attitude. So what about you? What's next?'

'That's something else I've thought about. Gran was right; I was hiding away here, taking the easy option. Don't get me wrong, I love this shop, but it's time to move on. I've accepted Dawn's offer and I start working with her next month.'

'Oh wow, congratulations! Does that mean you're selling up and moving on, then?'

'I've sold the business to Maria, but I'm going to stay on the island for now. I know Dawn would rather I was up in

London with her, but she's said she's happy for me to work from here if I don't want to move just yet.'

Maria appeared from the back room. 'Sold, huh, this bloody fool has practically given it to me. She needs her head looking at.'

'If you're selling the business, why aren't you moving to London?' Jenny asked. 'Bars, nightlife, theatre – it's the perfect place for a young woman. You'd have a great time,' Jenny asked frowning.

'That might have something to do with the fact that you're not the first police officer we've had in here today,' Maria replied, smirking.

'Maria!' said Amelia, looking daggers at her assistant. Maria's smile broadened, and her eyes gleamed with mischief.

Before Jenny could ask what she meant, the shop bell tinkled. She glanced round and did a double take as she saw DC Bancroft standing in the doorway. He spotted Jenny and started to fiddle with a button on his jacket, flushing pinker and pinker.

A large grin spread across Jenny's face as realisation dawned. 'Have a nice time,' she told Amelia. Then she turned and left the shop, winking at George as she passed.

Epilogue

Amelia leaned against the bonnet of her car and smiled as the last of the day's sun caressed her face. A gentle sea breeze rippled through her hair, and the only sounds were the cries from the gulls lazily circling the nearby cliffs. She closed her eyes and let out a small sigh of pleasure.

She was brought out of her reverie by the sound of a car moving along the track. She opened her eyes and looked over her shoulder just in time to see it pull into the secluded carpark, the gravel crunching under its wheels. After a moment's hesitation, Sam switched off the engine and climbed out. He looked Amelia up and down; she wore frayed denim shorts, a white linen top and white sneakers, and her legs, shoulders and face were tanned from long, lazy days at the beach. Sam, on the other hand, looked haggard, sporting nearly a week's worth of beard growth.

'Hi,' he said, and ran his hand through his unkempt hair, making it stick up even further. 'You're looking good.'

'Thanks,' Amelia replied. She made no effort to move from the car, turning her face to the setting sun once more.

Sam shifted uncomfortably. 'You wanted to see me?'

'Yeah. I thought we should talk.'

'That would be good.'

'Shall we go for a walk?' Without waiting for an answer, Amelia pushed herself away from the car and began walking through the long grass.

Sam hurried to catch her up before falling into step next to her. 'I see you've sold the shop.'

'Yeah, it was time to move on.'

'So what are you doing now?' he asked.

'I'm working with Dawn. I told you she came to see me after that night out together and offered me a job. Well, I accepted it.'

'Congratulations.'

'Thanks. After everything that's happened recently, I decided I needed a change. What about you? How've you been?'

'OK, I guess. I'm getting tired of being stuck at my parents' place, though. They're doing my head in.' Sam looked at her. 'Look, when are you going to get over the whole Megan thing? I admit I made a mistake, but she came on to me and anyway, I don't think that I'm entirely to blame in all of this. Our relationship had grown stale. Do you know how long it had been since we'd had sex? Maybe if you'd shown me more affection, instead of giving it all to that bloody cat, I wouldn't have been tempted to look elsewhere. But I don't think it's too late, you know. We've both made mistakes, but I think we can be stronger because of it. I still love you, and I've even forgiven you for kicking me out.'

Amelia kicked at a loose stone and glanced around. Apart from a couple of bored-looking cows, they were alone. The only signs of civilisation were a couple of houses, a distant inn, and Yarborough Monument. In front of her, the English Channel seemed to stretch to infinity; you could almost believe that if you kept going you would reach the edge of the world. The sea was still and calm, empty except for a couple of heavily laden cargo ships lazily drifting past in the distance.

Amelia breathed in the sea air and smiled. 'I love this view,' she told Sam, 'it's so peaceful. I can sit here, stare at the horizon and lose all sense of time. It's a great place to come and think.'

'What on earth are you talking about?' Sam asked.

Amelia looked him up and down. 'I asked you to come here to see if you'd changed. To see if our time apart had taught you any humility, compassion, or empathy, but you're still the same old Sam. Still the lazy, self-centred loser you always were, still quick to blame everyone else for your own shortcomings. I was too stupid to see it then, but not now. It took me a long time to realise, but Gran was right. You're a parasite, and I'm so much better off without you.'

'What the fuck's your problem, Amelia—'

'No. You don't get to talk to me like that anymore. Gran was right, and I should have listened to her. In some strange way, I owe my sister a small measure of thanks. If it wasn't for her, I'd still be sitting at home listening to your whining. We're done. I don't want to see you ever again.'

Without waiting for a reply, Amelia turned and walked back to her car, leaving a dumbfounded Sam staring after her, his mouth hanging open. She breathed in the sea air, and smiled.

Made in United States
Orlando, FL
05 June 2025

61806068R00198